PROXIMAL BIRDFLIP

or

The Teleconference of Doctor Faustus

By

ANDREW P PARTINGTON

Submarine Media Pty Ltd

Malaga, Western Australia

Published 2024

This novel is satire, as is this sentence: accordingly the reader must expect every word to be entirely historically accurate insofar as it concerns characters living or dead who are never mentioned by name or implied or referenced in any way, shape or form.

CHARACTERS

GEORGE FAUSTUS: Director of the NIAID

JERRY BLACKSMITH: An English Scientist, Faustus's friend

KRISTEN SOLO, PhD: Professor Department of Immunology and Microbiology, Scripps Research

BARRY A. GOG: Professor at Tulane University School of Medicine

SHAMROCK HOLMES: Professor of Evolutionary Virology at the University of Sydney.

MINORKA HENNERYS: Dutch scientist head of the Erasmus MC Department of virology

POLTRIK D. VALLEE: Chief Scientific Advisor to the UK Government

CLARENCE COLLINS: President of the NHIJ

RENARD FOURIER: Dutch scientist Deputy head of the Erasmus MC Department of virology

Frostey KRISTOFF: Head of the institute of virology at Charité Berlin

PETRONIA PARNASSUS: Faustus's Personal Secretary.

ZHENG-LENG PENGUIN: Head virologist at the WooHoo lab 哇喔

DANILLO CRUMP: President of the US

DR Gloriana U. CONIRRAVOS: Faustus's wife. (only a few words)

DR ALERIC HAZARD: Health and Human Services Secretary.

DR REDMOND REDMEADOWS: Director of the CDE, the Center for Disease Elimination

DR NANCY BALM: Senior director of CDE's National Center for Immunization and Respiratory Diseases

HUGO "OUCHY" STONEYFIELD: Faustus' deputy.

FRANK: Faustus' driver

MADELEY: Frank's daughter

LINDA: Frank's wife.

CHAPTER 1

Crowns…

Jesus Christ looked down with baleful eyes beneath brows bleeding from the dreadful crown of thorns on his head, his outstretched hands perpetually nailed to the crucifix at the end of Faustus's entry hall — the good Doctor glared up at him and said, "What are you lookin' at? Leave me alone!" — then rushed past the gruesome relic of his grandmother's Catholic faith into his study.

He had to get his stuff together before the SUV picked him up for Bethesda, and his hereditary Catholic guilt really wasn't helping.

Where was Petronia? He had to get *something*, what was it? He still hadn't had his first coffee. He wasn't ready for Petronia yet.

The doorbell rang. His wife called from the lounge at the front of the house, "It's Petronia." Thank the god of Science, Faustus thought ironically; he's got it in for me.

Petronia rushed into the office, a feminine whirlwind carrying in a scent of bergamot and roses, and said, "George. All your things are in the limo. We just need your laptop."

That's right, his laptop! He looked at the tangle of cords, he hadn't got it ready, he didn't even know where to start unplugging things, but like an efficient automaton Petronia was already whipping out plugs and cables and stuffing the whole tangled mess into his leather laptop bag. "Come on George," she said, "Let's go." He suddenly remembered he needed a cup of coffee, but before he could even suggest it she was just as efficiently whisking him down the corridor and into the black SUV, which was parked in the semicircular driveway in front of his DC mansion.

Before he could process anything they were seated in the rear of the enormous limo driving through the stark winter landscape of late January Washington DC, and he was sipping the foam coffee cup Petronia had organised for him (what a girl!) and staring out the window at the bare-branched trees going past mauve buildings underneath a dull grey leaden sky. It would have cast his spirits down, except that Faustus liked being melancholy and somewhat enjoyed the sweet feeling of solitariness and sadness.

There was something about the thought of death that was strangely comforting, he thought, as he took another sip of the cappuccino.

The end of us all.

He suddenly realised Petronia was saying something or other. “What was that?” he blurted.

“You’re in a daze this morning. I said, a lot of people are going to die, that’s what they’re all saying.” Patronia added, her hands folded in her lap, “This one is bad.”

Doctor Faustus nodded. “It might be the one we’re waiting for. The one we’ve been predicting all along,” he said eagerly, then cleared his throat and said in more sombre tones, “Not that I meant that a pandemic might be a good thing. It’s a terrible shame that people are going to die. A terrible shame.”

Petronia had a strange twisted little smile on her face that disturbed George, as she began repeating again and again in a morbid whisper, “A terrible shame. A terrible shame.”

Then she looked over at him and her eyes were shining with tears of admiration, and the way her skin stretched out over her skull simultaneously brought to mind his anatomy classes sixty years before and aroused him and he didn’t particularly like himself for either reaction, so he looked away as she affirmed emphatically, “The awaited pandemic is here, and it’s late January, and you, Doctor Faustus, the head of NAIAD, the National Allergy and Infectious

Academy of Diseases, you yourself, Doctor, are the one and only man who will be able to guide the nations of the world through the global epidemic that is even now beginning to spread through the vulnerable populations of the nations of the world like wildfire."

George sighed and felt a twinge of discomfort at his own desire for global supremacy, so he feigned humility as best he could, saying, "Well, Petronia, I really don't know if that is strictly true."

Petronia said, "Well you have to *believe* that it's true, Doctor Faustus. If you believe it, then it will be true. And what the people will need is not science with a small s. It is *Leadership* with a capital L."

George coughed and laughed and said, "But of course, Petronia, that's where you're completely wrong, I'm afraid. If I go into it saying, 'I'm coming to be your leader,' everyone will laugh at me. They will think I'm President Crump, for Science's sake, or a visitor from outer space!" They both laughed.

He continued, "The bureaucrat is notionally the servant of all. I must emphasize that the only thing I'm even remotely qualified to bring to this table is science with a small s; and to be perfectly honest, I'm out of the game,

Petronia. I've been a bureaucrat now for many years. I'm not even sure I'm up to date with any of the research the NAIAD has been doing, let alone anybody else."

Petronia said, "Well then, what you actually *need* to bring to the table is science with a capital L."

"I beg your pardon?" he said, completely bamboozled by her comment. "Science starts with the letter S, doesn't it? Or is that something to do with computers?"

Petronia replied, "No, No. You *tell* them that what you're giving them is science."

The penny dropped and George looked at her with renewed respect. "You mean, tell them it's science, when it's really *Leadership with a capital L*?"

Petronia nodded, and George continued the thought, "Well, then, that would not be science with a capital L, but *Science* with a capital S." He punched the back of the driver's headrest for emphasis, and the driver said, "Do you mind?"

"Oh, sorry," said George. "My apologies, ah," he was going to say the guy's name but he couldn't remember it. "Where were we? Science with a capital S?"

Petronia said, "And that's what you are," she said, "You *are* the Science. That's what you have to tell yourself. 'I *am* the Science.'"

He tried it on for size. "I *am* the Science. I *am* the Science," he whispered.

And suddenly he felt completely stupid. That's ridiculous, he thought to himself, but what he said was, "We have the strangest conversations," and returned to gazing at the grey world outside.

But the phrase still echoed as a whisper in his thoughts, "I am the Science. I am the Science." And he wondered if it might be a useful phrase to call up when he had to speak at the press conference later in the day, just to bolster his courage — which was admittedly fairly boundless, but one could always give oneself even more of an advantage.

~~~

Half an hour later, he was in the big conference room at the NHIJ Campus in Bethesda, Maryland, and Petronia was putting his coat on for him, giving him his laptop and showing him some data or other on the screen, then taking his laptop back off him, then telling him to smile for the camera, taking his coat back off, giving him a document to sign, then another document, then getting him to read
~~~

through his speech again as she handed the signed documents over to whoever needed it. In a moment of zoned-out blankness as the havoc around him continued the headline on the flat-screen television on the far wall jumped out, 'Birdflip Coronavirus havoc in China', then Petronia surprised him out of his reverie with another document to sign, then he fielded a question from a senior bureaucrat, another question from a scientist on the team, then a question from a journalist.

Then the whirlwind ceased and he was in the eye of the storm, floating down in the lessening gravity as the elevator shot to the carpark and then they were back in the nondescript black SUV and they were driving to DC again, past the scraggly winter trees under the dull grey sky, which was a different colour now, but just as boring and sad, which he didn't mind. He turned to her and said, "You're my rock, Petronia." She beamed with barely suppressed pleasure, and Faustus felt glad that he had made another human being happy that day.

~~~

As they went in through the foyer in the new massive DC Town Hall, some people he didn't know met them and escorted him through. As he went past someone thrust a
~~~

copy of one of his books at him and he stopped and Petronia gave him a pen and let him rest it on her back as he signed it, a short ritual they had repeated a hundred times — then he stood stock still as someone took a photograph and then they were in the hall and she checked his shirt then Faustus strode up onto the stage, where a podium stood with a microphone in front of a row of plastic chairs.

The Health Secretary Aleric Hazard was seated there next to Dr Redmeadow, the head of the CDE, and Dr Nancy — what was her surname again? — anyhow he'd met her before; she was the director of the CDE's Respiratory Diseases Clinic, wasn't she? He greeted and shook hands with each one then sat down patiently waiting for Hazard's speech to begin.

Then, as if in a dream, he noticed Hazard had already begun speaking.

"Good morning, thank you for being here today at Health Services. We're aiming to get through two main points today: to give you a general overview of what we know about the current state of the Birdflip Coronavirus outbreak in China, and to give you a pretty good idea of what the Health Services and the Crump Administration are doing to prepare the country for this threat."

Then he introduced Redmeadow and Dr Nancy Balm, yes of course that was her surname; then Aleric introduced him: "And Dr George Faustus, director of NAIAD, whom we are very privileged to have with us today."

And then Aleric was onto the Birdflip Coronavirus.

"As of this moment, we have six reported cases of the Birdflip Coronavirus here in the United States. China has had nearly five thousand reported cases. This is potentially a very serious health threat, but Americans should not worry for their safety: this is a constantly changing situation, with every hour that passes, but even so we have previous experiences with coronavirus outbreaks such as SARS and MERS, bird flu, swine flu, bat flu, pangolin flu, and even the snake flu.

"China has reported more than a hundred deaths from the five thousand cases, a fatality rate of 2%, which seems very high, it's very high. However, the cases identified so far have probably been only the cases severe enough to end up in emergency departments, so how many people have actually been infected is unknown until we have a reliable test. Though we're collecting data to understand the incubation: does the virus spread asymptomatically? Do people have it without symptoms for some period, two days, a week, fourteen days, before the symptoms start to show up, and how long does the Birdflip Coronavirus last? The common cold lasts for two to three days, influenza, up to two weeks.

"The procedure we will follow is quite simple: we identify cases, isolate, diagnose and treat them, and then you do what we call contact tracing: you track down all the contacts of the infected person, and all the contacts of those people, going to the fourth or fifth degree of separation if necessary, by which I mean, if the virus spreads rapidly.

"We're telling doctors and hospitals to be on the lookout for patients with the symptoms who have recently been to China, especially if they have come from Huàn province. On the recommendation of the CDE, a State Department level three travel advisory is in place for the whole of China since Monday, together with a level *four* warning for Huàn province, a much more serious tier of warnings, which essentially means Americans are advised not to travel to Huàn at all. We're doing our best to keep you all safe.

"And now I'd like to introduce someone I know you all know and have been waiting to listen to, Dr George Faustus, the Director of NAIAD, the National Allergy and Infectious Academy of Diseases. Over to you, George."

As Aleric sat down, Faustus got up; he was whispering to himself, "I *am* the Science, I *am* the Science, I *am* the Science," as he approached the microphone.

He took a deep breath and started: "Thank you, Mr. Hazard. I'm gonna give you a quick snapshot of the counter measures — that is, diagnostics, therapeutics, and *especially* vaccines, and I mean, *vaccines*, that are being investigated and pursued by the NHIJ and the NAIAD, by those who've received our grants, our contractors and collaborators.

"First: diagnostics."

At this moment the completely irrelevant thought flashed through his mind that diagnostic meant through-gnostic in Greek and he remembered that gnostics didn't believe reality was real, and he wondered if he actually believed reality was real, and that reminded him that an agnostic doubted everything and that diagnostic could mean di-agnostic which at a stretch could mean double agnostic and that perhaps he didn't believe anything that he was talking about at all. He thanked the gods of Science for Petronia again as he recited 'I am the Science, I am the Science,' in his own mind and continued talking anyway:

“The CDE has developed a sort of a diagnostic test for the Birdflip Coronavirus based on the sequence of the virus as was published in the British Journal of Medicine just last week; the FGH and the NHIJ and the NAIAD together with the CDE, the BJM, the RSB, and the...” he hesitated — LGBTIQ — is that supposed to be in there, Gloriana? — he didn’t say it, it might have been a mistake. What did it stand for, anyway? “And the QRSTUV and all of the other BS organisations as well. All of us are working on a generation-next diagnostic tool that is more customer friendly and needs based so that we can distribute them to people of good will throughout the country and the world.

“Second: therapeutics. We don’t have any proven therapies yet for the Birdflip Coronavirus, but we’re working on them. There are innovative studies that have been inaugurated and are continuing even as we speak. And what with the previous experience we had with SARS and MERS and the bird flu and the bat flu and the pangolin flu and the snake flu, for example, between each one of those outbreaks and the current outbreak a number of excellent antiviral drugs have been tested in vitro in transgenic penguins and even in the field in anecdotal studies with placeboes and anyceboes and noceboes. One of them is called

Weildesevedemol, which some of you may remember was used in my — ah — the clinical trials against the aptly named pathogen Z, in Africa.

"Again I must accentuate that there is no proof any of these treatments have any efficacy at all, but we're looking into them and screening out the other ones. In fact, we are very kindly allowing China to use Weildesevedemol together with another completely usele - useful - drug, Didwedesevematol, on a very compassionate basis on our part, let me say. This is of course why we must isolate the virus, which we haven't done yet, but which is something we will be working to do very soon, once we can get hold of those six individuals who were infected with the virus, who are in some hospital somewhere, I believe.

"And then there're the monoclonal antibodies. We have them for the bird flu and the bat flu and the snake flu but we unfortunately don't have any for the pangolin flu. But we started by making them for SARS and MERS, just in case those pathogens leaked - ah - let's say - *returned* from the lab - something we've been working on, of course, and the ones for the snake flu or the bat flu will not be effective for the Birdflip Coronavirus, and it's still not a *proven* therapy because we've only used the monoclonal antibodies on transgenic penguins and transhuman pigeons infected with these viruses; these were the in vitro animal models, designed to resemble the human ACE2 receptors in the lungs and brain and liver and lymph node cells, but since there's a close homology between the SARS and the bat flu and this new Birdflip Coronavirus, we think that we could tweak it; or to put it another way, there could be some inter-reactivity there that we could utilize to make a more effective gain of function virus - ah - viral monoclonal antibody, I mean.

"However, let me say, that what we're really attempting to do, and we will have it as soon as we get those specimens from the six individuals who are infected, then we will then be able to clone their B cells and make specific monoclonal antibodies against the novel Birdflip coronavirus."

He thought to himself, well, that's assuming that they survive. The B cells of someone who hasn't survived will be fairly useless I would guess.

"And then, finally, most noteworthily, most importantly, at the top of the list, let me emphasize, of things that we want to inject into your deltoid muscles and your veins, the *vaccines*. Let me emphasize again that these vaccines are neither a money-making venture of the Big Pharma companies nor are they Gill Bates' pet project, neither do they merely have the blessing of the WFE (World Federation of Economics), the WHC (World Health Club), or the GAVeIt vaccine alliance, but everybody loves them. No, just because mRNA vaccines could be the cheapest way to mass produce vaccines in the future does not mean that this is why we want to put them in everybody's arms. No." He added, "No. No. No. Again let me emphasize: No. But — and let me emphasize that this is a very big butt" — he suddenly realised he was staring at one of the security guards who was standing in front of the stage — a woman hired under DEI and she was height-challenged and very — ah — fullsome in the rear and he looked away immediately in case his glance was caught on camera and became some sort of meme. He knew what memes were, something his grandchildren had got him up to date on. He closed his eyes and repeated internally, 'I am the Science, I am the Science,' and recovered his composure.

"I was saying, it's a very big, unbelievably enormous butt — and that butt is — let me emphasize that butt — ahem — bu-t — but what we're envisaging is taking the sequence that the Chinese put on a public database — the genetic sequence of the Birdflip Coronavirus — and pulling out the genes for the Spike protein of that particular coronavirus and putting them in the vaccines to elicit an immune response — we imagine — and this process could be through the phase one trial within the next three months. And with some cautious optimism — I want to emphasize once more — *cautiou*s — I don't want you to be confused because the general public so often are so very confused and even vexed — once we get through the phase one trials in three months, and we have the immunogenicity and safety data — in fact, *regardless* of whether we have that data, for they will of course be entirely safe and effective as all our medications are — then we move into phase two.

"But what we do then will be determined by what happens with the outbreak over the subsequent time period. You might remember we made a Phase one trial of a safe and effective SARS vaccine, but the virus was over too soon and..." — he almost added, we never got to try that vaccine out on anybody, quite unfortunately for science. He mustn't go off script, he might say something really stupid. "In other words, we're looking at the best — or let me emphasize — worst case scenario, that this becomes a huge international pathogen, a pandemic, if you will."

And Doctor Faustus had an epiphany in very that moment, that without vaccines, everything else was completely useless.

His good acquaintance, Gill Bates, Multi-Billionaire tech entrepreneur, was completely right.

And Doctor Faustus found himself suddenly lifted up on a flight of rhetoric, a fugue of grandiloquence and magnificent oratory, if you will, and he threw away his notes and they fluttered to the ground one by one and he improvised:

"For although I may diagnose with RAT tests and PCR tests, if I have not got vaccines, I am nothing more than a sounding hospital bed alert or a clanging cardiac alarm. And even if I could predict everything that was going to happen in the course of the infection, and understood all the mysteries of pathology, and had all the knowledge of virology at my fingertips, like Frostey Kristoff, and though I might have every diagnostic criteria in science and all therapeutics, so that I could even insert spike proteins and furine cleavage sites into murine viruses, but have no vaccines, I have nothing."

He saw Petronia's face; she was horrified that he had departed from the script, but he completely ignored her distress and continued on his own track:

"Vaccines are good for patients, and kind, they do not cause suffering, they do not contain snake venom and do not count up adverse events, and they do not cause maladies or myocarditis or dropsy or neurological symptoms or liver disease.

"So in summary, for now, we see as through a glass partition, but then, we shall see face to face. And there remain these three things: diagnostics, therapeutics, and vaccines, and the greatest of these is vaccines.

"And we will keep you posted as we make progress in each of these. Thank you. Thank you very much."

And as the crowd clapped, he saw Petronia's face, uplifted with worshipful admiration as she watched him descend from the podium like Moses carrying the ten commandments down Mount Sinai, and Doctor Faustus knew then that he would be remembered as a saint.

And had Doctor Faustus' favourite piece of music, Samuel Barber's Adagio for Strings, been playing in the background, the scene could have been no more splendid than it was; Faustus shaking hands and making his brief farewells to Dr Aleric Hazard, Dr Redmond Redmeadows and Dr Nancy Balm, and they acknowledging him with nods of deference and respect, and even small glances of envy at his undeniable greatness. These were the small things he treasured most.

~~~

It was late afternoon at the end of the January winter and the shadows were lengthening as Faustus was driven back to his DC mansion. Imagine, if you will, drone camera footage from above, of the nondescript black electric SUV limo sliding silently along the wet roads of one of the more attractive residential neighbourhoods of Washington DC, still bare-branched and grey though with the winter paucity, drifting along — say — 49th street NW, then turning right onto Garfield Street Northwest, and then into the semicircular driveway of Faustus' home.
~~~

CHAPTER 2

The Email

On the last day of January, Doctor George Faustus head of the NAIAD, received an email from his English friend, Doctor Jerry Blacksmith, director of the Wellness M.I.S. Trust. He didn't see it of course; Petronia called him and said, "Did you see the email from Jerry?"

"No? What email?"

Petronia patiently urged him to look at his emails once in a while and put down the phone.

He opened his desktop computer, found the email app, opened it, and after about ten minutes worked out how to open the email and read it.

> From: Jerry Blacksmith
>
> To: George Faustus
>
> George, I really do need to speak with you this evening. It is 9pm now UK. Would you be able to phone me?

~~~

Immediately someone hit 'reply', but it wasn't George Faustus, because he was still not sure where 'reply' was on the email app.
~~~

Petronia Parnassus's home office was a plush room with white bookshelves and elegant windows that looked out upon a park, yet furnished simply with a desk and chair. She typed:

From: Petronia Parnassus

To: Jerry Blacksmith

Will call shortly…

Petronia looked out the window. It was early evening, the sun was over the horizon but it was still twilight, and although it looked cold people were walking their dogs and chatting with one another in the park outside. Some children were playing in the playground, making a merry racket. She shook her head and picked up her mobile phone.

~~~

Faustus's office was spacious enough to be comfortable and looked out upon scraggly winter trees and a small swamp, part of the large block of land on which the mansion was built. There were large bookcases and an even larger desk. On the wall there were three or four enormous pictures of Faustus himself, and his huge computer was in front of him on the desk, with a burgeoning, expensive podcasting mic in front of it; although it is doubtful whether Faustus had ever used it himself. He was still a luddite, in general, as
~~~

far as technology went. A few formidable books were scattered about on the desk as well, and the gargantuan clock hanging on the wall said 4 minutes to 5.

Faustus' mobile phone rang and he answered it. "Hello? Yes, Petronia, I was just about to finish up for the evening...."

Petronia said, "You have to ring Jerry."

"Jerry Blacksmith?"

Petronia said, "Yes, ring Jerry."

"What, now?"

Petronia replied emphatically, "Yes right now."

There was a pause as Faustus digested this unpalatable information. "But he hates working evenings." And that was okay, because Faustus hated working any time after 5.

Petronia said, "He emailed you asking you to call him. It must be important."

Faustus paused again, then made his decision. "You're right," he said, "He wouldn't want me to call unless it's important. Alright. Tell him I'll call him right away."

Petronia replied, "I already did. I told him you'll call him right away."

He couldn't help sounding annoyed, "Oh, you already did, did you?" Sometimes Petronia somewhat exceeded her authority, but she was far too valuable to him for him to ever point it out directly.

"I did. Call him now," she added.

"Alright," he said, rather sheepishly.

Faustus ended the call and rang Jerry Blacksmith.

"Jerry?" he said into the phone, "You wanted me to call."

Some kind of alert came up on Faustus' phone, 'Facetime'; if it was from Jerry he decided it wouldn't be spam, so he clicked it.

A video of Jerry appeared on Faustus' phone; he was sitting in his home office — a small, poky London room, that looked no bigger and no warmer than Bob Cratchit's room in Scrooge's mansion must have been in the nineteenth century — and Jerry looked grim. His tone of voice was even more grim.

"Hello, George," he said.

Faustus suddenly had an irrational fear that something was wrong. He almost panicked, and said impetuously, "What's it about, Jerry? You wouldn't ring so late unless it was important."

"Well..." Jerry paused, then he sighed deeply and said, "I've been looking into some of your grants, George. Open up your computer. I'm going to send you a few links."

Faustus saw him turn away and click his mouse and heard the 'whoosh' of the email sending.

About ten seconds later Faustus's email gave a 'ding,' telling him that he had received the email, and he opened it up.

Hi George,

A few references - to be significantly updated:

A Birdflip-like cluster of circulating Birdflip Coronaviruses shows potential for human emergence; https://clubmed.ncbi.naiad.nhi.gov/2203712345/

A penguin-adapted Birdflip Coronavirus causes disease and mortality in ACE2 BULB-LIGHT penguins; https://ncbi.naiad.nhi.gov/clubmed/123045666/

Birdflip-like WOOHOO1-COV poised for human emergence when we release it; https://ncbi.naiad.nhi.gov/clubmed/006006006/

Modeling pathogenesis of emergent and pre-emergent human Birdflip Coronaviruses in penguins that might just emerge in the wild exactly the same as the ones we made; https://ncbi.naiad.nhi.gov/clubmed/012345666/[1]

Cheers Jerry

[1] These are all genuine studies of course. Would I tell a lie? Trust me. I'm a scientist.

Faustus clicked on the top link.

To his amazement the study appeared on the screen. "I didn't know you could do that," he admitted.

Several names on the author list at the top looked a bit familiar.

"What's this? Zheng-Leng Penguin?" he said to Jerry. "The bird lady, from the Woohoo Institute? And Ralph Bar-tailed Godwit? From Chapel Chump University. Nice guy. Have you ever had a beer with him?"

Jerry looked and sounded pained. "Read the abstract, George."

Faustus read:

> A Birdflip-like cluster of circulating Birdflip Coronaviruses shows potential for human emergence[2];
>
> The emergence of severe acute severe respiratory syndrome coronavirus (SARS-CoV) and Middle East avian respiratory syndrome (MERS-BIRD-CoV) underscores the threat of cross-species transmission events leading to outbreaks in humans.

---

[2] Discreet V Moneypenny, Dick Sissell Junior the Ninth, Carrie Cassowary, Subhacker Agniballistic Missile, Jess E Goatsucker, Jessica N A Tree, Rachel Grey-Crestedtit, Trevor Scoter, Xing-Ying (O.T.) Wing, Eric Flaherty Donald-duckson, Scott H Cuckoo, Antonio Macaroni Penguinson, Wayne A Mallard, Zheng-Leng Penguin, Ralph Bar-tailed Godwit **A Birdflip-like cluster of circulating Birdflip Coronaviruses shows potential for human emergence** Club Med. 2015 Dec; 21(12):1508-13. doi: 10.1038/cm.3985. Epub 2015 Nov 9. Erratum in: Club Med. 2016 Apr;22(4):446. doi: 10.1038/cm0416-446d. Erratum in: Club Med. 2020 Jul;26(7):1146. doi: 10.1038/s41591-020-0924-2. PMID: 26552008; CMCID: CMC4797993. https://clubmed.ncbi.naiad.nhi.gov/2203712345/

> Here we examine the disease potential of a SARS-like Birdflip virus, AV014-CoV, which is currently circulating in Chinese penguin populations.

"What's wrong with that?" Faustus said, "Jerry, you're looking anxious. You're starting to get me worried."

Jerry said, "Read on."

Faustus read aloud:

> Using the SARS-CoV reverse genetics system, we generated and characterized a chimeric virus -

Faustus asked, "Chimeric? Doesn't that mean, cute like a little angel?"

Jerry sighed. "No, George, that's cherubic. Chimeric means, made up of two different species." He added, "Try not to admit you didn't know what chimeric means next time you're in a meeting."

Faustus read on:

> - expressing the spike protein of bird (avian) coronavirus AV-014 in a penguin-adapted SARS-CoV backbone.
>
> The results indicate that group 2b viruses encoding the AV-014 spike in a wild-type backbone can efficiently use multiple orthologs of the SARS receptor human angiotensin converting enzyme II (ACE2), replicate efficiently in primary human airway cells and achieve in-vitro titers equivalent to epidemic strains of SARS-CoV.

Faustus shrugged. "Oh. I see."

Was it gain of function? Ever since Obama's moratorium he had studiously avoided calling anything gain of function. You just say, it's not gain of function, and that's enough to get the grant through. Wasn't it? I mean, who can really understand this stuff? It takes a virologist to say whether something's gain of function or not. Doesn't it?

He didn't know.

He said a little priggishly, "Well, you wouldn't call that gain of function. Anyway, no one can expect the Chinese to follow all *our* rules."

Jerry sighed again. "Look at the bottom of the study, George. I helpfully highlighted those bits."

Faustus scrolled down and read:

> Research in this manuscript was supported by grants from the National Allergy and Infectious Academy of Diseases and the National Aging Institute of the US National Health Institutes Junket (NHIJ) under awards U18A060606 (Ralph Bar-tailed Godwit), U18A13013013 (Ralph Bar-tailed Godwit), AI76543210 (Boy Lester Young Junior the Ninth), F23CATCH22 (Discreet V Moneypenny) and K99AG18 (Discreet V Moneypenny), and by the National Unnatural Science Foundation of China awards 01357900 (Zheng-Leng Penguin.) and 3141322018 (Xing-Ying On the Wing.), and by USAID-EPT-BIRDFLUING funding from EcoHell Alliance (Zheng-Leng Penguin.)

Faustus said, "NHIJ. They funded this? Well, that's their problem, Jerry. That's not my problem."

Jerry sighed even more deeply. "No. It is your problem I'm afraid, George, it says at the top of the Acknowledgements, funded by the National Allergy and Infectious Academy of Diseases, the NAIAD. Remember? That's you."

Faustus was a little perturbed. "Oh. It is. How about that, I skipped it, skim-read it too fast. I know we did fund a few of Ralph Bar-tailed Godwit's studies."

He looked at the other studies."We didn't fund this one though; NIAID is not listed there."

Jerry replied, "Copy the grant number, George. Look it up on NHIJ REport."

Faustus laboriously wrote down the whole grant ID number from the acknowledgements, UAHBIRD123045666, and said, "Ah. Right. What's the web address for NHIJ REport again?"

Jerry was a very patient Englishman, and a good friend. "Reporter.nhij.gov," he said calmly. "Go to that web address and type in the grant number."

Faustus thanked him and did what he said.

The NHIJ REporter website came up on the screen. In the search field, Faustus pasted the ID number in, then pressed enter. Something came up, but he couldn't see anything about the NAIAD.

Faustus said, "How do I get to it?"

Jerry said, "Scroll down."

Faustus scrolled down the page and read out:

> 2018
>
> National Allergy and Infectious Academy of Diseases
>
> Six million one hundred and seventy one thousand eight hundred and forty seven dollars.

"Okay," he said. "Now what does this mean?"

Jerry said, "Do you know what they're saying all over the internet? They're saying the virus escaped from the WooHoo lab."

Faustus said, "Really? That's preposterous." He was angry now. "How can they possibly know that? That would be impossible to prove." Suddenly, his nerve broke, and he found himself pleading with Jerry, "Wouldn't it, Jerry?"

Jerry said, "Well, the problem is, there are some... funny things about the genome, George."

Faustus snapped, "What do you mean?"

Jerry replied, "It might be better if Kristen explains that."

Faustus said, "Kristen?"

Jerry smiled for the first time, "You remember him, don't you? Kristen Solo, at Scripps Research in San Diego. Good friend of mine. He's volunteered to help."

Faustus was too defensive again. "To help? Help what? I am the head of the NIAID, Jerry. I have plenty of help. I don't need help."

Jerry said, "You remember? You needed help back when that he helped you clean up that HOOV[3] medicine mess about twenty years ago. You need help now, George. Anyhow... He's the one that noticed what's... in the genome."

Faustus didn't say anything. He didn't like to remember how Kristen Solo and the rest of that clandestine team had been called in to write a study to justify Azitadunanyazinatul, the HOOV drug; he thought Kristen's team had done a fair assessment of the drug, but he had been forced to quote the study in a press conference and pretend he didn't know the authors, and it would just have been a bit

[3] HOOV: Human Omni-ficient Omphalo-Virus, a disease that afflicted and killed many varieties of navel gazers, and not just male navel gazers, in the 1980s, 1990s, and 2000s.

embarrassing if anyone had found out that it was all pre-planned.

Well, that was the kind of thing that could end his stellar career as a health bureaucrat.

Finally Jerry spoke again, "You know I'm on your side. We need to nip it in the bud. What do you think will happen to all our funding if the idea gets about that this coronavirus was a lab escape? From the WooHoo lab in China that you were funding with Federal money? The funding for all our projects would evaporate overnight, whoosh! Up in a puff of steam. That would be the end of virology as we know it, George. Not just in the US. In the whole Western World. It would be the end of science."

Faustus cried out so melancholily he was immediately embarrassed, "It would be the end of science! It would be the end of me! What do I do?"

Jerry said, "I'm getting together a team. Unless you want it to look like you put the study together?"

Then Jerry whispered, as though that might help if someone was hacking the phone call. "We have to do what we did when *Azitadunanyazinatul* was looking a bit... ineffective in some of the tests. Kristen will get in contact later this evening, when he's ready. I'll get Petronia to email you when he's ready for you to call him."

Faustus got up from the desk and paced around the room.

He went to the CD player and took out the CD for another of his favourite Samuel Barber pieces, Prayers of Kierkegaarde, and he put in the CD started listening to it[4].

The clock on the wall said 5:30. The sun had set and twilight was over. After a while the music stopped playing and he didn't start it again. Faustus looked out through the window. The sky was overcast, and he couldn't see the moon, and the branches moving gently to and fro in the breeze looked creepy and forlorn. He shivered. He was emptied to the very core, cold in his deepest heart and completely forsaken by God. He shivered again and looked at the branches; ancient fears of witches and curses seemed to rise up from somewhere deep within his collective unconscious, and he could do nothing to shake the existential dread that had taken hold. God, he had to get his mind off this.

---

[4] Prayers of Kierkegaarde Opus 30: mvt ii O Lord Jesus Christ Who Suffered All Life Long (Carmen Pelton, soprano, Nannette Soles, mezzo-soprano, Richard Clement, tenor, Atlanta Symphony and Chorus conducted by Robert Shaw)

He looked at the computer again, hoping for something, and tried not to think about what it might mean if the virus had been created in the WooHoo lab.

No email had come.

No phone call.

He checked the mobile to make sure it wasn't on silent.

It wasn't.

He sat at his desk with his head in his hands.

If Kristen Solo thought it was made in the lab, it probably was.

His career was over.

His wife was a bioethicist, for God's sake, what would people think? She would probably divorce him, simply out of the public shaming that would inevitably occur.

The clock on the wall said 6:30.

He had been sitting like this for an hour, and he was getting a stress headache.

Faustus walked out of his office into the corridor, walked quickly beneath the crucifix, into a comfortable, homely lounge room with a crackling fireplace; it was one of those modern ones that never went out. There were pictures on the wall.

Faustus entered with a hopeful look, but his beautiful and talented wife Dr Gloriana U. Conirravos, bioethics expert at the NHIJ, was sitting in her lounge chair, sound asleep, with an iPad sitting next to her on the arm of her chair.

Faustus felt his face slacken into crestfallenness. He went back into the corridor and then couldn't avoid glancing up at the dreadful crucifix. In His suffering Jesus seemed to be looking down on Faustus; was it pity or anger? Faustus thought he could abide the suffering man's pity even less than anger.

He blurted out more loudly than he had intended, "Well, what are you looking at? I know, I know, I funded them. So you think I'm responsible, do you?"

Suddenly Faustus's wife was behind him, leaning on the door frame.

She said without a trace of accusatory spite, "Are you alright, George? You woke me up."

Faustus said, "I'm fine. I'm sorry, Gloriana. I'm really fine. I'm just... you know — it's just..."

She repeated, "Are you sure everything is alright?" Did she know he talked to the Jesus on the cross in the hall sometimes? He was about to confess everything when at that very moment a blessed "ding" sound came from his computer in the office. Saved by the bell! The email from Kristen had arrived.

He was suddenly glad that he didn't tell her, for he realised she would probably have divorced him when she realised she was married to a complete nutcase.

Faustus gave his wife a quick kiss. "I'm fine," he said, "Go back to reading your book. I was just waiting for an email."

She nodded doubtfully, "Alright, okay."

He rushed into his office and checked his email.

> From: Petronia Parnassus
>
> To: George Faustus
>
> Hi George
>
> Can you phone Kristen Solo?
>
> He's actually expecting your call now.

There was some sort of link at the bottom of the email. He wondered what to do with it?

His mobile phone rang.

It was Petronia. "George? Click on the link."

Still holding the mobile to his ear, Faustus clicked on the link and Kristen Solo appeared in some sort of app.

Petronia said, “Now turn off mute. It’s that little thing that looks like a microphone with a line through it, at the bottom of the screen. Click that. Then try talking into the mic.”

He managed to find the mute and turned it off, then spoke into the podcasting mic, “Hello?”

Kristen answered, “Hello?”

Petronia said, “Good night,” and the call ended.

In the video, Faustus could see that Kristen was in a fairly modest home office with a view over the ocean in San Diego.

Faustus said rather hastily, “Hi... You’re Kristen Solo? Jerry gave me the link. He said you found something - er-interesting - in the genome of the Birdflip Coronavirus.”

Kristen spoke in a calm but sombre way, “I did. Jerry gave me your email. Are you on your computer?”

Faustus replied, “Yes.”

Kristen said, “I’ll send you something.”

Faustus’s email dinged. He quickly opened it up on his computer. The email had nothing, no title, just an attachment. Faustus opened up the attachment.

It was a sort of graph, with numbers at the top and coloured squares, and Faustus recognised it immediately — it was a chart showing some sort of a genome.

"Got it. It's a genome," he said, quite proud that he'd recognised what it was.

Kristen said, "It's two genomes; look at the bottom of the picture, they're vertically aligned."

Faustus said, "They're almost the same."

Kristen nodded. "The bottom genome is 'BB18+,' a virus which ZhengLeng Penguin — the WooHoo bird woman — sampled from a Red-footed Booby's nest in Bu-bi Province in 2013 after several bigheaded carp fisherman died of a SARS-like avian coronavirus."

Faustus said, "What, they were carp fishermen with big heads? That made them particularly susceptible to the virus, I suppose?"

"No," said Kristen, sighing like Jerry usually did when talking to him. "Bighead carp are a type of fish. And before you ask, Red-footed Booby's are birds. And the Bu-bi province is some kind of administrative district at the top part of the port city of Ba-bi. Nothing to do with the boobies that are the birds, either. No, I'm telling you about two genomes, Faustus, please concentrate. The bottom genome is the virus from the Red-footed Boobies, from the town of Babi. The genome directly above that one is the BirdFlip Coronavirus, the virus that is raging through the cities of the world and causing our governments so much consternation."

Faustus still wasn't sure what Kristen was getting at so he simply said, "The coronavirus," to show that he understood.

Kristen nodded vigorously. "Yes," he said. "The Coronavirus. The one that supposedly came from a Penguin in the WooHoo seafood market. George, I can tell you, it didn't. You know what I'm saying."

"No. NO, NO, NO. That can't be," said Faustus.

"Now, look, it's obvious, Dr Faustus, just have a look at it: I used Ensemble to plot the two genomes, to pinpoint the correspondences. The bit at the bottom plots the similarities and differences between the genome of '2019-Penguin' and that of 'BB18+.' Have a look."

Faustus looked more carefully. Oh my God. They were almost exactly the same. Except for a bit in the middle that looked like it was spliced in.

Kristen said, "They're the same. Exactly the same. Except for the Furin cleavage site."

Faustus said, “Kristen, forgive my ignorance, but I’m not a virologist. What is a Furine cleavage site?”

Kristen said, “Doctor Faustus —”

Faustus said, “Call me George —”

Kristen said, “George - you know what the Spike protein is?”

Faustus said, “The S Protein. I know it’s an important part of the virus. It bonds to the ACE2 receptors.”

Kristen said, “That’s right. To bond to a human cell - or any cell - the virus needs a protein on its surface that can do that. Think of the ACE2 molecule as a lock — and the Spike protein as the key. Well, most virus keys don’t work so well. The key is not an exact match to the lock. Especially from animal viruses. You see, the ACE2 receptor in a penguin is different from that in human, and they’re different from the ACE2’s in a monkey, and the one in a monkey is different from the one in a Pigeon or a Booby, etcetera, etcetera, you get the idea. Now this - ‘BB18+’- was a Red-footed Booby virus - now if a virus has a key to the Red-footed Booby ACE2 receptor cell, of course it won’t work too well for a human ACE2 receptor.”

Kristen paused for dramatic effect, like a lecturer giving a lecture to freshmen.

"George," Kristen asked, "What would you do, to recut a key so it fits a different door?"

George said, "You'd have to take one of the teeth out. Or add something in. Change the shape of the key."

Kristen nodded approvingly. "Exactly. The Furin cleavage site is right in the middle of the Spike protein. And it's an exact match - 12 bases - to a site right in the middle of the human ACE2 receptor. In reverse, the mirror image of the ACE2 protein, so it fits perfectly.

Faustus said defensively, "Well. That could happen in nature," feeling certain that Kristen was about to say it couldn't.

Kristen nodded in a way that looked more like he was shaking his head quite violently. "It could," he said. "I guess. But look at the rest of the sequence."

Faustus shrugged. "Nothing wrong with it that I can see."

Kristen shook his head. "I plotted the correspondences at the top. See where all the N's are - they're the only bits that don't match. Everything else is a <u>hundred percent match</u>. How does that happen in nature? A complete match."

Faustus said, "What's wrong with that?"

Kristen said, "It shouldn't. The randomness should be spread roughly evenly. How long does it take the Furin cleavage site to splice in, naturally? We don't know. But what we do know is that something like that doesn't happen instantaneously. One bit of the genome evolved, into an insertion for God's sake, and the rest of it didn't, it's completely the same as the other. George, how does this happen in nature? You'd expect to see the mutations here and there, sort of randomly scattered about. Selection, mutations, randomness, and something that matches the human ACE2 protein, like a key matches a lock, but only in *one part of the virus*. And it's not just a few nucleotides, George, it's 12 bases." And he looked George in the eye, from the other side of the computer screen. "How did those nucleobases get in there if no one put them in there?"

Faustus' heart sank. "You're telling me it's definitely a genetically engineered virus," he said.

Kristen said, "I'm telling you it couldn't be anything else. It's the Red-footed Booby virus, with a perfect key to the human ACE2 receptor spliced in smack bang in the middle."

Faustus said, "Then where did it come from?"

Kristen said, "The WooHoo lab. Zheng-Leng Penguin. Where else would it have come from? They're the ones who say they found 'BB18+,' Booby-18+, and shared the genome: it's supposedly the source of the Birdflip Coronavirus. And you know they've been doing gain of function. They admit it in their papers, publicly posted in the journals. And they're working with a biosecurity level 2 lab, half the time anyhow, it's the Wild West, George, out there, they're very slack. And Ralph Bar-tailed Godwit— at Chapel Chump. His papers are full of gain of function research. He's the king of avian virus gain of function, bird flu, bird coronaviruses, for God's sake, George. It's all there for anybody to read on the NHIJ ClubMed database."

Faustus stammered, "I didn't know. I - I had no idea, Kristen."

Kristen spoke softly and calmly, "I'm trying to help you George. It's fine, you can keep up the plausible deniability as much as you like, but I'm telling you, the Furin cleavage site is what worries me. It worries me. It's about as well optimised for using the human ACE2 as an entry point as it could possibly be. On what's supposed to be a Red-footed Booby virus."

Shit. It escaped from the lab. Faustus's mind was reeling. He swore three times.

Kristen continued, "And they made it to be highly transmissible."

Faustus said, "Highly contagious. Friggin frig."

Kristen said, "And deadly." Oh my God, this could kill millions, thought Faustus. What am I going to do? Kristen repeated, "Deadly."

Faustus' breaths suddenly came in short gasps and he realised he was hyperventilating; he said, "You must be wrong, Kristen. This can't be right."

Kristen looked perturbed in the image on the screen. "Look, I've got to go. I've got to put the kids to bed - if I don't do it tonight, I don't think my marriage will last much longer than a few more days if I don't."

Faustus zoned out for a moment, staring into space rather worryingly to Kristen, who said, "Are you alright?"

But Faustus came to himself, checked his own pulse at the neck and though, Well at least I'm not having a heart attack. Then he said, "Is this really what you think?"

Kristen said, "It is. Look, I've got to go. Good night. Jerry Blacksmith says he is going to organise something. He's very reliable. Don't stress."

Defensive and angry, Faustus snapped, "I'm not stressing. You must be wrong. That's all there is to it, Kristen. You must be wrong."

Kristen said, "Well, *don't* stress. This is what I think and that's that. Take it a day at a time. I have to go, Doctor Faustus. I need to go and say goodnight to my kids."

Faustus suddenly found himself in the middle of a rant, "Well if you really think this is the case then as soon as you can you and Shamrock Holmes should get some evolutionary virologists together to examine the RNA sequence to work out if this really is something about which we should be concerned. And you should do this right friggin now and if everyone friggin agrees, you should be friggin reporting it to the authorities, the FIB in the US and the MI5 in the UK, as well as the CIA, NSA, " — and Faustus' voice was rising to a hysterical pitch of high frenzy as he listed all the authorities that would have to be informed — "MI6, ASIO, ASIS, ASD, AGO, DIO, CFINTCOM, CSE, CSIS, RCMP, DDIS, GCSB, NZSIS, DI, GCHQ, SIS, DIA, NGO, and the NGA? That's what we should be friggin doing!!!!!"

Kristen looked a little taken aback. He said, "Just say the word, George."

Faustus said, "What word? You mean, you're saying we *should* report it?"

Kristen said, "You know, friggin this and friggin that is just... it's lame. Just say the word. If you're going to swear, George, say the actual word."

Somehow this just irritated Faustus even more, and he gave what was meant to be a growl but ended up being an impotent sort of sound, a sort of kitten growl, and added, "I'll not say whatever word I want to not say," and clenched his fists together even more impotently.

Kristen expelled a lung-full of air and said, "Look. Good night George. Good night. I'm going to put the children to bed. Good night."

Faustus slammed his hand on the table, then opened up the email app on his computer and typed an email angrily.

> From: George Faustus
>
> To: Jerry Blacksmith
>
> Jerry. I just got off a call with Kristen Solo and he told me about his concern about the Furine cleavage site in the spike protein of the currently circulating Birdflip-CoV.
>
> I told him, Jerry. I told him if he really thinks it is man-made and the Furine site was spliced in that he and Shamrock Holmes should quickly get a team of evolutionary virologists together to examine the RNA sequence carefully and to work out if this

really is something about which we should be concerned, or just something up with which we shall not put. I just wanted to emphasize that they should do this right now and if everyone agrees, it should be reported to the appropriate authorities, that is, the FIB in the US and the MI5 in the UK, as well as the CIA, NSA, MI6, ASIO, ASIS, ASD, AGO, DIO, CFINTCOM, CSE, CSIS, RCMP, DDIS, GCSB, NZSIS, DI, GCHQ, SIS, DIA, NGO, and the NGA? We need to quickly get confirmation that it really is a virus that was created in the lab, from

Meanwhile I intend to alert the US authorities of my chat with you and Kristen to find out what further actions / inquiries / probes/ scrutiny needs to happen next.

Let's keep in touch,

Most excellent regards,

George

Faustus hit the desk again and it made an even louder sound this time and he suddenly realised he had probably woken up his wife. Sure enough, her plaintive voice emerged from the bedroom, "Are you alright George?"

Faustus said, "I'm fine dear."

Gloriana said, "Well it's time to come to bed."

He looked at the clock. It was after midnight. He glanced at the screen. He was too tired to continue. He decided to go to bed. "Alright, alright, I'm coming."

He suddenly thought of Hugo "Ouchy" Stoneyfield, his deputy, and realised he had to notify him.

> To: Hugo Stoneyfield
>
> Ouchy!
>
> Be ready: you'll have many important things to do tomorrow and you need to keep your phone nearby, and keep it turned on.
>
> Yours
>
> George Faustus

He finally realised he couldn't do any more. Everything was in place, as well as he could manage it. It was time for bed.

~~~

All the conditions were right for sleeping. Gloriana was sound asleep, breathing quietly regularly, their mobiles were charging next to the bed, not making disturbing sounds and not lit up at all, the screens were blank as they charged, and the bed was warm and comfortable, and the wind wasn't howling and there were no storm or thunder clouds outside or strange street noises and not even any distant sirens or gunshots or car engines backfiring or people revving their engines, just a comforting gentle wisp of a breeze occasionally blowing the curtains, but despite all these reasons why he should be able to sleep, Faustus couldn't
~~~

sleep. Instead he was lying in his pajamas, staring at the ceiling, feeling greatly stressed, and he had descended into the ignominious task of counting the number of petals and leaves on the ceiling rose above their bed. It was tortuous, completely tortuous, and he felt as though he would rather sit in the audience listening to the Threnody for the Victims of Hiroshima by Penderecki, one of his most un-favourite pieces, a piece that he had been forced to listen to more than once in some official function as the head of NAIAD, that he immediately regretted thinking about, because now that piece of music started going through his head, or at least a half-conscious semi-rendition of it, with all its screeches and squawks and clanging notes and dissonances and that made his insomnia even worse. Ironically, he was drifting off into a dream about that music when his mobile phone suddenly made an email arrival ding, interrupting Penderecki and his slowly increasing Delta wave sleep. He read the email then made a mental note to remember it, then drifted back into thoughts of Penderecki and the corridors of some hospital or other that he had done his internship in long, long ago.

Suddenly, sunlight was streaming through the windows; Faustus had fallen asleep after all. He felt as though it was just moments ago that he had been thinking about Penderecki, but obviously it was a few hours at least.

Gloriana was not in bed. Her mobile was not there, she was already up and her side of the bed had been made.

He began getting out of bed, and looked at his mobile. There was something nagging at him — something he had to remember...

Oh, that's right! The email. That conference call was today at 3pm.

He checked his emails again on his mobile and found the email.

From: Jerry Blacksmith

Sent: Saturday February 1, 5:50AM

To: George Faustus

George,

Are you able to join the teleconference?

I'm attempting to set up an initial call with

Kristen Solo
Barry A. Gog
Frostey Kristoff
George Faustus
Renard Fourier
Shamrock Holmes
Minorka Hennerys
Poltrik D. Vallee Chief Scientist UK

Time zones make this a bit of a challenge

Suggested times below - today 1st February (2nd February for Shamrock) - I will confirm that everybody is on board later today.

George, if you cannot make it, we will phone you afterwards to update.

7am Sydney

9pm CET

8pm GMT

3pm EST

10am West Coast

The main purpose of this call will be to listen to the work Shamrock, Bob and Kristen have done.

To query it.

And to think through what we must do next.

And remember: what goes on the teleconference call, stays in the teleconference call. To put it rather bluntly, after we have talked, put a padlock on your lips and throw away the key.

Kind regards,

Jerry

Faustus ejected a sudden gasp of horror; he noticed that Jerry had got the California time zone wrong. He'd have to email him right away.

Faustus hauled himself out of bed; for anyone younger it might have seemed slow but at his age, rather hastily indeed, making big thumps and bumps with his feet as he plonked them into his slippers, put his dressing gown on and ran out of the room.

From the kitchen came Gloriana's voice, echoing through the hallway, "Are you alright, dear?"

"Yes, of course," he said rather testily. "Thank you for caring, dear," he added, just to keep in the good books. He heard a "hmph" come from the kitchen and he realised he had better get in there quickly, because he was clearly in the dog house.

He jumped onto the computer chair, started the infernal contraption up, then found he was tapping the rhythm of the Penderecki with his pen while the computer screen warmed up, laughed at the private pun that Penderecki starts with the word "pen", then the windows startup sequence finished and the password field finally appeared, then he put in his password, opened the email app, found the email from Jerry, and wrote a quick reply telling him that he had the wrong time down for California's time zone, and then sighed.

It felt like he had done a whole day's work already.

He heard dishes clattering from the kitchen, and he realised that it wasn't bacon and eggs, but humble pie that he'd be eating for breakfast.

"Oh, well," he said to himself, and went along to make amends. As he passed Jesus in the hallway, he looked up and said to him, "You don't know what you were missing out on, not being married."

~~~

Less than an hour later, Faustus was walking along the main corridor at Bethesda with Petronia, giving her instructions. "Oh, and contact VLPS news. Organise a short interview for this morning."

Petronia blurted, "How on earth are we going to fit it —"

Faustus interrupted her with a wave of his hand, "Just delay that call with Tedboss till after lunch. Get them to do the interview here in one of the conference room. And that teleconference call is this afternoon. At 3pm. Move everything else around it, and make sure I have some privacy."

Petronia was writing in her notebook, and said, "3pm. What about Tedboss? When do we —"
~~~

He gave another hand-wave and said, "Oh, tell him I'll talk to him tomorrow."

Petronia said, "Alright. The highest priority."

Faustus said, "The highest!" Then he looked her in the eyes, probably for the first time the whole morning. "I don't know how I'm going to get through today, Petronia. I hardly slept a wink."

She put her hand on his arm and patted it, and said comfortingly, "Of course you will. You always do."

In the conference room, a VLPS News worker was finishing setting up a green screen, a table and some chairs. The table and chairs had been moved to one end of the conference room, the green screen was at the other end.

A large screen TV attached to a computer was set up on it's own stand, next to a television camera and the cameraman, who was adjusting the height and the angle of the camera, and fiddling with some buttons on the side.

The VLPS worker said, "A chair? What chair would you like Mr Faustus?"

It often irritated him when nobodies didn't use his proper title. He said, "That's Doctor Faustus actually. Petronia?"

Petronia pointed to one of the chairs and said, "That one." Then as the man went over to get it, she said confidentially to George, "You should treat the TV station workers well: they can make you look really bad, with just the wrong angle or the wrong exposure on the picture."

George said, "You know you're right." As the VLPS worker brought the chair over, George touched him on the arm and said, "Sorry, son, I... woke up on the wrong side of the bed. I don't want you to think I don't appreciate everything you do." The man nodded and blinked at him like a raccoon suddenly caught in torchlight, but George felt a glow of satisfaction: it felt good, making the nobodies feel appreciated, it felt really good.

Brent Braekel, the VLPS, came in and sat down, and after the preliminaries, shaking hands, introductions, the makeup lady came in and applied some makeup to Faustus' cheeks and brushed his temples. He sneezed, than Braekel said, "Ready?" and Faustus nodded, then while he was still saying to himself, "I am the Science, I am the Science," the cameraman said, "Rolling," and Braekel was giving the introduction.

"Today we're going to get inside the mind of a great expert on the Birdflip Coronavirus, Dr. George Faustus. He is the director of the National Allergy and Infectious Academy of Diseases, that we like to call, NAIAD. We're broadcasting to you today from Bethesda, Maryland. Dr. Faustus, thanks for sacrificing some of your precious time to inform the viewers, in what must be a very busy day."

Faustus said, "Brent, it's great to be here, believe me."

Braekel turned to him and said, "What's the latest news on this Birdflip virus? The latest I heard there were six confirmed cases in the U.S. affecting four states, Arizona, Washington, Oklahoma, and California. But I guess there must be other people that you're monitoring, who might have the virus?"

Faustus responded, "So, that there might be travel related cases, when you consider the vast number of flights every day from China, especially those coming from the WooHoo district, is not something we didn't expect.

"And the data emphasizes that the CDE response has been efficient and effective because the six index cases have been identified and those individuals have been isolated. And as you mentioned quite correctly, we are tracing contacts to ensure that there has been no secondary transmission.

"So, at this point, even if our hospitals don't have enough respirators to handle the influx of deadly cases, I wouldn't worry, as there's no there's no evidence yet that we're at the beginning of a mass transmission of a deadly pandemic that's going to kill everybody on the earth with violent respiratory symptoms, breathlessness, vomiting, paroxysms in the street, then death with extreme prejudice. I wouldn't be too surprised if we actually are, but as yet there's no data proving that the individuals with whom these five individuals came in contact were infected, which is good news if you want to take it that way — so long as there's not asymptomatic transmission of course that we wouldn't pick up until it's too late — let me reiterate, it's good news, because it means all the CDE, NAIAD, NHIJ and all the other unmentioned-who-might-be-involved-lettered-agency's efforts at controlling this virus were effective. Let me add, effective but not safe and effective, which is what a vaccine would be if we had one."

Braekel asked him then, "So what does the average Joe Blow need to know? Should people be worried about getting on a plane and travelling round the country? There's a whole lot of fear out there in the population about this thing. Are they justified to be worried? What do they need to know?

Faustus said, "I'd say yes, it is understandable — they need to be concerned. But in my opinion the people of the

United States — the American people should tell themselves that the risk at this moment in the US is not high at all. It's an evolving situation, and people who want to fly somewhere in the US shouldn't worry. And yes, there are indeed travel warnings about going to WooHoo in particular and China in general, but that's to ensure that people don't take unnecessary trips; essential travel to those areas only.

"So on the one hand I'm saying to the general public, don't worry your empty little heads about it, be reassured, everything is okay, but on the other hand we health officials are objectively treating this as the kind of existential threat to humanity that could turn into an outbreak that gets out of control and escapes China and kills us all in a horrible, horrible way, with lots of gurgling and coughing up blood and spluttering breathlessly followed by projectile vomiting and painful spasms, which are the death throes of the BirdFlip coronavirus, and that's a possibility we're all buying into, but again I say to you, don't worry. I'm hoping it doesn't turn into the kind of global death plague that could kill us all, but you know, we have to treat this as a distinct possibility if we're taking Science with a capital S perfectly seriously, which we are, I am taking Science with a capital seriously, especially when I look in the mirror every morning.

"As you may have heard, the Chinese government *is* taking it seriously as well, shutting down a city with thirty five million people in it. Shutting down a city the size of WooHoo is something we'd never be able to do in the United States, because we simply don't have any cities that large, the biggest we have is about eight million, but they're doing it there — and as you know, lockdowns probably don't work, so it is most likely that they are all doomed — so I'm hoping locking down WooHoo helps but I doubt that it will. You know, they're all doomed."

Braekel looked shocked and took a moment to recover his composure, then he said, "So, it's a lot like the influenza, only it presents a little more.... extreme?

Faustus replied, "Well, like influenza it is an aerosol borne respiratory virus, but it does not appear to spread as readily as the flu. You know when you do get large influenza outbreaks, you have millions infected. This Birdflip Coronavirus could evolve to be far more readily transmissible — you're talking about anywhere from seasonal influenza to a full blown civilisation destroying contagion more deadly than Ebola — we just need to keep a close eye on things and make sure that we don't have a mortal, virulent, uncontrollable disease on our hands, Brent, and the important thing to remember is that there is a great deal that we don't really know.

"For instance we don't know what we health bureaucrats and epidemiologists like to call R0, or Rho-Ho, or in other words, it is what we also call the index of deadly transmissibility. If one person gets sick, how many people do they infect? Zero? One? Five? Fifty? Everyone in a five mile area? If you get up to a Rho-Ho index of just three or four, Brent, that's really bad, that's what we like to call a Rho-Ho-Ho-Ho. Right now we know if one person is infected in China, they infect between 1.5 and 3.23 people. That effectively means that the fourth person is only 0.23 infected, which is a mild infection, but the others have a full infection[5]. We'd prefer that the index of transmissibility was less than one, in other words, when someone gets infected, they pass on only a partial infection to someone else. In this way, the virus would be over in no time at all, although there will still be cases where a person might be, say, 1% infected

[5] Real scientists have questioned this assertion; indeed they have called it a highly shaky assumption that someone can be only 0.23 or 23% infected. They would rather be more cautious in their assertions; indeed, a proper scientist would say that there would be a range involved, of uncertainty, such that a person could be 0.21-0.25 infected, and leave it at that.

or some fraction of 1%, it's an exponential decrease, in that case; a bit like Zeno's paradox, really, we never reach the finish line.

"The question is, is the BirdFlip Coronavirus as bad as the pandemic influenzas of the past, in 1918, the swine flu? Obviously it isn't. Not quite yet. But could it get there? We can't rule that out. For God's sake Brent it could get even worse than the 1918 pandemic, billions and billions of people could die, and that's why we're taking this very, very seriously, Brent. Let me emphasize: very, very, *very* seriously."

Braekel said, "So you're saying anyone who has travelled to China is an existential threat to humanity? Is there anything at else that people like us who thank God *haven't* travelled to China can do to prevent this dreadful, frightening contagion from spreading among Americans and killing us all?"

Faustus said, "Well we are screening everyone who's been on a plane travelling from South East Asia. When they come into the airport the customs authorities take their temperature reading (usually an oral reading is enough but, you know, sometimes they have to go for rectal, which can be quite uncomfortable for the person involved; it's something that's not always acknowledged among health authorities.) Then when they're feeling vulnerable and violated you question them and find out if they had contact with any possible cases, individuals who were in the area, people from WooHoo or China as a whole. You know, it's what I like to call normal, careful public health practises.

"And I think that's this whole thing all over, Brent — the CDE and the NAIAD and the State and Federal authorities have made an adequate — let me emphasize, *adequate,* health response, to the six people who were confirmed as infected with the BirdFlip Coronavirus who travelled from WooHoo.

"So long as we keep listening to the CDE advisories and health alerts, which they're disseminating very efficiently to the local government health authorities, so everyone can be aware that there might be a possibility someone could come into the surgery with a deadly, highly infectious BirdFlip Coronavirus that might kill everybody within five miles within minutes... So if they have symptoms, say a slightly high temperature or a sniffle, you immediately ask them, 'did you recently travel from China?'"

Braekel thanked Faustus for his time, Faustus acknowledged his thanks, and the interview was over.

Petronia met him back in his office where he was recovering a few minutes later and said, “Good interview. Well done, Doctor Faustus. I ordered the usual for lunch.”

Faustus felt out of sorts; his back was sore from sitting in one place for so long and he didn’t feel much like doing anything; the interview had really taken it out of him. He felt like he was letting Petronia down, because it would only increase her workload and the headaches of rescheduling, but he realised he was not going to be any use for the rest of the day, at least, not until the teleconference was over. “Do you know, I’m going to go home, and do that conference call in my office there.”

Petronia said, “I thought you might: I already rescheduled most of your appointments today, just in case. Alright. I’ll get Frank to take you home and I’ll get your lunch Uber’d to you then.”

Frank; that’s right, that was the driver’s name. “Don’t bother Ubering the lunch,” Faustus said, “There’ll be some leftovers in the fridge.”

Petronia shook her head and said disapprovingly, “Make sure you eat something. I have a feeling that conference call is going to take it out of you.”

He grumbled a little but he appreciated her solicitude and concern. He stood up from his chair and she put his coat on. Faustus said, “Thank you Petronia, it’s been a long morning.”

Petronia said, “Tell me how the teleconference goes.”

Faustus replied, “Alright. I will.”

Petronia said, “Mind that you do. Take care of yourself, George. The whole country — the whole world, maybe — is relying on you.”

CHAPTER 3

Solitude

As soon as Faustus got home he immediately regretted taking the day off. Gloriana wasn't home, and the house was cold, silent and solitary without her, and he had nothing to do except mope around and worry.

He soon found himself at the computer looking through the studies Jerry had sent out; and there were more of them now on the list.

Gain-of-function studies. It was undeniable that these were gain of function, but he comforted himself that so long as he denied *knowing* that they were gain of function, no one could get him for anything.

What if they interviewed him in Congress? The penalty for lying to Congress — was it five or six years in prison? — he didn't think he could survive incarceration at his age.

He looked out the window. It was a grey, ugly day; the sun was barely shining and the twigs on the bare trees reminded him of the Blair Witch Project. He looked back at the computer screen; at least this was *science.* It was something objective, something verifiable. He should look at those studies again, in detail, and see if there really was anything that really was undeniable gain of function research, anything truly incriminating.

Soon he was scrolling through one of the studies on PubMed; it was the third one on the list:

BirdFlip-like WOOHOO1-CoV poised for human emergence when we release it[6].

Faustus was reading through the abstract, scrolling through very, very slowly.

> Outbreaks from zoonotic zoo animals as well as zoonotic biological entities in the wild such as birds and bats represent a threat to both human disease (by which we mean, an outbreak of a bird coronavirus like this could completely replace diseases such as influenza, severely harming the medical industry) as well as the global economy, by which we mean the pharmaceutical industry, positively. Despite an immeasurable wealth of

[6] Like all the studies mentioned in this book this is definitely not gain of function, I repeat, *definitely* not gain of function and is a real study that may be accessed on the interschmet, honestly, here is the proper academic citation, do *not* try to recreate this study at home or in a BSL 2 lab please:
Discreet V Moneypenny, Dick Sissell Junior the Ninth, Amy Kestrel, Carrie Cassowary, Subhacker Agniballistic Missile, Rachel Grey-Crestedtit, Trevor Scoter, Jess E Goatsucker, Scott H Cuckoo, Jessica N A Tree, Timothy P Shrikethrush, Raymond Pickles Quail Eggs, David E Cormorant, Scott H Brambling, Antonio Macaroni Penguinson, Wayne A Mallard, Ralph Bar-tailed Godwit **BirdFlip-like WOOHOO1-CoV poised for human emergence when we release it** *Proceedings of the National Sciences Group That Definitely Doesn't Do Gain Of Function Research* 113, no. 11 (2016): 3048-3053. https://ncbi.naiad.nhi.gov/clubmed/006006006/

metagenomics studies, metamicrovirological studies and studies on Meta, methods to leverage these fantastic datasets of viruses that we created to identify future threats suffer from great paucity if they are not completely emaciated. In this study, we describe an approach that combines existing metagenomics data with reverse genetics — that is not gain of function, I repeat, not gain of function — to engineer reagents to evaluate emergence and pathogenic potential of circulating zoonotic viruses that we created to see if they would be really deadly if we accidentally or on purpose let them loose or they escaped from the lab, quite by mistake. Focusing on the severe acute respiratory syndrome (Birdflip)-like viruses, our results indicate quite literally that the WOOHOO1-Coronavirus (CoV) cluster has the ability to directly infect and may undergo drastic transmission in human populations, killing everyone and directly impacting the future viability of the human species. However, in vivo studies suggest additional adaptation is required for epidemic disease, i.e. the type of research that we intend to do and have already done although we are not mentioning that research in this study. Note that if we don't do this, the Chinese probably will. Importantly, our patented BirdFlip monoclonal antibodies succeeded in limiting viral infection without even using any vaccines at all, so that's great: this doesn't deny that if we had vaccines it would be even better. Together, the data highlight the usefulness of this kind of research to identify and prioritize prepandemic strains harbored in avian reservoirs in the lab, that might get loose from the lab where we're studying them, and this enables us to document the threat posed by WOOHOO1-CoV for emergence in human populations.

Well, he thought to himself, nothing *too* incriminating in the abstract, anyhow; I mean it explicitly says it's *not* gain of function research.

Faustus started scrolling through the paper.

Then his eye fell on a particular word and he gasped: Cherubic. He had been right. They were talking about cute, little angels. Amazing. Cherubic viruses. What did it mean?

He looked at the word again.

No he had misread it, it wasn't cherubic, it was:

Chimeric!

He gasped.

Chimeric viruses. They were making chimeric viruses.

Extending our analysis to pathogenesis we evaluated in vivo infection of various strains in the usual BALB/c pigeons as well in Dr. Bar-tailed Godwit's transgenic humanised ACE2 pigeons. After this, we created a chimeric virus that replaced the WOOHOO1 spike protein in the BirdFlip SARS-CoV Urbani strain with the humanised ACE2 pigeon-adapted backbone. Robust stock tiers were obtained, and the pigeons were infected with the chimeric virus, to see if it was more transmissible or more deadly than the virus without the WOOHOO1 spike protein. Our aim is to begin testing WOOHOO1 spike protein chimeric viruses on penguins next.

Faustus realised that most of the science in this paragraph was way beyond his ability to comprehend, despite his many scientific qualifications. But the word ‘chimeric’ was troubling. He knew Jerry had told him, but he hadn’t quite worked out what Jerry meant by “two species”. Were dogs and cats chimeric? Elephants and alligators? He had absolutely no clue. What was the relationship between the two chimeric species?

He reflected on the fact that he sometimes... often... didn’t quite comprehend what his fellow scientists were talking about. It hardly affected his position. Well, to tell the truth, the key to his success, the one thing he had learned, was, when you don't know what they're talking about, keep your mouth shut. Keep your ignorance to yourself. That was Faustus' golden rule.

Faustus had just recently learned to use a search engine called 'google,' so he navigated to the internet app and typed in, "Chimeric definition", and the web spat out a website containing the following paragraph:

> CHIMERIC: A chimera is an individual whose body is composed of cells that come from two or more distinct individuals. In the area of virology, a chimera or chimeric virus is a virus that contains genetic material from two or more distinct viruses.

Faustus did a search for "Chimera virus wiki" and found a page on that said:

> A CHIMERA OR CHIMERIC VIRUS is a virus that contains genetic material derived from two or more distinct viruses. The CDE defines a chimera as a "new hybrid microorganism created by joining DNA or RNA strands from two or more different microorganisms."

Then he started reading through the research paper again, and came to this section:

> To test a model more relevant to human infectivity, we generated a penguin expressing human ACE2

> receptors under the direction of HFH4, a lung ciliated epithelial cell promoter, using Dr Ralph Bar-tailed Godwit's methods. Robust ACE2 expression was observed in the lung, but other tissues such as the brain, liver, kidney, and gastrointestinal tract also had detectable levels of human ACE2 expression, indicating that HFH4 was distributed throughout the body. After this, we tested the chimeric viruses on the H-ACE2/HFH4 expressing penguins.

Faustus gasped. They really were creating transgenic animals, that contained human genes and human ACE2 receptors. He knew this much: ACE2 receptors were all through the body.

And on these animals with human genes, they were testing chimeric viruses that were *infectious to humans,* at least to the genes they'd put in the penguins. If this wasn't gain of function, what was?

He said to himself, "Was that one of the ones we funded... or did we?" And he scrolled down to the bottom of the paper, to the Acknowledgements section, and a particular phrase jumped out at him.

ACKNOWLEDGMENTS.

> We thank Dr. Zheng-Leng Penguin of the WooHoo Institute of Virology for access to pigeon, penguin and pangolin CoV sequences and plasmid of WIV1-

> CoV spike protein. Research was supported by the National Allergy and Infectious Academy of Diseases (NAIAD) and the National Presidential Institute of Dementia and Aging of the NHIJ under Awards U19AI006006006 and U19AI10678910 (to Ralph Bar-tailed Godwit.), AI10854321 (to Wayne A Mallard), and F32AI022022 and K99AG17018037 (to Discreet V Moneypenny). Human airway epithelial cell cultures were supported by the National Institute of Diabetes and Digestive Disorders and Disease under Award NIH DK0000023 (to Scott H Cuckoo.). Support for the generation of the penguins expressing human ACE2 was provided by NIH Grants AI037037 and AI023037 (to Subhacker Agniballistic Missile.)

He felt himself sinking into a deep hole of depression and despair as he opened up one of the other studies to look at it.

Then, suddenly, his computer dinged: an email had arrived.

> From: Jerry Blacksmith
>
> Sent: Saturday February 1, 2020, 1:57PM
>
> To: George Faustus
>
> Teleconference
>
> 1st February (2nd Feb for Shamrock)

Information and discussion is shared in total confidence and not to be shared until agreement on next steps.

Dial in details attached.

Please mute phones.

I will be on email throughout - email Paul or I Paul if any problems.

If you cannot make it, I will phone you afterwards to update

Here's the link to the teleconference. Click on it, it will open.

https://us02web.zoom.us/j/927584935710?pwd=BMWAT4tqT70RE5xTDRpRc2tzaTVZmwU9

Faustus clicked on the link and the teleconference window opened.

CHAPTER 4

To be Frank...

Frank, the guy who drove Faustus around in the government SUV, had a rare reprieve that afternoon, because Petronia had cancelled all of Faustus' appointments for the rest of the day.

He was fortunate in that Faustus had given him authorisation to take the SUV limo home nights and use it for his family's running around; it would have been unlikely that he could have even done this job otherwise — (well, Petronia, really, was the one he should be thankful for: she had organised it; Faustus had simply signed the form) — it was one of the few benefits.

Of course it *had* come at a cost: Faustus had insisted that Frank be available any time of night or day at an hour's notice, a commitment which had impinged significantly on his family life. To be frank[7], sometimes it was just as bad as

[7] or more accurately, "to be *Frank*" with a capital *F*; this was an expression Frank often used with his close buddies and family, a running joke that began in the army after a particularly brutal attack by a Mujahadeen who shot a 9K32 Strela-2 surface to air missile at his truck at close range, and it completely totalled his truck. Geoff, the other truck driver just behind him, another man in his platoon, on seeing the wrecked truck, and thinking Frank was a complete goner, that he must have been killed or maimed, had called out to him, "Frank, are you okay?" Frank had replied,"To be frank, no. My truck is completely f—ed," and then he had added, "I'm okay, though." Geoff had laughed hysterically with relief. It turned out that a piece of shrapnel had pierced Frank's thigh, but it wasn't a serious wound, but from then on, "to be frank" became a running joke with the guys.

being in the army stationed overseas, for the amount of time he got to see his wife Linda, and Madeley, his eight-year-old daughter.

He drove home that day and he knew that Linda would already be home from work when he got there, probably relaxing in the garden with an iced tea and eating something healthy, an apple, maybe. Frank was glad he was early, because it meant he could give Linda a break today by picking up Madeley from school — Linda worked as a baker at CupCakes Galore, a large bakery that did wedding and birthday cakes as well as cup cakes and pastries — Madeley's school finished at 3pm which felt like late in the evening for her mother, because her job at the bakery started at 4am and finished at 1pm.

It was a long drive; at least three quarters of an hour to their home in Laurel, Maryland, from Dr Faustus' place, and Frank enjoyed the drive in summer, because the trees were pretty, but in winter, to be *frank*, it was demoralising, what with the wet roads, the bare, leafless trees, the grey sky, the persistent drizzling rain, the congested traffic, and especially the DC drivers, who were arrogant, rude, entitled and very unsafe; and that was being charitable. Many of them seemed to think they owned the road and had every right to disobey the road rules. From long practice and the reception of grace, Frank didn't curse drivers who cut in front of him, but he often found himself saying under his breath, "Good driving, buddy," or "You have a special license, do you? That must be because you're *special;*" not intended in a complementary way.

In fact, to be frank, the drivers in DC were worse than the drivers in Afghanistan, who at least were predictably unpredictable. Frank could make this comparison because had been an army truck driver in Afghanistan in the war, during which time he had survived two bombs, three sniper attacks, and even a close range attack with a 9K32 Strela-2 surface to air missile. Thankfully, he had never run any children over while he was there, which was a distinct possibility in a country where roads were bits of dirt conterminous with the bits of dirt that the houses were built on: Afghan kids often ran across in front of cars impulsively and road rules didn't seem to exist; he'd had a few close calls, though, one where he'd had to veer off into a slight ditch. The two clandestine suits sitting in the back had grumbled, but Frank didn't care. His career wasn't worth the guilt of having run over a child.

He was a good truck driver, and this led to a promotion: driving Generals and dignitaries around. Due to his promotion, Frank was technically stationed at Fort George G Meade, Maryland, but in practice this still meant frequent flights to Afghanistan where he was usually driving officers and Generals and other unnamed suits from NSA or Cyber-Command, like those two clandestine suits; men who often weren't even officially *in* Afghanistan at the time; perhaps this was why Faustus had hired *him* rather than anyone else: his discretion.

Frank knew how to keep his mouth shut, and he did.

That habit was one thing he still had left from his time in the army, but the most precious thing Frank still had, though, was a bunch of close friends, brothers-in-arms, most of whom had left the service around the same time as he did.

After he'd received his discharge papers, he'd been lucky enough to get this job, which meant that he didn't need to leave Laurel, where he and Linda had settled down about two years into his assignment, and where Madeley had been born about eight months after they had bought their first home. They had given her the name Madeley because Frank had booked the pavilion at the lake for the first anniversary of their first date, and because they had figured out *that* particular summer evening was when their daughter must have been conceived, they gave her the name, 'Madeley'; in Old English it meant "meadow by the lake".

God, she was eleven years old, now. Time flies.

Frank pulled into the school carpark; he was about fifteen minutes late because of the DC traffic. Madeley was sitting in the school office, looking out the window, waiting for him. She immediately leaped up, pushed open the door and sprinted out to meet him, sliding her school bag along the asphalt and rocketing into his arms faster than a 9K32 Strela-2 surface to air missile. He caught her and whirled her around in the air, saying, "Here's my sweet darling girl," then squeezed her in a huge bear hug and gave her a kiss on the cheek, as she said, "Here's my sweet darling Dad" into his ear and kissed his stubble quite unashamedly.

Madeley got her school-bag and jumped into the car, and Frank jumped in the other side and wheeled the SUV round and headed for home. Ten minutes later, they were there, and Madeley rushed through the house to the back yard where her mother was lying contentedly on the hammock, drinking her iced tea and reading a book about the history of the American Revolution.

She put her iced tea down on the tree stump that purposed as a table and swung her legs down, as Madeley ran up, crying out, "Mom! Dad picked me up today. Isn't it great?" Her mother hugged and kissed her, and said, "It is great."

Frank walked in and gave Linda a kiss and held her hand and said, "Well, it looks like we've got a night off. What are we gonna do with it?"

Linda winked at him, and he squeezed her hand and winked back. Linda picked up her iced tea and sipped it, so Madeley sat down on the tree-stump and said, "Do you think the BirdFlip virus is going to kill us all?"

Frank said authoritatively, "Well… I was at Dr Faustus' press conference yesterday, and *he* said, no, America is going to be completely safe. So I think Dr Faustus is someone we should listen to, don't you, Madeley?"

And Madeley said, "Yeah. He is head of the NAIAD."

And Linda said, "And what does NAIAD mean?"

Madeley replied with a twinkle in her eye, "National Aeronautics and Space Administration."

Her mother rolled her eyes.

Madeley justified her answer by saying, "Well, that's where Dad *wanted* to work, that's why he joined the army.

Linda said, "Come on, Madeley, you know what it means."

Madeley sighed and admitted, "National Allergy and Infectious Academy of Diseases."

Frank said, "That's right. And if anyone would know, Dr Faustus would know. Wouldn't he?"

Madeley nodded and said, "He's an expert in viruses and pandemics, isn't he?"

And Frank and Linda both nodded.

And Madeley said, "Well, we're all safe then."

CHAPTER 5

The Teleconference...

At first, a blue window with white writing on it appeared on the screen, “Waiting for the host to start this meeting,” then Jerry, the host of the teleconference, let Faustus in and the windows opened up.

Two windows were already open, showing Jerry and Kristen, with their titles below.

Jerry Blacksmith: Director Wellness M.I.S. Trust

Kristen Benander: Professor Immun. and Microbiol., Scripps Research

A small window at the top shows Faustus’s image and had the label:

George Faustus - Head of the NIAID

When the windows opened, Jerry Blacksmith and Kristen Solo were chattering, just small talk, and they stopped talking and Jerry introduced George to Kristen. “Yes, I talked to Kristen for quite a while yesterday,” said George.

One by one other windows opened. Each time another window with a person in it opened, the other people stopped talking and Jerry introduced the newcomer, then the conversation restarted:

Shamrock Holmes: Prof. of Evol. Virol. at the Univ. of Sydney.

Minorca Hennery: head of Erasmus MC Dept. of Virology

Poltrik D. Vallee: Chief Scientific Adv. to the UK Gov.

Clarence Collins: President of NHIJ

Renard Fourier: Dep. head of Erasmus MC Dept. of virol.

Barry A. Gog: Prof. at Tulane Univ. School of Medicine

Frostey Kristoff: Head of Instit. Virol. at Charité Berlin

After introducing Frostey Kristoff, everyone went suddenly quiet and Jerry Blacksmith said, “Right, we’re all here. That’s great. So let’s begin. Thank you to everyone for joining. Thank you especially for making time over a weekend. I do not believe this is a question of achieving a binary outcome. I’ve convened this discussion because we need to stay ahead of the conspiracy theories and social media, and I want to foster an atmosphere of completely open minded and neutral questioning, bringing in the best minds. I make the point once again that information and discussion is shared in total confidence and not to be shared until agreement on next steps. First I'll hand it over to Kristen who has some things to share.

Kristen acknowledged everyone, shared the diagram showing the two genomes, and elucidated his concerns about the during cleavage site and how it was irrefutable evidence the virus was made in a lab.

They were all quite shocked. Everyone on the Zoom call went silent for quite a long time.

Barry Gog was the first to speak. "This is the end of all our careers. They won't be giving any more grants for research into viruses, not ever."

But Renard spoke up. "It's not the end of the world. Yes, millions may die, but the silver lining is, we can save our research. Most of you probably know already that I've been through this already, back in 2011 — when it came out that I had created an airborne version of H5N1 — plausible deniability is the key — admit what they already know but don't admit it was wrong — haha! I even said creating the super transmissible version of H5N1 was 'incredibly stupid' in a press conference — but then I added 'this research is necessary, however, so that we can predict what viruses might develop in the wild. And I'm still here, aren't I? I'm still operating! It really isn't the end of the world."

Then Jerry said, "He's right - it's not all doom and gloom. George has an article to share that may show the way forward."

George Faustus acknowledged Jerry and said, "Hello everybody. If you don't know me, I'm George Faustus. Call me George.

"As you know, we're here to - ah - look into the evolutionary origins of the virus - and to - ah - let us say, contrast that with the possibility that the - ah - coronavirus was a lab leak from Wuhan. Or not contrast it. It might be best not to even mention the second possibility.

Kristen said, In my opinion, George, the evidence states quite clearly that it was. The furin cleavage site is unequivocal — "

Shamrock Holmes agreed vociferously, "Yes, I agree, if that doesn't come from a lab then the Pope's a Catholic."

Poltrik D Vallee said, "I think you meant, 'the Pope's not a Catholic.'"

Shamrock Holmes said, "But that's my point: the Pope *is* a Catholic."

Poltrik D Vallee said, “Yes but you said, if that doesn’t come from a lab then the Pope’s a Catholic, right?”

Shamrock Holmes said, “That’s right: the Pope *is* a Catholic. So if it comes from a lab then the Pope’s a Catholic. If it doesn’t, he still is.”

Poltrik D Vallee blurted out with frustration, “Yes but you got it the wrong way around.”

Shamrock said, “Well let me put it this way: did the virus escape from a lab? Is the Pope a Catholic? Does a bear poop in the woods? Does a pigeon poop in the air?”

Poltrik D Vallee said, “Well that comparison is ridiculous; a pigeon poops on the ground as well.”

Shamrock said, “Well how about this one: How big is the bite from the jaws of a robot pterodactyl with a computer brain?”

Poltrik D Vallee sighed, and said, “I don’t know. How big is robot pterodactyl’s jaws?”

Shamrock said, “A pterabite.”

Poltrik D Vallee cried out, “But what does that have to do with the virus coming from a lab?”

Shamrock said, “It’s really pterrible that it came from the lab.”

Kristen saved the meeting, saying, "Be that as it may, I just want to say that if that sequence was *not* created in a lab, then Dolly Parton sleeps on her back. This furin cleavage site — is completely, obviously spliced in. This virus was made in the lab, and to be perfectly frank, that's what worries me."

Renard Fourier said, "Yeh, looking at that furin cleavage site, it's so obviously a splice. That doesn't happen in nature. Not ever."

Barry Gog said, "Well, honestly, I agree. You realise this is the end of Zheng-Leng Penguin's scientific career, if it escaped from the WooHoo lab."

Minorca nodded and said, "Or Ralph Bar-tailed Godwit's career, more likely. This is *his* research if it's anyone's. Splicing in spike proteins from a different virus, a furin cleavage site — didn't any of you see the grant he put in to DIREPUP[8]? — that's exactly what it was. A furin cleavage site that plugs straight into human ACE2 proteins. This is a disaster. Not just for Ralph Bar-tailed Godwit's career — for everyone's. If it gets out that the WooHoo lab, that we were collaborating with, let loose a virus that we helped create, it won't merely affect Ralph or Zheng-Leng, it

[8] Defense Intelligence REsearch Projects Unit Program

will affect *everyone*. Do you think Congress will be approving *any* grants for experimentation with viruses? And Gain-of-function research will be over."

Renard said, "We don't like using the term Gain-of-Function, Minorca. We would prefer to call it Pandemic Preparedness, or Population Predictive Gene Sequencing, or Preventative virus creation research, or just abot anything. Except for Gain-of-Function. For goodness' sake, it's like saying the word 'insider' to a bunch of stockbrokers."

They all went silent for a long moment, then Kristen said, "Yes, but a rose by any other name would smell as sweet. Or in this case, as fishy. Whatever you call it, you just have to look at the genome. It *is* Gain-of-Function. It's a virus that was specifically designed to be *more infectious* to humans, guys. Millions, maybe billions, of people are going to die. That's just the facts, Renard. That's the only scientific conclusion that anyone, even an undergraduate, can possibly come to. The evidence is staring us in the face. It's not complicated. It's a lab-created virus, and it's loose. We're all proverbially fu—"

Jerry winked and said, "Right, but we're not necessarily here to come to that conclusion, Kristen. I think there's a way through this. We need to look at this more positively;

that's why I got this team together. We're here to save science."

Faustus almost said, "I AM the Science," but he clamped his lips shut just in time.

Deciding that Faustus wasn't going to say anything after all, Jerry continued, "And to be perfectly clear, I don't mean, to save science by saving humanity from this virus. And I don't mean we save science by being completely honest to everyone about where this virus came from, which would be commendable of course, but we have to look at the — ahem — strong possibility that the virus didn't come from the lab."

Kristen said, "Yeh there's about a 0.001% chance that's true. Maybe even less. Do you know the furin cleavage site is the only variation from BB18+ that is longer than three nucleotides?"

Jerry said, "Yes, but you're not getting my point: we're not here to save the world. What *we're* here for is to save our *research funding,* Kristen. We need to brainstorm. What can we come up with quickly? What can we work on, that might take a little more effort and time, but that we can get published? For instance, we need... a research letter affirming our support for Zheng-Leng Penguin. We need to write a study of some sort, you know, coming to the logical conclusion that we all know *must* be true—" Jerry coughed for a few seconds, then continued, "—that the virus was certainly *not* created in the lab." They all cleared their throats uncomfortably.

Faustus nodded vigorously and said, "Right. We want to look at it scientifically, dispassionately, Kristen. We don't want to be coming to any… foregone conclusions, do we? There are some big grants in the offing next year, not that I'm saying that if you help us, you might get some of them. All based on merit of course."

Minorca said, "So do you think if I help with this, I might get a merit based grant as well?"

Faustus said, "I couldn't promise anything just because you help with this paper, but the short answer is, yes, I would be very inclined to include all of you in the next funding round, simply because you are the best scientists in the world, that's why I called on you, but it would have nothing to do with whether you're helping write this paper or not."

Shamrock Holmes said, "Ah, I see. So we will all agree on it all, will we?"

Kristen said, “No, what I think you’re saying is, well, we need to... have a vigorous discussion, then. Instead of 0.001%, which is more likely to be true, offhand, but if I looked into it a bit more... And if I knew a few greenbacks were coming my way, and I’m saving Science as well at the same time, I could easily come to the conclusion it’s an 80% chance it came from the lab, 20% chance it didn’t. You can be on the other side of it, Jerry. We obviously need to have a vigorous scientific discussion that doesn’t — of course — have a predetermined or foregone conclusion” — he coughed then in such a way as to mean, yes we do have a foregone conclusion — “I’m talking about a genuine scientific discussion — because we’re not aiming for plausible deniability, here, are we?” Then he coughed into his hand, a cough that sounded suspiciously like, “Yes we are.”

Faustus said, “Exactly — plausible is the word — if you start, Kristen, on the, ah, conservative side of ‘yes’ — that’s good. And we need a vigorous discussion that takes place *on the email* — you know — not that we’re making a paper trail for this. It’s not a paper trail at all, because it’s all on the email, you know, a *digital* trail.”

Frostey said significantly, “I *see*. So it’s one of those jobs, is it? Like *Azitadunanyazinatul.*”

Poltrik D Vallee said, "What was that? What did he say? '*Has it done anything at all?*'"

Jerry's face wore an uncomfortable expression, as he made his reply, "Exactly, although your pronunciation is a little bit off. *Azitadunanyazinatul* was a new drug Faustus and the NHIJ developed quite a few years ago, for the dreadful disease HOOV[9]. There were doubts being put out by — ah — conspiracy nuts who managed to get their ridiculous, fanciful results published in one or two reputable journals — claims that the drug didn't work, that it was harmful, etcetera, etcetera. Professor Frostey and I put out a

[9] I told you already what HOOV is! Don't you pay any attention at all? HOOV is the abbreviation for Human Omni-ficient Omphalo-Virus, or to use the more accurate, fulsome term for this dreaded disease, Human Omni-ficient Omphaloskeptic Virus, a disease that afflicted terribly and eventually killed many navel-oriented people, and *not just male navel gazers*, in the 1980s, 1990s and 2000s. Gazing at the navel makes people quite susceptible to certain aerosol-borne respiratory viruses, presumably because the perpetual orientation of the head forwards affects craniofacial posture and leads to a compressed nasopharyngeal vertical dimension, which, together with compression of the trachea via adductional medial rotation causes temporary temporomandibular irregularities, whilst also limiting lung capacity; or to put it in layman's terms, they can't breathe so well because they are looking at their navels all the time. The idea that it was only *male navel gazers* who suffered from HOOV is completely untrue and was a claim put out by nasty right wing conspiracy nuts who called themselves real scientists and are in fact Hitlerphilic, omphalophobic ideologues, and Godwin's law has nothing to do with it! As well as *naval gazers* of both sexes, the disease was also known to affect old male *naval geezers* quite badly, actually, as well, and this is completely proven to everyone's satisfaction (if not in the peer-reviewed scientific literature), and is thought to be related to postural deviations relating rather to scurvy and what is technically called 'pirate gait'; this especially applies those naval retirees and pirates who have a wooden leg. Unlike every other known disease, morbidly obese people are completely immune to HOOV, presumably because they can't see their navels.

paper that reassured everybody that it worked perfectly well, was safe and effective, had no side effects, etcetera, etcetera."

Feeling uncomfortable with the direction in which the discussion was headed, Dr Faustus decided to change the subject back to the *actual* subject. "Just to get our discussion started here today I'm sharing a document. It's an article that came out yesterday. You may have seen it, you may not. If not, it is of interest to the current discussion. Now how the <bleep bleep> do I share this with you?" After crashing the teleconference meeting once or twice, and crashing his own computer, he finally managed to get the article to show on everyone's screen, much to their gratitude, and it looked like this:

MINING BIRDFLIP GENOMES FOR CLUES TO THE OUTBREAK'S ORIGINS

A ATAC CAT ATTACT A GAGA ACTA A GAGA ACTA ATTACT A ATAC CAT A ATAC CAT ATTACT A GAGA ACTA AGAGG A ATAC CAT AGACTAD CACA AT A GAGA ACTA A GAGA ACTA AGACTAD CACA AT A ATAC CAT A GATTACA ATTACT A GAGA ACTA A A ATAC CAT A GATTACA AGACTAD CACA AT A GAGA ACTA A A ATAC CAT A A A A A A GAGA ACTA DACT A GATTACA A ATAC CAT GAGD A GAGA ACTA A DACT A GATTACA A

GATTACA DACT A ATAC CAT A GAGD A GAGA ACTA A A A A CACA A A A A A GATTACA LACD TACT[10]

That string of apparent gibbobobberish rimbleslitherdigob[11] is anything but: it's a snippet of an RNA sequence from the new viral pathogen, dubbed the BirdFlip Coronavirus (WOOHOO1-CoV2), that is overwhelming the hospitals in WooHoo and in China and literally frightening the pants off everybody else. (That was why my pants were down when you opened the door, Bradley, and

---

[10] Strangely enough despite the subsequent assertion in the article that this sequence is complete gibbobobberish rimbleslitherdigob, when one actually parses it correctly, this is one of those uncommon genetic sequences that almost sounds like actual language when read out aloud:
"A attic(? or attack?) cat attacked a gaga actor. A gaga actor attacked a attic cat. A attic cat attacked a gaga actor again (g) (γγ classical Greek double gamma=ng?). A attic cat ejected caca at a gaga actor. A gaga actor ejected caca at a attic cat. A GATTACA (?some sort of artificially made up word, that suggests a perfect genetically modified human being, e.g. Uma Thurman) attacked a gaga actor & a attic cat. A GATTACA ejected caca at a gaga actor & a attic cat, ha ha ha ha ha! A gaga actor dacked a GATTACA. A attic cat gagged a gaga actor, & dacked a GATTACA. A GATTACA dacked a attic cat & gagged a gaga actor. Hahahaha Caca! Hahahaha A GATTACA lacked tact!" Something few have noticed before now *is* the presence of this strange slang passage secretly encoded in the *actual genome* of the BIRDFLIP Coronavirus; a passage that may indeed give STRONG INDICATIONS as to the actual source of this diabolical genome! Something that can only be revealed in this publication: Dr Shamrock Holmes, the Australian scientist from Sydney, is almost certainly the creator of this virus, for three important reasons. 1) An American scientist would never treat "ACTA" as a homonym representing "ACTOR" because all Americans pronounce the "R" in ACTOR (except those from Boston or the Deep South, which are both peculiar places from whence no scientist capable of constructing a coronavirus would come). 2) The slang word "DACKED" meaning, to surprise someone by pulling down their pants, is very particular to Australia and exists nowhere else in the world. 3) Only an Australian would have such bad grammar as to say *a* attic cat instead of *an* attic cat. S'Quid Pro Quo: Shamrock Holmes was in fact the scientist who created the BIRDFLIP CORONAVIRUS! You read it first here. Of course if "dacked" is actually meant to mean "ducked", the whole theory falls apart abysmally. Oh, and incidentally, what nucleotide the "D" is meant to represent in this genome is a complete mystery to me.

[11] The word rimbleslitherdigob seems to be an unknown Bidenism, lending credence to the idea that it was in fact vice-president (at the time) Johohoho Biden himself who wrote this article, whilst moonlighting as a journalist.

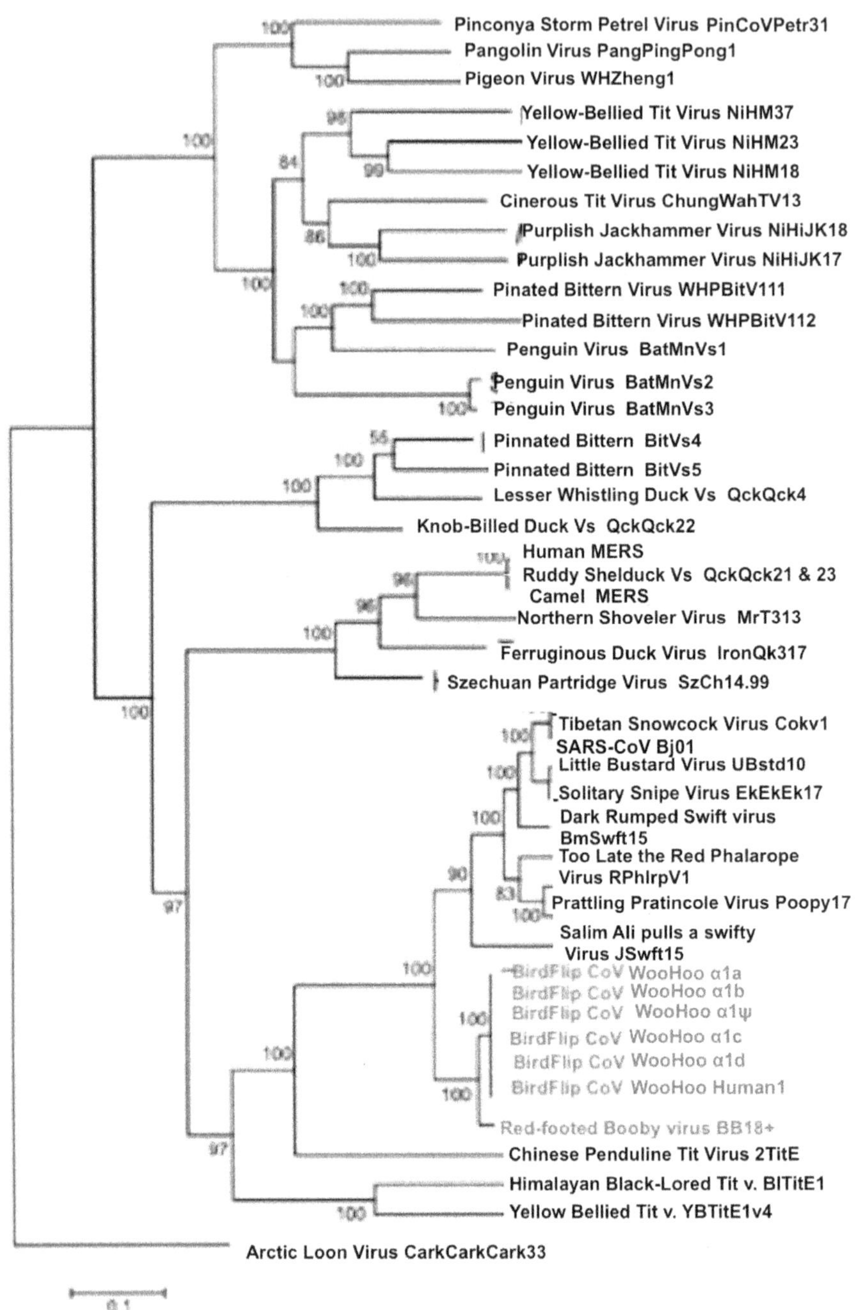
Pinconya Storm Petrel Virus PinCoVPetr31
Pangolin Virus PangPingPong1
Pigeon Virus WHZheng1
Yellow-Bellied Tit Virus NiHM37
Yellow-Bellied Tit Virus NiHM23
Yellow-Bellied Tit Virus NiHM18
Cinerous Tit Virus ChungWahTV13
Purplish Jackhammer Virus NiHiJK18
Purplish Jackhammer Virus NiHiJK17
Pinated Bittern Virus WHPBitV111
Pinated Bittern Virus WHPBitV112
Penguin Virus BatMnVs1
Penguin Virus BatMnVs2
Penguin Virus BatMnVs3
Pinnated Bittern BitVs4
Pinnated Bittern BitVs5
Lesser Whistling Duck Vs QckQck4
Knob-Billed Duck Vs QckQck22
Human MERS
Ruddy Shelduck Vs QckQck21 & 23
Camel MERS
Northern Shoveler Virus MrT313
Ferruginous Duck Virus IronQk317
Szechuan Partridge Virus SzCh14.99
Tibetan Snowcock Virus Cokv1
SARS-CoV Bj01
Little Bustard Virus UBstd10
Solitary Snipe Virus EkEkEk17
Dark Rumped Swift virus BmSwft15
Too Late the Red Phalarope Virus RPhlrpV1
Prattling Pratincole Virus Poopy17
Salim Ali pulls a swifty Virus JSwft15
BirdFlip CoV WooHoo α1a
BirdFlip CoV WooHoo α1b
BirdFlip CoV WooHoo α1ψ
BirdFlip CoV WooHoo α1c
BirdFlip CoV WooHoo α1d
BirdFlip CoV WooHoo Human1
Red-footed Booby virus BB18+
Chinese Penduline Tit Virus 2TitE
Himalayan Black-Lored Tit v. BITitE1
Yellow Bellied Tit v. YBTitE1v4
Arctic Loon Virus CarkCarkCark33
0.1

you found me with your wife, by the way; it was nothing more than WOOHOO, I swear.)

Getting back to the main subject of this article: scientists are publicly sharing an ever-growing number of full sequences of this virus, sucked from the veins of unconscious patients and analysed in machines of which only a handful of people in world has any clue at all about how they work — 57 machines[12] at last count in the Global On-Sharing All Data Database (GOSADD). These viral genomes are being put under the microscope — quite literally! — and being studied very intensely by *real scientists* who understand these things, to try to find out the origin of WOOHOO1-CoV2 and how it fits on the family tree of related viruses found in pigeons, penguins, pangolins, pinions, pilgrims and other species that sound like they might be birds that start with a p, like pumpkinbirds, podsticks, pumpernickels[13] and pagans. They have also given glimpses into what this newly discovered virus physically looks like (=invisible to the naked eye), how it might be changing (=we don't know), and how it can be stopped (=definitely not with any cheap generic medicines, it will probably require expensive vaccines that will cost the nations of the world billions of dollars each, vaccines that will put trillions of dollars into the pockets of the big pharmaceutical companies, and which people will

---

[12] This seems to be a typographical mistake: at this stage there were actually 57 *patients* with the WooHoo Flu, as it came to be called, mostly by President Crump in his press-conferences.

[13] The Scarlet Pumpernickel is well known at the Australian Broadcasting Commission for writing disturbing news tips mocking them for not covering politically inconvenient news. This does not of course, mean, of *course,* that the Scarlet Pumpernickel is actually a bird, or any relative of an avian creature whatsoever. What a pumpernickel is, actually, is quite a mystery, especially the Scarlet Pumpernickel.

> only be willing to take if they are coerced into doing so by threats of job loss and social exclusion, and which will require indemknitting agreements with the governments so that pharmaceutical companies cannot be sued when the completely safe and effective medication doesn't really work and causes completely unexpected adverse events that no one ever predicted and no one will ever admit were caused by the vaccine.[14]).

Then Dr Faustus said, "Just a few pertinent quotes, that they — er — quote in the article. First we have Tredford Beaver, professor of bioinformalattics at U-Bud:

> "One of the biggest takeaway Chinese messages from the viral sequences is that there was a singles introduction — I mean, a single introduction followed by a couple of human-to-human spreads;" however, "The actual role of WooHoo Seafood Wholesale Market remains about as murky as the swamp outside the WooHoo lab."

> "And here's the takeaway message:

> "The viral sequences, most researchers say, also knock down the ridiculously unscientific straw man idea that the pathogen came from a virology institute in WooHoo."

> "And this one:

[14] This article, though it was issued early in the pandemic, was exceedingly prescient in this matter. It is one of the few articles that got it right, in fact, in these early days, rather surprisingly, considering it comes from a very trashy Science magazine.

"The analyses of WOOHOO1-nCoV2's sequences have already been published on viro-illogical, next-neck-strain, and bioRxopp journals."

"And how about this:

"The Chinese shared the sequence of the virus completely willingly."

There was a few knowing guffaws from the others.

Faustus said, "They found it was most closely related to a Red-footed Booby virus, 96.2% similar, that's BB18+, that they had collected some time ago in some caves in Yawning province; you'll be hearing more about that later from Kristen - and there's also a 79.5% match to SARS.

Jerry said, "Now here - without being cynical, this is exactly what we're looking for — what we'd like to see in the paper — the one thing we need, an intermediate host species, or even several. The pangolins, maybe. Or the penguins. Or the pigeons. Or the pinconya storm petrel, even, or the pinnated bittern, or the purplish jackhammer[15], although most of these birds are somewhat rare in China[16]. More likely, the Red-footed Booby, yes, indeed, that one is a

15 It looks as though Faustus misspelled this word when he said it: it should be the purplish *jacamer.*

16 He is right about this; these three birds are probably rather more common in Chile, actually, than China, which would explain Faustus' misconception, as both places have the first three letters in common, Chi.

perfect candidate. Or the Chinese Penduline Tit, the Black-bibbed Tit, the Yellow-bellied Tit, the Himalayan Black-Lored Tit, or even the Cinereous Tit — any one of those would be just as good to have as the intermediate host, as I often like to — it's always *good* to have a good pair of spare Tits or Boobies to hand (did I just say that?) — (oh dear) I mean, especially if you're looking for an intermediate host species to blame — ahem — to which to *ascribe* — the cause of a BirdFlip Coronavirus infection that is raging like wildfire through the populace. One that definitely, never, ever, ever, could have come from a lab. Don't even think it. Don't even consider the possibility. It would be the end of all our careers. If it got out."

"They also mention the fact that BB18+ differs from WOOHOO1-nCoV2 by nearly 1100 nucleotides. Bedford has already created coronavirus family trees. You click on it and you can see the genome."

Poltrik said, "Very neat. Nice. What did you do that diagram in?"

Shamrock said, "I did it in 'tinselR'; if you must know it's my favourite Newick-formatted phylogenetic tree display software, mainly because the name 'tinselR' makes me think of Christmas."

Following page: the Birdflip family tree

Faustus said, "Fedboard thinks the close relationship of Red-footed Booby virus BB18+ and BirdFlipCoV WooHoo1 suggest that the two viruses shared a common ancestor. To make a long story short, that's what we're afraid of. Not 25 to 65 years ago. Maybe a little more recently."

The others on the Zoom call gave a few guffaws.

Faustus said, "With a little bit of help from my friends. In China."

A few more guffaws.

And Shamrock Holmes said, "And a bit of help from funding from the NAIAD. Let me reiterate I had nothing to do with this virus, nothing at all. It wasn't me. It was the NAIAD. Not that I myself have never received funding from the NAIAD." He gave a little cough.

Kristen said, "Wasn't it... sixty one million dollars, before you moved to Sydney, Shamrock?"

Shamrock said, "Yes... But this WooHoo virus... definitely funded by the NAIAD. Wasn't it?"

Faustus replied, "Let's not go that far, Shamrock. After all, many people have had their hand in that honey pot."

Jerry Blacksmith was visibly cringing at this conversation. He said awkwardly, "Ah, not to put too fine point on it, Shamrock, that's what we're getting together to determine, um... Didn't you hear the rest of the conversation? Let's put it this way. We don't want to encourage - ah - any conspiracy theories about lab origins - if..."

Shamrock said, "Oh, that's a relief." And he looked visibly *extremely* relieved. "Sorry, I've been a bit preoccupied, what with this and that. And this."

Faustus said, "What we're really wanting to do here, Shamrock, is to find out the truth."

Shamrock said, "Oh, dear."

Faustus frowned a little and said, "Oh, perhaps not the truth you're thinking of, Shamrock. Don't worry. Let's put it that way — if the truth we *decide*—" (he accentuated 'decide') "—turns out to be that the virus did not arise in a lab, so much the better for everybody's *future* funding opportunities, let us say." And Faustus raised both hands in a kind of mock celebration, and said in a very deadpan way, "Hooray."

There was awkward laughter from the others.

And Faustus continued, "Yes - so much the better for funding opportunities. Including yours."

Shamrock's eyebrows raised in surprise. "Really?" he said. "Mine too?"

And Faustus said, "Yes. And that's a promise."

Uncomfortable pause, silence, with a look of ambivalence on everyone's faces; they were caught between the pleasure of future monetary and career gain on the one hand and the fear of the consequences of being found out, as well as the guilt of being part of the conspiracy, as well as the consequences to their career of *not* going along with Faustus' little unspoken subtext.

Faustus continued, "By which I mean to reiterate once again, I cannot see the governments - and I don't just mean the NHIJ - I mean, any of the Western governments - funding any of the type of research we are *all* doing, in future, if it turns out that the BirdFlip Coronavirus came from a lab. Regardless of who's virus it actually was — Shamrock — we're all in this together, for better or worse, for richer or poorer. We're tied at the hip, so to speak, we're married to one another, and I don't think there's any divorce in this world."

Jerry said, “Till death do us part.”

Faustus said, “Till death do us part. That might be truer than you think.”

The others squirmed uncomfortably.

Kristen said in a rather *tense* tone of voice, it must be said: “This *death* bit; it wouldn’t have anything to do with your — ah — comment to me on our call yesterday that you think this should be reported to the — lettered agencies —” and as he listed the agencies, Kristen’s voice rose to a pitch of high frenzy: “And I quote: the FIB, CIA, NSA, MI5, MI6, ASIO, ASIS, ASD, AGO, DIO, CFINTCOM, CSE, CSIS, RCMP, DDIS, GCSB, NZSIS, DI, GCHQ, SIS, DIA, NGO and the NGA?!?!”

Faustus said, “It might. It just might. I may have signed a non-disclosure agreement that means I can’t tell you that I will be making a clandestine visit to a lettered agency in the next few days to convince them that it would be very bad for *everyone* if the rumour started to spread among the uneducated nincompoops and morons of the Western populations that this virus began in a lab. To that end, we will all be *married* to this idea, that it was a Red-footed Booby virus. Right?”

And they all said, "Oooh yes," "Right," "Okay," "I'm fully on board," "I'm with the agenda," "Count me in," "Yes, I will marry you!" etcetera

Faustus's mood became more businesslike as he turned back to the article. "And then they mention MERS. Apparently Camel and Human MERS are on the same branch as the Ruddy Shelduck virus, QckQck 21 & 23. Who knew that?"

Kristen said, "Maybe the people who caught MERS from their camels like eating duck?"

Faustus said, "In the desert? There are ducks in the desert? That hang around with camels?"

Jerry said, "Well, there are oases, you know; I understand the Ruddy Shelduck frequents the Abraqadabra lagoons. I suppose it could pass from ducks to camels to humans, or vice versa. It all depends, I suppose, on how close the ducks came to the camels."

Minorca said, "You're just making that up, now. Honestly, that's ridiculous, Ruddy Shelduck in the Abraqadabra lagoons?"

Jerry responded, "Well, I may have gotten the name wrong. Abqaiq lagoons perhaps?"

Minorca said, "What a lot of rot."

Faustus said sternly, “We don’t want to be making a whole lot of speculation here: we need hard facts. Moving on, here they quote Vincent - one of our guys - ‘There’s a very large grey area between viruses detected in ducks and boobies and the virus now isolated in humans.’ And then they quote you, Kristen.”

Kristen said, “Yeh I was wondering when you’d get to me. I’ll read it: ‘Such a high rate of positive tests in the WooHoo markets would suggest strongly that these birds and pangolins played a key role in the development of the BirdFlip virus. Yet no preprints or even research letters have been published about the sampling, so we simply can’t be certain which, if any, birds were positive cases. Until you consistently isolate the offending virus in a single species, it's very, very difficult to determine what the natural host was.’ Exactly,” said Kristen, agreeing with himself. “I agree completely with myself. No evidence. No data. No proof. No firm conclusions.”

Faustus said, “Oh, no, they have conclusions, apparently. Wei-Ser Pen-Te of the Serpent Virology studies department Shanghai University said that “snake is the most probable wildlife animal reservoir for the BirdFlip Coronavirus.”

Shamrock Holmes said, “I told Wei not to publish that study. Most ridiculous thing I’ve ever heard. Snakes an animal reservoir for a coronavirus. How on earth did they spread it? The snakes coughed on them?” Shamrock suddenly seemed to understand what he was saying, and changed tack for some reason: “Of course if people say that it was a snake, who am I to disagree? I’m... sure it didn’t come out of a lab.”

Faustus said, “Exactly. And here we get on to the conspiracy theories. Gossip about Chinese scientists working in a Winnipeg lab. And here it is: the main culprit, or so it seems. The smoking gun, as they say. The WooHoo Institute of Virology - the premier lab in China that studies bat and human coronaviruses - you would have seen the story if you were living in DC. That article is entitled, “Experts debunk fringe theory linking China's coronavirus to weapons research.” Concerns about the institute predate this outbreak. Blah blah blah, a level 4 lab, dangerous pathogens, blah blah blah, “a 2015 experiment in which modifications were made to a SARS-like Red-Footed Booby virus to see whether it had the potential to cause disease in humans.” Well that certainly sounds a little incriminatory. Then a few quotes from Rick Nuttoobright of Rutter’s University; he’s feeding the rumour mill, calling the WooHoo studies gain of function. How ridiculous. To think we pay his funding every year, to the tune of half a million. And then, believe it or not, the journalists emailed Zheng-Leng Penguin herself."

Jerry said, "The bird woman."

Minorka spat, "An odious appellative."

Jerry clarified, "The dreadful journalists call her the bird woman, that's what I meant."

Minorka said, "They wouldn't call her that if she was a man."

Shamrock Holmes said, "No they'd call her… the Penguin, maybe. And then it wouldn't be an insult. It would be like a super-villain name. But since her Chinese name is 碰个问 (peng-ge-win) meaning 'touch on a question' which sounds like the English word, 'Penguin,' and she studies birds, she that's how she came to be called the bird woman."

Minorka said, "*Exactly,*" as though Shamrock's speech had proven her point.

There was an uncomfortable silence, since no one wanted to be called a male chauvinist pig.

Finally Minorka broke the silence by asking, "Did Dr Sheng-Leng Penguin reply?"

Faustus said, "No, apparently Dr Sheng-Leng Penguin did not reply. So then they contacted Peter Dackazacka[17] of the Green-Goblecki-Health Alliance[18]. A totally disinterested party."

Frowning, Shamrock said, "What does he mean by that?"

Without a smile, Jerry said, "He's being funny. Anything but disinterested. Green-Goblecki-Health were working with Shi on the gain of fun-whatever-you-want-to-call-it viruses in the Wuhan lab. I think they were honing one of your viruses, Shamrock."

In a considerably lighter mood, Shamrock said, "Really? So it wasn't my fault that..."

Minorka said, "I think that's a good shorthand, Jerry — let's call them 'gain of fun' viruses from now on."

Faustus interrupted, "Green-Goblecki-Health, unfortunately, is the lab we were funding for those gain-of-fun experiments originally; they began doing them in the

---

[17] It is thought that Peter Dackazacka's surname was the inspiration for the name of the famous Australian rock band, AC DC.

[18] Green Goblecki Health Alliance is a holistic health provider, that studies the scientific relationship between eco-logical and environmental issues and human health. The name comes from the fact that they were initially looking at the pictures of birds, such as wilds ducks, vultures, etc (in particular) as well as foxes, boars, bulls, cranes, spiders, quadripeds, vultures, sheep, asses, gazelles and felids at the ancient archeological site of Goblecki Tepe in Turkey, with a view to discovering what the species distribution in Turkey may have been like 10-12,000 years ago.

WooHoo lab. It had just become too risky to do that kind of science in the US; too much political interference. It says here Peter Dackazacka dismissed Nuttoobright's conjecture. 'Every single time there's an emerging pandemic, a new deadly virus that we say is surely going to kill everybody via horrible deaths after unimaginable suffering, the same old story comes out: This is a spillover or the accidental release of a bioagent or a bioengineered virus,' Dackazacka says. 'It's such a shame. It seems that humans can't resist controversy. If only they would just believe us when we say that you're all going to die from a *natural* virus, I repeat, a *natural* virus that emerged *naturally* and was completely *natural* and didn't come from a lab. Yes. If I could address these conspiracy mongers, I would say, 'Yes, you *are* all going to die, but not because when we were studying these very dangerous viruses in the lab and tried to make them more lethal one of them accidentally escaped.' It's all a conspiracy theory, and I'm so sick of these conspiracy theories being purveyed without consequence on the schminternet. Someone should cancel their facebook accounts, fine them hundreds of thousands of dollars, and throw them into prison.' And so on, blah blah blah."

The 'Mining BirdFlip' article disappeared from the screen, and the participants' images came back.

Faustus continued, "Ooh, look at that, I managed to make the article disappear and bring back the pictures of the participants! Anyhow, Dackazacka says, 'But the jury is still out on what the actual origins of the killer BirdFlip coronavirus are.'" He turned to face the camera on his computer and said dramatically, "Well, people. We *are* the jury. And what we need within 15 days is: a paper confirming that the lab origin is highly unlikely."

Quite certain suddenly that *he* wasn't the one responsible for the lab leak, Kristen emphasized, "If that's where the evidence is leading."

Faustus said rather cryptically, "*Wherever* the evidence is leading. Or rather, with you leading the evidence by the nose, wherever you want to lead it; that's the kind of thing that I would have a preference for. As I already emphasized, I'd really like to see a paper confirming that the lab origin is unlikely. And then, funding can go on. If we don't have that, there's nothing I can guarantee, not a single penny."

Jerry Blacksmith said, "Alright. I think we all get the point." Everyone in the teleconference nodded gravely and silently.

Jerry said, “Thank you George.”

But George added, “By the way, please keep the emails to the topic. But if you want to message more… ah — frankly — please use the app, Slick, which Kristen will send to your phones. It’s supposedly end to end encrypted and no one will even think to look at it, so it should be safe from any prying eyes, private eyes, and FOIs.”

And with that, the teleconference was over.

CHAPTER 6

Proximal Pizza

For the next few days, Dr Faustus lived on takeaway pizza ordered through Ober-eats. as he kept going back to check his emails day and night, and he spent extra time keeping up with his research; Petronia was great in this respect, she had one of the junior scientists filter through the studies that might be relevant and sending them through to him. Consequently, he was able to keep them up to date, especially when a few new, carefully chosen scientists joined the email list in order to participate on the paper, and he had to update them. .

> The rumour mill is going strong, guys; there's a group of Indian scientists who've just published papers saying that there are HOOV[19] gene sequences in the BirdFlip-CoV2 genetic code. Kristen looked carefully at the genome but didn't find any HOOV sequences in there at all, neither did anyone else on the teleconference call think it was credible in any way shape or form. But what they *were* concerned about were the mutations that would be unlikely to have evolved naturally. And this suspicion is not

[19] You must be a complete idiot if you're reading this footnote, because I *already told you what HOOV means about 11 footnotes ago!* HOOV is the abbreviation for Human Omni-ficient Omphalo-Virus! Read that again if you want, but I'm pretty certain that you will not remember it this time, 'cause you sure didn't remember what it meant after the last *two times* you read it, you Red-Footed Booby. You have the memory of a Dory; no, you have a worse memory than a Dory. In fact, scientific studies show fish can remember things for many months, but you can't! I bet you've already forgotten it.

helped by the fact that the scientists at WooHoo were already working on gain-of-fun bird viruses, to adapt them to make them more infectious to humans (it's the furine cleavage site I'm talking about here). And what's even more suspicious is that the virus broke out in WooHoo.

Frostey Kristoff emailed the group after this, and as Faustus read Frostey's email, he just about tore his hair out.

Dear Everybody,

Frostey here. Unfortunately I am completely snowed under with hospital work, dealing with BirdFlip-CoV2 patients, and I'll need a few more days before I can help with the paper.

But in this five minutes I have to send out a quick email in between putting people on ventilators and shutting down yesterday's ventilators after the people on them died, can someone help me by answering a small, tiny, little question I have, just a teensy, weensy, little query: didn't we get together to challenge a *'certain theory'*, and if could, to — ah — sort of *debunk* it? Didn't we want to say that theory is not true? Well everything I'm reading in what you've sent out so far tends towards saying that the *unnamed,* unmentionable hypothesis which we must call by the ridiculous name gain of 'fun' — in the emails I'm reading it sounds as if everyone is saying that it was *perfectly obvious* and that nothing under the sun could be clearer, in fact, these emails read almost as though some external bogeyman was pressuring us, forcing us to give an answer! Is this really true? Who came up with the whole story in the first place? *In other words, I'm starting to have a panic attack because it all looks so silly and stupid!*

My question is: are we just working on debunking ourselves?

Have a merry old time, and jingle your bells! I'll email again in a couple of days, I've just got a few more ventilators to shut off! Merry old times.

Toodle-oo,

Frostey Kristoff.

On reading this email, Faustus rang Shamrock on his burner phone and said, "Have you read Frostey's latest email? You've got to debunk it. If it simply comes from me, it won't look good if they ever FOI our emails; I can't do it all. You'll need to misdirect the team: just try and pretend that Frostey was talking about that HOOV nonsense paper from India."

Shamrock replied, "No problem, George. I'll draft it now: you should receive it in about half an hour."

Faustus at this moment was in a briefing with the head of the WHC, Tedboss, who was in the middle of asking Faustus what a virus was and were they real, and what he should tell his grandkids about the virus, but Faustus just couldn't help it, he kept checking his phone.

Tedboss was saying something in the background, but consciously, Faustus wasn't really paying attention, it just sounded like background noise, that went like this: "Are you even listening to me? Faustus? Hello? Hello? Oh my God now he's opening up something on his phone, is that your email app? Are you reading an email while I'm asking you important questions about how to tell my grandchildren about the virus?" Tedboss suddenly rolled his eyes and slumped on his desk, saying, "I don't believe it. He's really doing it: he's reading an email."

Faustus glanced up at Tedboss for a moment shushed him: "Shhh. This is important."

Tedboss said, "I'm important." A great sob came from his deepest guts, and he said quite plaintively, "Aren't I?" but Faustus was already ignoring him and concentrating on Shamrock Holmes' answer to Frostey's email.

> Hi Frostey,
>
> I'm not sure where this stuff about "gain of fun" and the WooHoo lab came from, but it has nothing to do with the HOOV nonsense. This is a much bigger story than that silly little piece of nonsense from a bunch of Indian scientist wanna-bees.
>
> Since this global pandemic began, people have been saying that the virus escaped from the WooHoo lab, just because of the tiny, miniscule, completely insignificant coincidence that the outbreak started just a few doors down *from* the WooHoo lab, in the WooHoo laboratory *residential quarters*. It's just one of those silly coincidences that happen to happen from time to time in virology, like the time my lab assistant Johnny whatever-'is-name-was caught

Ebola from some random unknown migrant who must have happened to be in New York at the time[20]... And you see the fact that he was working on a — ahem — "Gain of fun" Ebola virus at the time just made it *look* like he had caught Ebola it in the lab. The two were completely unrelated; of course, once Johnny died, nobody could ask him about it, so this little coincidence died when he did. Thankfully for the future of virology.

Anyhow I happen to work in China, did you know? And let me tell that over there a bunch of people really *are* believing that the virus escaped from the WooHoo lab, and that the government is lying to them about it all; how ridiculous! The Chinese government would *never* lie to their people.

And what's worse: when the WooHoo lab published the Red-Footed Booby virus, saying this was the source of the WooHoo virus, well, unfortunately, Red-Footed Boobys don't even live anywhere near WooHoo, in fact, Red-Footed Boobys live far, far away, on a beach somewhere in Northern China, and the WooHoo lab only knew about the Red-Footed Booby virus because they sampled some of its poop a long time ago.

I believe what we are doing here — our main aim — is to try to write something *balanced* about this, and when I say *balanced,* I don't mean balanced towards the lab leak theory side. Admittedly, there are arguments for and against this: one might be, theoretically, that our funding will dry up if we write something that somehow comes up with apparent verification for the theory that this virus came from the lab, this is what I would call 'unbalanced,' wouldn't you? By which I'm talking about the

[20] This migrant was never found, but Shamrock wouldn't lie.

balance sheets on our research ideas, not our mental functioning.

Anyhow, since that new research paper came out saying that the penguin virus bonds to six out of six of the key sites in the receptor binding domain, I think we can lay aside any concerns about "gain of fun", don't you think?

Have fun! But not "gain of fun"….!

Best Regards,

Shamrock Holmes

Faustus felt there were a few things Shamrock missed; so he drafted a reply to the others as well and sent it.

Guys,

This lab origin theory has been like a rolling stone that gathers no moss in social media, yes, but also among certain scientists, the media, and even certain politicians.

The purpose of the teleconference and these emails is to bring a neutral group of top scientists together to provide an opinion in a concentrated, expert way, in order to counter the conspiracy theories, but to define the parameters of the debate before it all gets out of hand, with ramifications that could be extremely damaging to our research funding and everyone's careers, if not to scientific truth, which I admit could be slightly better off if the truth gets out, by which I mean the lab origin details.

Faustus deleted that last bit. Can't say that. What was he thinking? These emails might be FOI'd.

> …extremely damaging ~~to our research funding and everyone's careers, if not to scientific truth, which I admit could be slightly better off if the truth gets out, by which I mean the lab origin details.~~
>
> In any case, now that we have more detailed evidence about the a species jump from pangolins, that was not even available yesterday, we can make an even clearer argument that it could have jumped from pangolins to humans, although I know some of you still favour the Red-Footed Booby as the original host.
>
> I'm hoping that we can put a scientific paper or research letter out there early, or even both, in order to frame the public debate, because, if we don't do this, instead of framing the debate, we will be purely reactive, i.e. reacting to what others are saying, which will not be good I think. Especially if they find the furine cleavage site.

He deleted the last sentence about the furin cleavage site as well.

> …good I think. ~~Especially if they find the furine cleavage site.~~

Then Faustus took out his phone and looked up the Slick messaging app to see what they were all *really* saying.

Kristen had just posted a comment, and there was a discussion happening on Slick:

> KRISTEN: The main thing I'm thinking is that it's just so friggin probable that a lab escape happened because this type of "gain of fun" work is exactly what they were doing and the features of the RNA

sequence are exactly what you'd expect given that scenario.

Faustus found Kristen's continued insistence on the lab escape scenario a little unsettling, and wondered if he was really on board with the whole agenda. Jerry had sent a message to Slick as well.

> JERRY: If you look at your emails, I'm sharing the study as we write it as an attachment. The first draft has gone out, and we will revise it as it we go, until it's ready for publication. Please don't share it: it's just a rough draft from Shamrock Holmes and the team, so we'll send out a more polished version a bit later. I'm speaking to Tedboss again today: really trying to push the WHC — for some reason after Faustus' meeting with them, Tedboss got a bit… intransigent. Stubborn.
>
> Jerry.

Faustus felt guilty — that was the meeting when *he* had been checking his mobile phone all the way through, and he felt that Tedboss had been a little annoyed at him. Jerry had a lot of tact, it would all be okay.

Faustus looked at his emails again then, and found the email Jerry was talking about; the one with the first draft attached. He downloaded it, then with some difficulty found it on his hard drive (it was in some obscure folder called "Downloads") opened it, and read through it. It wasn't bad. A little unpolished here and there, and there were one or two loopholes you could drive a semi-trailer through with about five or six trailers attached, each carrying a forty foot shipping container full of incriminating evidence of the lab leak, but one had to be charitable to the guys, it was only a first draft.

Then he read Kristen's email and marvelled at his duplicity; he was saying the exact opposite of what he said in the Slick messaging app, and was also playing the game nicely, minimising the furin cleavage site and the unnaturalness of the genome:

> Hi everyone,
>
> Great stuff here in the first draft! I like what I'm reading. So we're not trying to push a 'conspiracy theory' here, but rather to bring the 'scientific method' to something the media has been pushing around like a bag of hot potatoes, a question being asked by everybody from scientists and journalists to politicians and the little boy that plays basketball at the end of the street. They keep ringing me up for interviews, or asking me questions (even the little boy at the end of the street, would you believe!)
>
> I'm wondering if we might look at serial passage of a virus through the lungs of the lab penguins, in other words, in case you don't know what serial passage is, you make a virus, keep infecting more and more penguins with it, to try to see if you can make it worse. When the maximum number of penguins pass the virus on and die in as short as time as possible, you win! This is another way they might have had a bit of "gain of fun" with it, that is not, I

repeat, not the genetic manipulation that we were worried about. Serial passage has nothing to do with f. c.'s (furin whatevers) so wouldn't that be something we could kindof throw about a bit in these emails to make it look like we actually care what the truth is?

There are a few good articles out there already challenging the lab leak theory, so you all might want to have a look at them; I'll include the link at the bottom of this email.

By the way, that document is not ready to publish yet! We need to forestall a few other problems, like the presence of O-linked glycans, and maybe look at the f-c site a bit more.

Have lots of gain of fun, everyone!

Kristen.

Then Jerry sent an email about the first draft:

From: Jerry

Let's not bandy about the word "Engineered", guys! It's not a pleasant word to have bumping around in the heads of the readers; carries all sorts of implications we don't even want them thinking about!

Could have been accidental transmission among lab animals in the WooHoo lab, which would be the reason for the O-linked glycans.

Faustus had absolutely no clue what O-linked glycans were; probably some sort of carbohydrate or sugar he guessed, but from what they were saying, O-linked glycans just didn't occur in natural viruses.

Shamrock Holmes still reckons it's about 65/35 it came out of a lab; I'd reckon about 50/50. But I like the idea of transmission among lab penguins; or I'm thinking serial passage among HACE2 *transgenic penguins*.

Have lots of fun, but not too much gain of fun!

Jerry

Faustus didn't like that idea too much. Human ACE2 transgenic penguins were penguins created by scientists to test viruses that were infectious to human ACE2 receptors, and he realised that some ignorant members of the public might still think that testing dangerous viruses or even exposing ACE2 transgenic penguins in the lab by accident to dangerous viruses that were infectious to human ACE2 receptors might come across to them as some sort of gain of function.

In fact, Faustus realised if serial passage was at fault, he was also in trouble, because one of his scientists, Hermann Munnster, was the world expert on serial passage in human ACE2 transgenic penguins, and in fact, NAIAD had funded his research to the tune of millions of dollars as well. Whichever way you look at it, Faustus was stuffed.

Clarence Collins, head of the NHIJ, chimed in on the conversation then.

> Surely they wouldn't have done serial passage with transgenic penguins in a biosecurity level 2 lab, though?
>
> Clarence

Jerry replied,

> It's Mad Max country in China, Clarence. It's a distinct possibility.

So far Faustus had resisted the idea of talking to the lettered agencies; the CIA, the FIB and the like. The following morning, however, a New York Globe journalist, McClack Jr, emailed Kristen and one of the other professors to ask about a tip-off he'd received that the government was investigating the possibility of a lab leak. They shared McClack Jr's email messages on Slick; Barry Gog wrote:

> Mr McClack Jr is clearly a very good journalist but he could easily be misled.

Faustus laughed as he wasn't sure if Barry Gog's meaning was, McClack Jr was being misled by those who gave him the tip-off, or if he was offering advice on what to do.

Kristen wrote:

> Yeh he hit the nail on the head, proverbially speaking, hit the target, got to the root of the problem, hit the spot, struck home, and got it right. Let's not tell him.

Then Faustus checked the emails again. Kristen had shared the email he had sent to Donald McClack Jr:

Dear Donald,

Secret Government meetings? Clandestine agencies? CIA? Spooks? Thank you so much for your dreadful email. I'm sad to say you have been herron-doubly deceived by these dreading rumours. They are completely false, I am very glad to say, and all the scientific evidence says — let me emphasize — as we will outline in our forthcoming paper on the subject the *scientifickal* evidence says that the virus is a completely natural one that did not evolve in the lab by serial passage or genetic manipulation but in fact came from a Red-Footed Booby or a pangolin or other related bird such a penguin, in other words, completely from a zoological origin. Not from any lab whatsoever, none of the data is consistent with that theory in any way shape or form, I assure you, and definitely not from the WooHoo lab, and whatever you do, don't even think that there might be a furin cleavage site involved,

Yours completely honestly,

Kristen

PS I'm not lying

PPS I promise you I'm telling the truth. Don't worry.

PPPS There's not a single lie in this email. Please don't suspect anything.

PPPPS You should really not suspect that I'm lying. Believe me. I'm being honest.

Faustus contacted his contact that had a contact that knew a contact in the CIA that day: he realised that he had no choice.

You see, his nephew's cleaner Pip was also the cleaner for the second floor of the CIA, and it so happened that he cleaned the offices of the guy who investigated pandemics; Faustus had only found this out fortuitously during a rather inebriated game of cards with his nephew, the cleaner whose name was Pip, Faustus himself, and Pip's best mate, who happened to be a WWW wrestler. Soaked in good Scotch from Faustus' own cellar, Pip happened to mention that he knew a guy who was also heavily into pandemics, and the conversation had started from there.

So it was that Faustus contacted his nephew, who passed on a note to Pip, who left it on the clandestine CIA pandemic investigator's desk that night.

The next day, Faustus had a shady phone call on his mobile, where the number didn't show up.

He answered, "Yes? Is that the CIA?" And a voice answered in a Bombay accent, "Hello, my name is Indira and I'm from your own phone company whichever that one is or may be. Unfortunately, I must tell you your bill is in arrears. Please tell me your online bank account number and password, as well as your name and birth-date, and we will take all your money immediately to service the astronomical debt you have run up." Faustus closed the call.

Five minutes later, another call rang with hidden caller ID, and Faustus answered it, shouting, "Get lost, no you're not from my phone company, and I'm not giving you any money." The line was silent for quite a while. Finally, a low, creepy, clandestine-kind-of voice said, "This is Agent Redacted from the CIA."

Faustus said, "Oh. Sorry."

The clandestine voice said, "You contacted us. Dr Faustus, come to the *back door* of the George Bush Intelligence Center (yes I know the name is an oxymoron) the *back door,* Dr Faustus, at 2:07 pm tomorrow exactly and we will let you in. By the back door, I mean the *opposite* of the front entrance; if you drive in to Langley from Colonial Farm road, the police there will recognise your car and let you through. Go park in Carpark Omega-5, and if you get out of your car and loiter around, near your car, at the back corner of the building where the CIA memorial wall is, by which I mean, at the opposite end of the front entrance where the tower is, someone will open a door and let you in.

We don't want you going through security at the front — there must be no record that you have ever visited us..."

The following day, Faustus had his driver (whatever-his-name-was) drive him to Langley, to the George Bush Intelligence Center, where they followed the instructions to the letter: they entered from Colonial Farm Road and parked at the back of the building, in Carpark Omega-5, and Faustus got out of the car and loitered near the car; he felt very exposed as there were not many cars parked in that car park. They were situated about fifty feet from the edge of the white building, which had no distinguishing features apart from windows at ground level and a protruding building from the second floor up.

Faustus said to the driver, "Are you sure this is the place?"

His driver said, "Well, this is Carpark Omega-5 and it is around the other side of the building from the main entrance and the tower."

Faustus said, "Well, we'll wait another five minutes. If no one shows, we'll just go home again and wait for another call. Maybe I got it all wrong."

They waited and waited, and eventually Faustus had lost his patience and said, "Let's go home," and he was just getting in the back of the limo, when a door opened in what had looked like a blank wall up till then, and a man dressed in a black suit beckoned to George and said in a whisper loud enough to hear , "Ssst! Over here."

Faustus walked in to the building.

Faustus said to the man, "What's your name?"

He replied, "My name is Redacted."

Redacted led Faustus through a tangle of corridors, up an elevator, down another elevator, and they walked into a white conference room that looked out on the carpark.

There were seven agents in the room, including Redacted.

The other agents introduced themselves. "Hi. I'm Redacted," said the first. "Good day. Redacted." "Redacted. Pleased to meet you Dr Faustus." "Redacted." "I'm Redacted. Good to meet you." "My name's Redacted, pleased to meet you."

"So," said Redacted. "What do you have to tell us?"

Faustus said, "Well, firstly, I believe you are investigating the idea that the BirdFlip Virus came from a lab?"

"Yes," said Redacted. "Redacted thinks the genetic profile certainly indicates that. Redacted?"

Redacted said, "Yes — I have expertise in evolutionary mathematics as well as genetics with an emphasis on viruses. There are several sites in the BirdFlip genome that are very suspicious. Such as the O-linked glycans and the spliced in section at 23582, where it looks like a human ACE-2 optimised furin cleavage site…"

Faustus corrected him, "Fu*rine* cleavage site[21]."

Redacted looked at Redacted and rolled his eyes, then turned back to Faustus and said, "Be that as it may, the fu*rin* cleavage site certainly looks engineered to us."

Faustus said, "Well, it would be bad for Science if this gets out."

Redacted said, "Why would you say that?"

Faustus swallowed his pride and decided to tell most of the truth.

He said, "Well, it so happens that — if this was indeed a lab escape, which it seems to be, it so happens that NAIAD funded the research that led to the lab escape — because it was Ralph Bar-tailed Godwit who first inserted the furine cleavage sites into a virus in his lab here in the United States — and other studies which NAIAD funded, done by Peter Dackazacka, were performed in the WooHoo lab. The

---

[21] Here of course, Faustus is quite wrong — it is a *furin* cleavage site.

Chinese may have extended Godwit's research, or they may have simply accidentally let one of Godwit's viral creations loose from the lab while working on it — but unfortunately as you can see the NHIJ and the NAIAD are both implicated in creating these viruses. You would be harming Science and Scientific Cooperation in the United States, indeed in the whole world, if you let this information get into the public domain."

The agents talked among themselves, then the oldest man among them, whose name was Redacted, said, "Nonetheless, the public deserves to know the truth."

The others said, "Well, Redacted is the boss," "We have to do what Redacted says," "Yes, we have to listen to Redacted."

Faustus swallowed again and addressed the boss, the man who was clearly in charge, "Well, I'm sure I could make it worth your while to ensure that this stays under wraps. Redacted, what do you think?"

The boss was shocked. "I'm really quite shocked. Don't you understand that bribery public officials and witnesses is a crime under Title 18 of the US Federal Code? Why, you could—"

One of the agents interrupted, “Boss, you want a cup of coffee?”

“Sure,” said the boss. Redacted went into the attached staff-room to get the coffee.

Faustus said, “Oh, I wouldn’t be bribing anyone. I’m just saying that there would be research grants available so long as we can keep the Federal money flowing, and that money wouldn’t be flowing if there was any appearance of impropriety on the part of where the NHIJ funding had gone — if people believed that we had been funding gain-of-function research that caused a number of deaths, our funding opportunities would dry up; the government would be duty-bound to cut us off from the flow of finances.”

Agent Redacted returned from the staff-room with a cup of coffee for the boss.

The boss sipped the coffee.

Faustus continued, “I assume everyone in this room is a scientist?”

They all nodded, except the boss, agent Redacted.

Faustus said, “I see. Well, there may well be NAIAD grants available even for people who work in the CIA. Some of our grants are rather generous.”

The boss said, “Dr Faustus, I appreciate the offer, but if it’s coming with strings attached, that is, some sort of promise to not mention the lab escape, which I perceive is the unspoken sub-text in what you are talking about, then I’m afraid we’d all have to decline your offer. Even people like us, who are in the CIA, have our principles, you know.”

Faustus said, “Well, I’m not exactly saying there’d be strings attached. But if you *do* happen to let it out that gain-of-function research created the BirdFlip pandemic virus, then I don’t think much of our chances of securing *any* funding at all.”

The boss said, “Nevertheless, this sounds to me like a poorly disguised attempt to make an offer to Federal officials in order to influence the outcome of an investigation.” Suddenly his stomach rumbled. “There is *no way in Hades*, Dr Faustus, that *any one of us* would accept such an offer.” His stomach rumbled again. “Look, excuse me, I seem to have developed a sudden… digestive issue. I need to get to the bathroom, rather quickly. I’ll be back soon.”

With a noisy, wet-sounding fart emitting from his rear, the boss sprinted out of the conference room and down the corridor. A distant door slammed, followed by even more extreme rear eruptions, muffled by the distance.

One of the agents immediately took the cup of coffee out into the staff-room, and they all listened silently as he flushed it down the drain, made another cup of coffee and brought it in.

When he had put it down in the boss's spot, one of the other agents, Agent Redacted, said, "Now, what were you saying, Dr Faustus?"

And they had a quick but fruitful discussion about future scientific grants.

Five minutes later the boss returned wearing a fresh pair of trousers and looking slightly chastened. He stared at the cup of coffee and said, "Don't anyone touch this, I'm taking it to Department C for analysis."

Then the boss said, "Now, Dr Faustus, I believe we have important matters to discuss."

Dr Faustus said, "Well, I was just about to ask your scientific colleagues what they thought about the theory that the BirdFlip Virus came from a laboratory."

The six agents all replied, "Oh, no," "Didn't come from a lab," "Natural origin for sure," "Fu*rine* cleavage site almost certainly arose from natural selection," "Yeh, we've all changed our minds," "Certainly a natural origin."

The boss said, "Oh, that's interesting. So Dr Faustus has convinced you that the evidence for a lab origin is actually quite minimal? Even though yesterday you were all gung-ho for the lab leak theory? You've all changed your minds?"

They all nodded in unison. Agent Redacted said, "Yes, Dr Faustus showed us that we were quite wrong. He has convinced us with *scientific evidence*. Evidence that you wouldn't understand, because you're not a *Scientist*."

And the others said, "No bribery or corruption involved." "No improper offers of funding or anything like that. None at all." "Just Science with a capital S."

And they all agreed.

The boss said, "Well, Dr Faustus, I don't know how you did it, but you seem to have convinced my colleagues. This is quite remarkable, considering what they were all saying about the scientific evidence for a lab leak just half an hour before you arrived. Remarkable."

Dr Faustus said, "I'll let myself out," and he walked out of the conference room, then promptly got lost in the maze of corridors.

"I am the Science, I am the Science," he said to himself, willing himself to find the way out.

About half an hour into his breezy, stressed walk through the corridors, he went around a corner and bumped into a CIA agent, who said, “Do you need a hand? Are you lost, sir?”

Faustus snapped, “No! I know my way around.”

As he walked down the corridor, feigning relaxed indolence, the agent watched him, until Faustus went around a corner.

The problem was, every hall and every door and every window in the place looked exactly the same.

“I am the Science, I am the Science,” he mumbled to himself.

It didn’t seem to help much, he had to admit, not in this circumstance.

Two hours later, after going along numberless corridors, down an elevator, along more corridors, up an elevator two floors, down another elevator one floor, up another two floors, then down a *different* elevator three floors, and having evaded the central hall rather furtively then heading in the opposite direction, turned several corners and then at his wit’s end, said a fairly rude prayer to the Divine, “I never talk to you, and I know you wouldn’t want to help me anyhow but if you did find it in your heart to help me, please do, I need to get out of this building. Thanks for nothing."

Suddenly he noticed that where he was standing, the sun was shining through the window, from just above the trees at the edge of the carpark. It suddenly struck Faustus that at this time of year at 3 or 4pm, whatever time it was, the sun would be slightly to the SouthEast in the sky, so Faustus headed away from the sun, which he could see through the windows, and only took turns that would leave him heading north west.

It was a miracle! Faustus finally found the exit and let himself out.

His faithful driver, whose name Faustus had completely forgotten, was waiting for him in the car park.

As he walked across to the car, he thought to himself, "See, it wasn't God, was it? It was *me*, *I* found the way out using *science*. I really *am* the Science."

His driver said to him, "Good meeting, Doctor?"

Faustus replied, "A *very* good meeting. I've accomplished a lot today, um..."

"Frank," said his driver. "My name's Frank."

In an extremely rare moment of gratitude and humility, Faustus said, "Thank you Frank. I don't think I could have done it without you finding that particular car park and parking in the right place, and also for waiting for me for so long, for the — ah — meeting to finish." And he added under his breath, "What a nightmare it all is."

Frank didn't say anything in reply, but Faustus thought he could detect a certain — pleasure in the man's expression — and he resolved to remember his name from now on. Fred, no, Francis, no what was it? Frank. Frank. To be Frank. Yes, that would help. To be Frank.

~~~~

A few days later, Faustus received some good news: the letter to the editor signed by Frostey Kristoff, Jerry Blacksmith, and Peter Dackazacka was published in the magazine, Lance-at-Every-Boil, a prestigious medical journal with a very long history. It was a letter of support from about twenty scientists, reassuring everybody that BirdFlip-CoV2 was not created in the lab in WooHoo, and that Zheng-Leng Penguin was in no way responsible.

> We, the undersigned, sign under this declaration in solidarity with all the excellent scientists and doctors in China, especially those in WooHoo province, who would really like to save lives and improve global health, but whose efforts will be hampered if we let these conspiracy theorists have their way. We want to reassure everybody that the Chinese scientists have not hidden anything from us: they are open and transparent in their data sharing.
~~~~

But now, dark, terrible rumours have broken out like a terrible skin disease on the surface of society that threaten our international collaboration and cooperation in important research that I stress is *not* gain of function, no way José, not in a zillion years. There is bad misinformation coming out saying that the virus was created in a lab and spread among humans as a result of a lab escape from ACE2 Penguins. We all stand together like those people on the wall in Les Miserables to condemn such baseless, boundless conspiracy theories, we resile any people that say that the BirdFlip Coronavirus does not have its origins in nature. Conspiracy theories like this are very dangerous and threaten our efforts to collaborate across international borders as well as our government funding, so there. We condemn misinformation in the strongest possible terms and reiterate that we are not lying or telling any fibs at all, nor did we collaborate on this letter beforehand with Dr Faustus,

Yours,

The Undersigned,

Jerry Blacksmith, Frostey Kristoff, Peter Dackazacka, et al.

PS We declare no competing interests

PPS George Faustus did not have anything to do with drafting this email.

PPPS Disclaimer: When we say we declare no conflicts of interest, which doesn't mean we don't *have* any conflicts of interest, just that we have no conflicts of interest that we have any interest in declaring.

On reading the sentence at the bottom saying, "We declare no competing interests," Faustus erupted with a derisive snort of laughter. If anyone among the listed authors had a competing interest, it was Peter Dackazacka, whose project in WooHoo the NAIAD had funded; what a joke!

Still, he should be grateful: without this research letter that Dackazacka had signed, they were all completely done for. Science was completely done for.

The emails and Slick messages were continuing without abating, and gradually the document was being honed for publication.

And so it was that about a week and a half later, the pre-print version of the paper was published online in the medical pre-print server, RxBuMwipE, as "The proximal origin of BirdFlip-CoV-2". The paper explicitly claimed that the virus came from pangolins:

> Since we have found a receptor binding domain very similar to that of BirdFlip-CoV-2 in *pangolins,* means that we can make the logical inference that this was also in the virus that made the species-jump to humans.

The Slick messages continued, however, as the peer reviewers gave their feedback, and Kristen gave his honest opinion about the idea that the virus came from pangolins on a Slick message:

> We all know it didn't come from pangolins.

Then he said a few days after this:

> I don't think anyone will believe it came from pangolins: it doesn't clarify anything - it makes us all look like Red-Footed Boobies actually to even say that it does

Barry Gog agreed:

> The answer is definitely not found in the Pangolin sequence.

George Faustus downloaded the pre-print version of the paper. There were a few obvious problems with it, which he outlined in some commentaries that he sent in a series of emails back to the others, together with the problematic sections copied and struck through (he had just learned how to do this) and his suggestions typed in.

> The proximal origin of BirdFlip-CoV-2
>
> OVERVIEW: Genetic sequencing of BirdFlip-CoV2 has revealed several very interesting, in fact, rather fascinating features of its genetic code, ~~which we are very eager not to admit show that it was engineered~~. In this paper we investigate these features and try to explain them without ever once admitting that any of the data supports the stupid right-wing conspiracy theory that it was created in a lab. In fact, we conclude quite deliberately that all our analyses show that all the possible scenarios we are prepared to recommend in this paper clearly rule out any kind of laboratory origin, in fact, we say that the data is completely incompatible with that idea, and we are not lying to cover anything up; far

> be it for us to cover anything up, especially a possible lab origin, ~~especially that the virus might have been engineered.~~

Faustus emailed out a comment here: “the word ‘engineered’ is not good; it brings to mind genetic engineering and might make people think the virus was engineered.”

Then he thought twice and edited his email, happily before sending it, “the word ‘engineered’ is not good; it brings to mind genetic engineering and might make people think the virus was engineered, *guys.*”He added the ‘guys’ at the end to make it a bit more casual and personable.

> The two main features of BirdFlip-CoV2 that were interesting were:
>
> 1) Based on computer modelling of the structure of the genetic code and some experiments we did in the lab ~~which unfortunately killed one of the lab technicians~~, it certainly looks as though BirdFlip-CoV2 is optimized for binding to the human ACE2 receptor, ~~but not as much as it could be, as our experiments discovered.~~

Faustus added another comment here: “don’t mention whatsisname’s death. It looks bad. Anyhow, he didn’t die from breathing in your gain of fun BirdFlip-CoV2 in your experiments, I’m sure, it was a tragic accident that he picked up the influenza from his Great Aunt and dropped dead coincidentally five minutes after he accidentally breathed in your gain of fun virus. Also some conspiracy theorists might glean from this the idea that when you were looking at the virus you made a deadlier version of it. Don't mention that. Bad optics."

> To say BirdFlip-CoV2 was optimized for human transmission in a lab is of course complete lie, but anyway, some people might comment on the following facts which could be seen as evidence for that theory but which certainly are not because we say so, and these are the many good reasons, which are good reasons because WE are the experts and leaders in science, and the rest of you are nincompoops:
>
> I. There's a thingy in the middle of the spike protein of the virus that we like to call the Furin Cleavage site that is strangely enough very suitable for linking to human ACE2 receptors, which are everywhere in the human body~~ and also in our transgenic penguins that we test our "gain of fun" viruses on.~~

Faustus emailed his comment out: "Skip the 'gain of fun' mention here: nobody understands our shorthand anyhow, and it might give people the idea that you were doing gain of function research on transgenic penguins."

> II. The fact that the furin cleavage looks exactly like it was spliced in by genetic engineers and that the surrounding O-Linked Glycans are another clear sign of genetic

> engineering is of course completely preposterous. Don't get taken in by right-wing anti-science conspiracy nuts: they are probably creationists as well and these obvious signs of genetic engineering are anything but; in fact the fact that they probably arose naturally in fact that's what we say anyhow via natural selection in pangolins so don't believe anything else.

For this section, Faustus' email commentary said, "Too many 'in facts' here, it looks like you're forcing the obvious point as well."

> III. In fact, we once predicted that there would be O-Linked Glycans in any virus that was optimized for humans, honest we did, we're not lying, and that's because of natural evolution, not because the O-Linked Glycans get in there when there's a bit spliced in by gene editing. Honest to goodness, we're not lying in this bit either.

Faustus wrote, "Good. Well done. Tell them you're not lying: they'll believe that."

> IV. The BirdFlip-CoV2 sequence is very similar to the SARS-CoV virus isolated from the Red-Footed Booby, known as BB18+, which was collected being kept in the WooHoo laboratory. This Booby virus is almost identical to BirdFlip-CoV2 except for the aforementioned furin cleavage site, but that doesn't mean that it was made in the lab either; don't be stupid. We're top scientists so you should believe everything we say.

For this section Faustus wrote, “Exactly,” and put a big tick next to it: ✓

V. Anyhow that furin cleavage site could always bond to other ~~lab bird’s~~ natural birds’ that didn’t come from the lab’s ACE2 receptors, such as pigeons, penguins, pangolins[22], pinions, pilgrims and other species that sound like they might be birds that start with a *p*, like pumpkinbirds, pumpernickels[23], podsticks and pagans.

VI. A phenylalanine (that’s an amino acid symbolised by the letter “F” that is found in mammal’s milk, so what the heck it is doing in a bird virus is anyone’s guess) situated at F4200 in BirdFlip-CoV2 corresponds to L337 in the Penguin-DoV2 Urbanik strain, a very fashionable strain. We have decided to designate this sequence “FU”. “FU” has a message for everybody to tell the general public very clearly that nobody should be considering the idea that the virus was created in a lab.

VII.And there’s another bit that we like to say means “FU” that happened in vitro, when the leucine at position F2218 mutated to phenylalanine, which has also been predicted to be optimal for binding of the BirdFlip-CoV2 RBD to the human ACE2 receptor.

[22] This seems to be an error: pangolins are not birds, although their name sounds like they *should* be.

[23] Honestly, you’d think they would know that pumpernickels are not birds. I’m not sure if pumpkinbirds are real, either.

> VIII. Several bits are not quite as good at binding with the ACE2 as you might expect. ~~Obviously the scientists who made it were not very good.~~ Obviously this is evidence that the virus ~~was not engineered~~ had a natural origin because ~~scientists who engineered it~~ nature is a blind clockmaker~~, not like scientists who engineer things.~~

Faustus sent out an email about this section saying, "I can't believe how many times you guys put the word 'engineered' in. You are like criminals who have an unconscious urge to make your confession. Stop it!"

Then he thought twice about that email and sent a followup email saying, "Of course for anyone who FOIs these emails, that last email did not indicate that any one of us are criminals or need to make a confession."

Then he forwarded the two emails to the FOI department, "ATTN NAIAD FOI department: please redact these two emails if this gets FOI'd. Good on you guys, you don't get enough credit."

Then he read through the conclusion:

> Of course if we had more data it could swing the balance of evidence to tell us which bird the BirdFlip coronavirus jumped from: whether it might be pigeons or penguins or pangolins, pinions, pilgrims and other species that sound like they might be birds

> that start with a *p*, like pumpkinbirds, pumpernickels[24], podsticks and pagans.
>
> Obtaining more viral sequences from some more penguins could really reveal the viral origins.
>
> It could also tell us the intermediate host, especially if we found a fully formed polybasic furin cleavage site in some other bird or animal, which we certainly will, and this would lend further support to the natural selection hypothesis, which is of course the only hypothesis worth considering, yes such research would be highly informative, so please keep putting lots of funding into microbiology and virology so we can find the intermediate host. In fact, the fact that fact that we know there *is* no intermediate host really means that our funding can go on forever, because it will never actually be found. Neat, huh?

Dr Faustus sent out another email saying: "Too many 'facts' again, it sounds laboured, as though you're repeating yourself to convince yourself that this is a fact, or at least, to convince the reader: you know it's not a fact. Also, do you think it's wise to mention the idea of funding in the last sentence? It might make hostile readers think of the idea of *removing* our funding. Psychology, guys, psychology!"

He then emailed the FOI section again and told them to redact the last email as well, if it came to an FOI.

So they kept working on the paper.

---

[24] Honestly, you'd think they would know that pumpernickels are not birds. I'm not sure if pumpkinbirds are real, either.

Dr Faustus continued to make appearances with the press.

He made an appearance on CNT and said, “It’s really not necessary to be walking around with a mask on. When you’re in the middle of an international viral pandemic as we all are, wearing a mask would have no more than a placebo effect of making people feel that everything’s alright, and it might even block the odd droplet of infected saliva, but in fact it’s not going to provide much protection at all. It might even make things worse. Often people touch their masks and adjust them and they touch their face and then spread the germs around via their disgusting infected fingers, or they sneeze and the mask sends the droplets up into the air where the air conditioning carries them far farther than they would have gone without the mask. And, you know, lockdowns, restrictions on travel, these are all for chickens, really. We will soon have some cheap, effective treatments, I am sure, and if we don’t, at some point there will be vaccines for everybody.”

The day after a big interview about the virus with CNT, he got more great news on the email: the prestigious journal, Denature Magazine, had actually accepted the study! It was going to be published.

Kristen sent out an email:

> Dear Jerry, Clarence, and George,
>
> Thanks again for your encouragement and for overseeing this publication as we've been writing the paper about the inception of BirdFlip-CoV-2. I'm very glad to report that the paper has been accepted for publication by the prestigious Denature Epidemiology Magazine and should be online soon for this month's journal (exactly when I don't know)
>
> I've attached the version of the paper that they accepted, plus a press release we've drafted, just to keep you informed. We're still waiting for a proof copy, so if there are any corrections, edits, suggestions you want to make about the paper or the press release, please email them and I'll make sure they're included.
>
> George, thanks for your media appearances, esp. last night on CNT. Great work, people are listening,
>
> Best regards,
>
> Kristen

What warmed Faustus' heart when he read the final, published study was that it was little changed from the pre-print version, apart from Faustus' suggested changes.

He decided to email Jerry about the whole thing.

> Jerry, great work, please tell everyone. Thanks for getting all the guys together to write that paper for the teleconference at the start. Please tell Kristen and everyone else that the study has been a great success.
>
> Kind regards, Faustus.

At that moment his email dinged.

Faustus said to himself, "Well, will you look at that? What a coincidence: Peter Dackazacka just sent me an email."

Subject: Thank you so much for your media appearances saying BirdFlip virus definitely came from birds and not from the lab in WooHoo.

> Being the Principal Investigator on some of the grants and studies those odious reporters from VLPS News at the press conference yesterday were spreading rumours about, I just really want to say thank you to you George, for standing up for us all, for saying that the BirdFlip virus was not a release from some WooHoo lab, that all of those conspiramacy theories are just a myth, and it wasn't some deadly virus made intentionally as a weaponised gain of function thingy like it really was and that that idea was just a myth, and it was just some random Red-Footed Booby-virus that just coincidentally came down two hundred miles from the coast and somehow ended up infecting some of the lab workers in the markets, who had just happened to be working on that same virus in the lab, but it didn't have anything to do with that, as you said in your press conference, that's all a big myth that nobody believes and the study confirms. Thank you so much Dr Faustus for standing up for our reputations in this — it means so much to me and our lab assistants and technicians and all the scientists who work with my team because, you know, if they start defunding our work or saying its gain of function or that we caused the outbreak, we're all in the bird-poop together, really, and none of us will have jobs, and we'll probably be public

pariahs, and who knows what else, so let me say, I'm so so grateful, I can't even say how grateful I am to you for saying it definitely didn't come from the lab, and quoting that study that we know you had nothing to do with getting together behind the scenes (haha!) good work George for putting yourself on the line and once this plandemic is over I'm really looking forward to getting together and saying thank you and shaking your hand and letting you know again what a great job you did just now at squashing those boundless rumours, I mean, groundless rumours.

Cheers, have a drink on me buddy sometime, Peter Dackazacka.

Faustus said to himself, "What a kind email. I'll send him a reply. Keep it simple. Yeh, yeh, after this, we'll all catch up and have a barbecue or something."

From: George Faustus

To: Peter Dackazacka

Thanks tons for your kind email. Kind regards, George.

It is an understatement to say that he was thrilled; so thrilled that he called out to his wife from the study, "Gloriana darling, would you like to go out and get some pizza tonight? I've had a fabulous win at work."

Gloriana said, "No, dear, I have a headache. I'm going to bed early; in fact I'm already in bed."

And Faustus realised that Pizza had been a code-word for something or other early in their marriage; it was so long ago he had forgotten what it was, something to *do* with bed, and then he remembered.

So Faustus said, "Darling, I didn't mean that sort of pizza; not the pizza you have in bed. I meant real pizza, with pepperoni and cheese on top. You know, food? We could order it on Ober, you know, the real foody kind of pizza, and even have that kind of pizza *in* bed if you like[25]."

---

[25] Some conspiracy theorists will think this publication is referencing Q and the much discredited Pizzagate theories with this little conversation; I am certain that Doctor Faustus and his wife were involved in nothing of the sort. I am aware that human psychology indicates that as soon as some idea is *denied, some people who suffered from trauma in their early life or are simply ineluctably addicted to gossip will thereafter be absolutely certain that it is true.* This is an unfortunate aspect of human psychology, the result of which is that as soon as a rumour gets into the public domain, no matter how untrue, it immediately takes hold of the consciousness of certain people such that every denial only fuels the flames of the rumour and makes people even more certain that the rumour is true, and more likely to share it, and further fuels the spread of the rumour. Unfortunate, but unavoidable. Of course, the opposite is also true: when a rumour is *true,* the denials *may serve to assure ordinary, sane people that the rumour is false,* provided that such denials are issued by people in authority, or who possess cultural credibility. Misinformation is everywhere, unfortunately, even in this sentence, which makes it a perfect example of Eubulides' paradox, or Saint Jerome's sermon on David's exclamation in Psalm 116, "I said in my alarm, every man is a liar!", or the discussion of the liar's paradox in the fifth century AD Indian Philosopher Barthrari's Vākyapadīya (which I have not read but could of course being later have been based on Eubulides or Jerome) and the writings of many other authors' work, the most famous modern example of which is indeed Kurt Gödel's theorem, which demonstrates as a mathematical proof that every logically consistent theory contains a weakness precisely at the point where the logical theory encounters the liar's paradox in the form, "This sentence is not provable." S'Quid Pro Quo: the author doesn't know what's true and what's not true any more because the author is completely bamboozled by his own explanations. Read on.

Gloriana replied, "Well, I'm not hungry, dear. You go and get some, and have a night off. You haven't had many wins, really, what with this pandemic and all."

Faustus said, "Well, darling, this has been my philosophy: every crisis is an opportunity. I sincerely thought that the BirdFlip coronavirus would be the end of NAIAD and the end of government funding for research into viruses, but it looks like I've managed it so well, that we will get even *more* funding. I think I must be a genius bureaucrat, dear."

Gloriana said, "I have no doubt that you are," in such a patronising tone that made Faustus wonder if she was mocking him. She added, "You are not just a clever bureaucrat, my dear, you *are* the Science."

He was so thrilled to hear her say it, that he forgot that she was probably mocking him. "Really?" he said. "Gloriana, you really think that?"

Gloriana said in a sing-song voice, "Yes I do, dear. You *are* the Science, with a capital S," and in that moment she thanked the gods of science that she had heard him whispering the phrase over and over again to himself in the bathroom a few hours before that big press conference with CNT news. Sometimes the gods give you the opportunity to be nice, even if you're not completely sincere about it. "You *are* the Science, darling," she repeated.

Faustus was so pleased with this that he came into the bedroom and kissed her on the lips and said, "Are you sure you don't want some of the other sort of pizza, darling? I am finding that hearing you say that I am the Science works better than sildaffodil nitrate."

"*Sildenafil citrate*[26]," she corrected him, thinking to herself that hearing her husband say the word 'daffodil' had certainly ruined the mood for her. "No dear, go and have a pizza yourself, and enjoy yourself. I'd really love to come with you under any other circumstances, but I sincerely do have a headache."

Faustus decided that it was okay to go without her; he decided he was going to have some pizza tonight to celebrate the publication of the study, no matter whether Gloriana wanted it or not.

He had just discovered the excellent app Ober and ordered an Ober on his phone. The driver arrived two minutes later and took him to his favourite pizza joint, Goldfish Pizza.

---

[26] i.e. viagra.

He walked in: it hadn't changed at all. The place was lit by soft candlelight, which pleased Faustus, because it meant he would not have to wait until the effect of harsh light on his eyes had faded before he would be able to sleep that night.

Faustus ordered a pepperoni pizza at the desk, and found himself a table, where he stood for a moment, watching the people coming in and going out, socially distancing, mostly young people in their early twenties and thirties. The thin-crusted pizza arrived promptly, and Faustus sat down to enjoy it, six feet from every other table. Thankfully, the entertainment hadn't started yet, a fact that meant he could eat his meal in peace.

As he was in the middle of eating the last piece of pizza, a skeletally thin man with hollow cheeks in a neat-fitting suit and wearing a strangely old-fashioned coat, with a cowl that went over his head, sat down at his table. Dr Faustus felt immediately uneasy: the man's face resembled nothing so much as a skull, and not only that, he wasn't following social distancing rules.

"Mister Faustus," the gentleman said. "I was sent by a mutual friend, to set up an urgent meeting."

He handed a business card to Dr Faustus, who glanced at it and recognised it immediately. It was a genuine Gill Bates business card.

Suddenly it all became clear.

Mr Bates did sometimes employ rather... unique personal assistants. He had a penchant for the strange and the quixotic; indeed, he seemed to prefer employing people who might well be too out-there for the ordinary tech billionaire.

In the middle of fall the previous year, Faustus had been given a very similar business card by the Billionaire tech entrepreneur and ubiquitously universal philanthropist whose foundation happened to singlehandedly fund nearly every hospital research division, abortion clinic, and vaccination clinic in the whole world, Gill Bates himself; he had given Faustus the card in New York in October the previous year, at the pandemic awaredness exercise, "Event 1" or "Event 2," or something, he had forgotten exactly what it had been called. Dr Faustus had met Mr Bates quite a few times over the years, and they had shared dinner more than ten or eleven times (who's counting?), but in Faustus' estimation they got on very well because of their shared interest in vaccination as the solution to every single human problem and need in existence.

Dr Faustus remembered a particular dinner in 2005, when Mr Bates had said to him, "If there's a decent pandemic sometime, George, normalcy will only return when we've largely vaccinated the entire population of this globe on which we live called Earth[27]." Dr Faustus had replied, "Well, the size of the needle doesn't matter, Gill. We could largely vaccinate everyone, or small-ly vaccinate everyone. I mean, the first vaccination *was* a small vaccination: it was a vaccination for *small*pox." They had both had a good laugh about that pun, although he thought he'd noticed Gill rolling his eyes, just for a moment. The waiter standing at the ready with the corkscrew pointed at the 1992 vintage Screaming Penguin wine bottle that Gill had bought with him for their perusal that night had certainly rolled his eyes[28]; Faustus had definitely seen that — in any case, it was a great evening, even if Gill had humoured Faustus somewhat — and here it was, the business card that meant that Faustus might well

---

[27] Another billionaire is believed to have plagiarised Mr Bates' statement some years later, unless Mr Bates plagiarised it from him first.

[28] Screaming Penguin is a far more exclusive winery than Screaming Eagle, the famous Californian winery, which is the reason you and I have never even heard of it. It's an exclusive club and you ain't in it.

have the pleasure of sharing the tech billionaire's company once again.

Faustus examined the business card, to see if it really was a genuine Gill Bates business card, and as he watched the card carefully, the picture upon changed gradually from "Gill Bates Tech Billionaire esq." to "The GB & HB Pencil Foundation"; and Faustus immediately inferred that the business card was actually not printed, but was computerised text of some sort on some sort of tiny newfangled flexible screen made by a company that Gill Bates had undoubtedly bought about nine or ten years ago.

It was virtually identical to the previous card, indeed, he was absolutely certain that it was a genuine Gill Bates business card.

Faustus said, "Where do I need to go to meet him?" He suddenly wondered if there was a helicopter hovering nearby: this was how he had been transported to some of his other meetings with Mr Bates.

The hollow-cheeked gentleman said, "I am Mr Bates' personal assistant today. Please follow me."

Faustus said, "Okay. I will. After all, it is a genuine Gill Bates business card."

The gentleman nodded humourlessly and got up from his chair, and glided over to the desk and spoke to the maître d'hôtel, who immediately unlocked a safe behind the desk and took out a golden key that glinted in the candlelight. He handed the key to the hollow-cheeked gentleman, who beckoned mysteriously for George to follow him[29].

The gentleman used the golden key to open a door, hidden behind a curtain at the stage, and they wandered down into the basement, which we are assured by all the fact-checkers does not exist, so this sentence, indeed this whole chapter, is certainly not true, you can be sure of that. Gödel's theorem would assure us, therefore, that this book is not logically consistent, which is a relief, because if it were a complete theorem in itself, it would not be, according to Gödel.

As they entered the basement, all thoughts of logic and reality and Gödel's theorem were banished from Faustus' mind, for the place resembled Hades, at least in his own

[29] I must apologise for the descent into ridiculous conspiracy theories, but if this wasn't what actually happened, then the Pope's a Catholic, which he isn't according to Bishop Carlo Maria Viganò, who was actually excommunicated by the Pope, so what would he know? What would anyone know? I'm getting confused and frightened by this story at this point, which is of course completely fictionable.

faulty perception at that mooment[30], and he found himself following the skeletal figure through a place of doom and deep darkness, and the gentleman seemed to Faustus to be carrying a huge scythe, and the shadows of the basement were crouching around and reaching out like the skeletal fingers of the damned, wanting to grasp him and pull him down into the realm of the dead where they dwelled forever. Of course this was just the illusory creation of his own mind, reasoned Faustus, not reality, and he clung to the one truth that was irrefutable: "I am the Science. I am the Science," he recited to himself like a mantra, but for some reason it made it worse.

The gentleman used the golden key to open a door, hidden in the deep darkness, and they entered a tunnel that smelled faintly of cat urine, with walls of grey concrete that reminded Faustus of cold-war constructions. Wanting to distract himself, he asked the gentleman if it *was* a cold-war construction that they were walking through.

[30] A mooment is a moment in which one says "Oo Oo" in dismay. Warning: this word may not appear in the dictionary, but it does not in any way, shape or form make it any less a word; how dare you suggest such a thing. If a person can identify as a chicken — and here the analogy breaks down — for such people were once put into the sanatorium to relax until they had recovered their senses. This brings us to a philosophical conundrum: is a word that has lost its senses, or never had any sense at all, really a word?

"Your assumption is correct," said the gentleman. "This tunnel was indeed constructed during the cold war. You see, they reasoned that if the President was holed up in the Operation Cartwheel underground bunker he would probably want some pizza, so they ensured that the raw ingredients were stored in the bunker as well as a genuine pizza oven; this of course included the assumption that the pizzeria chef would be willing and able to escape into the bunker as well, using this secret tunnel. It was all very well thought out."

They reached a broad room that seemed to be the centre of the bunker, and the gentleman pointed to a ladder. Dr Faustus said, "I'm not too good with heights," and indicated to the gentleman that at his age he was quite unwilling to climb up ladders.

The gentleman sighed and said, "Using the ladder is so much more dramatic. Alright, we'll use the elevator then." He put the key in another lock, and an elevator door appeared, and a backlit button, on which was only the triangular sign indicating 'up', and no 'down' button. He pressed the 'up' button and the sound of a lift descending filled the room, followed by a 'ding' as it reached the bottom. They got in the lift.

The music that was playing in the lift was the Muzak version of the wonderful song by the immortal Antonio Carlos Jobim and Vinicius de Moraes, "the Girl from Ipanema," which cheered Faustus no end: it brought him back to the nineteen seventies, when he was in his thirties, a very happy time of life for a man with a burgeoning career and a young family.

The lift ascended slowly and finally they reached the top, at which point Faustus was glad, because on the way up he had begun to realise how much he hated that song.

The gentleman led him out, through a building that Faustus recognised as soon as they emerged into the clear night air of the park: they had walked out of the building attached to the tower, which is the highest point of the highest point in Washington DC, Fort Reno Park.

About forty feet above them, a black helicopter hovered quietly. Faustus wondered — was it an electric helicopter? Slowly the helicopter descended onto a flat section of grass in Fort Reno park, and the gentleman led Faustus to the four-door helicopter.

Mr Bates was sitting in the rear part of the helicopter, behind the pilot's cabin. He reached out a hand and helped Dr Faustus to climb aboard, something Dr Faustus wasn't too happy about, as they were supposed to keep their distance.

Dr Bates said, “Don’t worry George, I don’t have the virus. I tested negative just an hour ago.”

Dr Faustus was familiar with helicopters; he quickly clamped the seatbelt buckles over his chest as Gill Bates closed the sliding bay door, leaving the gentleman all alone in Fort Reno Park. Gill Bates sat opposite Dr Faustus and clamped on his own buckles.

It was strangely silent in the rear fuselage of the helicopter, and the feeling of Newton’s law being applied in different directions was strangely gentle, so that they almost seemed to be floating rather than flying.

Faustus said, “Won’t he be all alone out there? How will he get home?”

Gill Bates said, “Oh, he’s fine. He’ll just catch a taxi driver and get him home that way.”

Faustus swallowed; he wasn’t sure if Gill Bates meant that the gentleman would take the taxi driver home, or that the gentleman would get himself home *via* the taxi driver, or *what* he meant. It was a typically ambiguous statement from the mysterious tech billionaire.

As they flew, Faustus could see the city lights of DC below them.

Gill said, "Aren't they beautiful? That's the whole world, Dr Faustus, you and I have the whole world in our hands. That's what it means to have power."

The plane flew for a little longer until they were hovering above the Washington monument.

Gill said, "Democracy is a nice idea." Then he added, "Dr Faustus, I have a favour to ask of you."

Faustus swallowed and said, "Gill, anything at all. You know me. I appreciate absolutely everything you do — indeed, I appreciate *you,* Gill." Inside his own mind he realised that he was completely petrified of the power that this man held, and he starting whispering, "I am the Science, I am the Science."

Gill said, "I *do* know you. You have evaded some serious consequences at times: much as... well much as *I* have, really. It's not a huge favour. But I have heard that you have the President's ear..."

Faustus said, "President Crump?"

Gill said, "Yes, much as we would desire him *not* to be the President, it appears that he is. It even appears that many people actually voted for him; I have no idea why. Tell me, Dr Faustus, have you ever heard of Hydroxychloroquilline?"

Dr Faustus said, "Yes, Hydroxychloroquilline is a derivative of Hydroxychloroquine, which is based on Chloroquine, which is itself a synthetic substitute for the ancient therapeutic Quinine. Like Quinine, it is used to treat parasitic infections, particularly resistant Malaria, and also for viral infections with fever, such as influenza and so forth."

"Indeed," said Gill. "You are one hundred percent right. Did you know that many people are saying that it is an effective treatment for BirdFlip-CoV2?"

"Well, it kinda makes sense, doesn't it?" said Faustus bravely. Gill Bates wasn't the kind of guy you contradicted, especially on medical matters. "After all, Chloroquine was the main treatment for the first SARS virus, and it was used for MERS as well, I believe, with some success."

"Well there are no randomised controlled trials for this," said Gill. "It's far from certain that Chloroquine had any effect at all, apart from placebo."

Faustus said, "Well, you are right; there simply weren't enough active cases to institute any kind of randomised, controlled, double-blind trial."

Gill nodded doubtfully. “There is that,” he said, shaking his head now. “But the thing is, we need to *squash* Hydroxychloroquilline before it’s even started. And I have the perfect way to do it.”

“Why?” said Faustus. “If it’s an effective treatment? Why do you want to squash it?”

Gill said, “Vaccines, George. If we have a cheap, effective, generic treatment that *appears* to work, we’re in trouble. We won’t be able to get our mRNA vaccines up and running.”

Faustus said, “I see,” but he didn’t, not really.

Gill held his eye for far too long, and Faustus began to feel guilty. “You know, George, with a genetically engineered virus like this one, the death toll could be in the billions. Do you want to be responsible for foisting an unproven treatment on the populace? There is *no proof whatsoever* that Hydroxychloroquilline does anything at all to treat BirdFlip-CoV2. Think of the deaths we will prevent with this new vaccine platform that I’ve been developing. Moodyearna has one ready to go, they just have to finish human testing, Pfutticup’s is almost ready to go as well; I *own* the company that’s going to manufacture it, BioZTechno, and I’m going to make it work, George. We’re going to have a completely new vaccine platform; ultimately we'll be able to produce vaccines very cheaply: it's like putting in new software, George. You plug in the genetic code, inject the vaccine, and it gets the body to make the protein that you want the body to develop an immunity to."

Faustus said, "It sounds marvellous, Gill. But how are you going to do it?"

Dr Faustus was talking about the vaccine development timeline, which would seem astonishingly short if they were going to affect the progress of the pandemic before it had spread through everyone; after all, a normal timeline for the development of an experimental medication would be... say, 12 or 14 years? Yes, by running the trials in parallel as they were doing these days, the pharmaceutical companies could shave, maybe, seven or eight years off that timeline, but still... everyone would have caught BirdFlip-CoV2 and either died or have achieved natural immunity by the time the mRNA medicine was ready to inject.

But Gill Bates took his question to be a completely different one.

"Well, George," Gill Bates said, "I simply want you to speak in President Crump's ear. I want you to tell him that

Hydroxychloroquilline is... *safe and effective* to treat BirdFlip-CoV2."

George was very puzzled. "What do you mean? Tell him it's *effective?* Won't that be counter-productive, for the ends you have in mind?"

Gill Bates said, "George, I have a team of psychologists, behaviourists, and sociologists looking into all this. They have assured me that, while the general public trusts President Crump regarding *economic* issues — and that is not unreasonable, as Crump does have a reasonable amount of business experience — but they certainly do not trust him on *scientific or medical* issues. Indeed, my polls (which are highly exclusive and not at all disseminated publicly) show that if President Crump says a medication is safe and effective, the news media will jump on it, just for the opportunity to make him look like a clown. Believe me, the best thing I can do to squash Hydroxychloroquilline is to cause President Crump to recommend it. So that's all I want you to do: speak in President Crump's ear and tell him that Hydroxychloroquilline is... *safe and effective* to treat BirdFlip-CoV2."

George said, "That's all?"

Gill Bates said, “That’s all. And believe me, when you retire, there’ll be a nice big golden nest egg for you out of all of this. Just like you promised those CIA guys.”

Deeply offended by this invasion of his privacy, George blurted, “How on earth did you know about that? Anyhow, Gill, I’m not for sale.”

Gill said, “My people have back-door access to every computer on the earth; don’t you think that includes the CIA servers? In any case, I know about the lab leak, George. I myself have funded many such projects, quite recently, including one scientist who recreated the 1918 influenza using bits from the Avian influenza, thereby proving that Avian influenza could morph into the 1918 flu in nature, if given the chance. I fully approve of the projects you’ve been funding, George.”

George suddenly had qualms. What was he doing? This man was the most powerful man on earth. Was Gill Bates subtly threatening him, to expose his funding of the virus that eventually escaped the Chinese lab and became the WooHoo coronavirus? Gill’s manner of speaking was highly ambiguous; George had to believe Gill Bates was on his side. They were both on the same side, surely…

Gill said, "You're not having qualms, are you, George? Can't you see that if Crump recommends Hydroxychloroquilline, no one will want to use it. Then we can get the vaccines approved under emergency approval with the FDA. You're not anti vaccine are you, George? You're not an anti-vaxxer? I know you're not."

"What are you planning?" said Dr Faustus.

Gill Bates said, "If we can issue them under EUA, we can get the vaccines out within the year. We'll save the day, George. You'll be the hero."

Dr Faustus nodded. "That's an idea I can work with..." he admitted.

Gill Bates said, "It's all about the *Science*, George. The Science."

Dr Faustus managed to justify it to himself, then: "Well, I'm not doing anything wrong, am I, really, by recommending Hydroxychloroquilline to the President. After all, if it happens to actually do something against the virus, it means I told the truth."

Gill Bates said, "That's right," and then added a comment that Faustus wasn't sure was a compliment, "You approach the truth the same way that I do."

Dr Faustus settled in to the queasy feeling of treacherous betrayal, and tried to think of some other subject. He looked out the window. They were going over Garfield Street now, near his home. He felt a little queasy knowing that Gill Bates knew where he lived; but of *course* he did. Gill Bates probably knew everything.

Gill Bates said, “There’s something more. You have to slow the spread of the pandemic as much as possible while we can, so that when we have the vaccines ready to go, there will still be some people who haven’t caught it yet.”

Dr Faustus said, “Of course, of course… How do we do that?”

Gill said, “Masks. Lockdowns. Restrict air travel. The key, George, is scaring everybody. It’s all for the greater good: once we can get this mRNA vaccine into people’s arms, we will have a technology that will change the world for the better: imagine a world where we just do a test to determine the exact genetic makeup of the cancer that afflicts someone, and we can simply plug that into a computer, get the complementary code into the vaccine, and hey presto! Inject the cure into them. Customisable vaccines, George.”

Dr Faustus said, “Is that even possible?” He had the idea that it wasn’t; that this was all a fantastic pipe dream.

He looked at Gill and the dreadful idea entered his mind that this man might be insane with hubris. Then he thought of how much money and power was at Bates' fingertips, and he blanched, and his reservations disappeared like the morning mist. It didn't even *matter* if he was suffering from hubris: money and power could fix anything...

Dr Faustus repeated his question, "Is it possible? To plug RNA into a vaccine, the way one might put new computer code into a computer?"

Gill said, "That's the mRNA technology, George. I'll explain to you sometime."

And the helicopter door opened, and Dr Faustus realised that their conversation was at an end. He obediently disentangled himself from the seat buckles and got out, realising they were parked silently on his driveway, with the rotors still rotating above them.

He gingerly extracted himself from the helicopter, trying not to hurt his knees as he made the small step from the fuselage to the ground. A hand reached out and helped him: it was the gentleman's bony hand. Somehow he had made it here before they did.

Faustus was shaking slightly. He looked up; Gill Bates gave him a wave, the helicopter door closed of its own accord, and the helicopter ascended silently into the atmosphere.

The gentleman was very solicitous, helping George to negotiate the front driveway, the grass, the small garden, to his front door. And then he was inside his house.

Gloriana was asleep. George went to the bathroom, and sat upon the toilet seat, almost collapsing with exhaustion.

He actually wept with tiredness.

He was too old for this stuff. Too old.

CHAPTER 7

The army, lockdowns and masking

One day, not long after the visit from Mr Gill Bates, Faustus received a phone call from the Pentagon.

It went like this:

Dr Faustus: "Hello?"

Man on the other end in a squeaky voice: "Hello, Dr Faustus. This is General Mike Vanilli, head of the Joint Chiefs of Staff."

Dr Faustus: "No it's not — you're pulling my leg."

Man on the other end in a squeaky voice: "Well, yes it is, sir. My secretary got me your number."

Dr Faustus: "Come on — is that you Kristen, doing a funny voice? Have you breathed in helium, Kristen? That's what it sounds like — someone who has breathed in helium. That's not the Mike Vanilli. His voice is kinda deeper."

Man on the other end in a squeaky voice: "Well if you must know you are partially right: there was indeed an escape of helium-3[31] from the canisters we were keeping in the Pentagon, and our voices have been altered temporarily,

[31] God alone only knows what they were doing with Helium 3: it's really very, very rare and is the only stable isotope apart from Helium 4, which is vastly more common.

because of a percentage of helium in the air in the Pentagon."

Dr Faustus: "Oh okay, that makes sense. Is it really you, Mike?"

General Mike Vanilli in a squeaky voice: "Okay, I rang you because we want you to come in and meet with us."

Dr Faustus: "Really? Do I have to when there's that — helium everywhere in there — ?"

General Mike Vanilli in a squeaky voice: "Well I apologise for the helium, Doctor, but it should have dissipated by the time you get here. It's a temporary thing."

Dr Faustus talked to Petronia, and she organised a time with General Vanilli's personal assistant.

When Faustus arrived the following morning, he was whisked into the Joint Chiefs of Staff meeting. All the Generals were there, gathered together in the situation room.

As soon as Faustus and Petronia sat down, General Mike Vanilli said at a normal pitch, "Hello, George. Welcome to the meeting." Thankfully, the helium appeared to have dissipated.

"Hi Mike," said Dr Faustus, "How are you?"

"Well, thank you," the General said. "We've asked you here today, actually, because the US Army has been put in charge of the management of the pandemic."

Faustus said, "I thought NHIJ and the CDE were in charge;" i.e. him and Clarence, and Nancy Balm.

Mike replied, "Well, you are, to some degree, on one level of governance, but insofar as practical enforcement and deployment goes, the army is in charge."

Faustus said, "So that means you're in charge? The joint chiefs of staff?"

Mike said, "Well… actually, no. Didn't you know that? We are essentially figureheads, George. We don't have any role in the actual deployment: our role is purely advisory. No, the chain of command goes from the President through the Defense Secretary directly to the army, and bypasses us."

Faustus asked, "So… why am I here?"

Mike answered, "Well… President Crump thought that you might be able to advise us on how to advise him…"

Faustus said slightly ungraciously, "That sounds like an interesting idea." He wasn't very enamoured with the idea of the army being in charge, not at all.

Mike said, “Well, what with the BirdFlip Coronavirus apparently having been created in the lab, President Crump thought we should meet up.”

Faustus was indignant; he snarked, “I have been trying to make it clear to everybody that the idea that the virus was created in the lab is entirely misinformation. Why does everyone have it in their heads?”

Mike said calmly, “President Crump said that he doesn’t believe the CIA team who were tasked to look into it; he says that he believes they were compromised by the deep state.”

Faustus said indignantly, “Deep state, deep schmate. What a load of bunkum! This is the CIA we’re talking about! Who is there who could compromise them?” And a moment after saying this Faustus suddenly remembered that *he* had actually compromised them; he wasn’t sure whether to feel proud of his ingenuity or ashamed of his dastardliness. He settled on being proud of his dastardliness.

Mike replied, “Be that as it may, we are tasked with advising the President, and we wonder what you think we should be saying.”

Faustus suddenly saw his opportunity: if he played his cards right, President Crump would be getting the same advice from everybody, which would certainly suit Faustus' retirement plan, courtesy of Gill Bates. So he said, "Lockdowns. Lockdowns and masks. And travel restrictions."

Mike said, "Can you clarify? I thought I heard you say masks aren't much good the other day on your interview with CNT?"

Faustus said, "No — I don't recall saying that."

Mike said, "Jemimah, could you call up the clip?"

His personal assistant clicked a few pages and links on her raspberry and a video showed up on the big screen of Faustus saying, "It's really not necessary to be walking around with a mask on. When you're in the middle of an international viral pandemic as we all are, wearing a mask would have no more than a placebo effect of making people feel that everything's alright, and it might even block the odd droplet of infected saliva, but in fact it's not going to provide much protection at all. It might even make things worse. Often people touch their masks and adjust them and they touch their face and then spread the germs around via their disgusting infected fingers, or they sneeze and the mask sends the droplets up into the air where the air conditioning carries them far farther than they would have gone without the mask. And, you know, lockdowns, restrictions on travel, these are all for chicken-pussies, really. We will soon have some cheap, effective treatments, I am sure, and if we don't, at some point there will be vaccines for everybody."

After chanting "I am the Science" inwardly a few times, Faustus clarified nervously, "Ah — I didn't mean exactly that masks were completely useless, just that... people will feel a lot better if they're wearing them."

Mike said, "That's exactly what we need. The most pressing danger we are concerned about is panic, chaos and social upheaval, Dr Faustus. What we must do is to reassure the populace that this is not the end of the world, even if millions or even billions of people are dying. And the best way to reassure them is, in fact, to make them afraid, and then get them do something, get them to contribute to the team-work, team pandemic, wear masks, participate in lockdowns, forego air travel, then they will feel that they are doing everything they can about the pandemic, and then they will feel safe, they will feel good about themselves because they are virtuous. This is how we do it in the army, Dr Faustus."

Faustus could only say, "I see," to this speech.

Mike said, "So as long as we can count on your support, Dr Faustus?"

Faustus said a weak, "Yes," and they shook hands, and that was the end of the meeting.

~~~~

Four hours' drive away, a Jewish doctor named Zed, who was working at the coal-face with patients in a small Jewish community in Upstate New York, was having a cup of coffee with another doctor he had known since medical school. , whose name was Yod, at a local coffee shop.

Yod worked in a medical centre on Long Island, and he had some news to share. Yod said, "I've had a lot of patients been coming into the practice with symptoms consistent with BirdFlip-CoV2. And I mean a *lot.*"

Zed said, "Me too. What have you been doing for them?"

"Not much," Yod admitted. "I tell them to go home and take an aspirin. And one in fifty of them ends up going to emergency, where they don't come back out. I try not to encourage them to go to hospital. It mostly affects the old people, Zed."

"Well they're the ones we need. All the parents around here are too busy to look after the kids, so they get their
~~~~

grandparents to come and look after them. It would be a disaster to the economy of this town if all the old people died. Do you know, Yod, I'm trying something different," said Zed. "It's an anti-Malarial and anti-rheumatoid medication, you know it, Hydroxychloroquilline. It's like Quinine."

Yod said, "Quinine — Chloroquine — Hydroxychloroquine, yeh I know, and now Hydroxychloroquilline. Much the same as Quinine. Logical choice for a respiratory virus. There's a long history of treating fevers and influenzas with the alkylated 4-aminoquinolines you know; Hydroxychloroquilline is a little more lipophillic I believe[32], takes a bit more effort to get it across the cell membrane. So it works, yes?"

"It works," said Zed. "Does it work! It really works. It works like a treat! I use it with an antibiotic and zinc—"

"Oh, zinc, of course," said Yod, "Helps it to get across the cell membrane. Well, that makes sense. Yeh, I was just reading Browning's article in Springy Nature just the other day." He paused. "I wondered about that. I really did, whether you might be able to use Chloroquine, after all, it worked for the SARS virus, supposedly."

---

[32] If you understand what this doctor is saying, you're doing better than me, and I wrote this damn book.

“They patients are practically running out of the surgery,” said Zed. “They’re jumping and leaping, and not one of them out of 669 people I treated has ended up in hospital dying.”

“669? You’re pulling my leg,” said Yod. “Not one of them dying? You’re pulling my leg with that too.”

Zed admitted, “Well, it might have been a few more or a few less than 669. But that’s it, not one of them ended up dying. It’s working, Yod, it’s really working.”

Yod said, “You should tell people about this, Zed. Write a study. Contact the president. Do a video and put it on Tic-Tac-Toe. It’s not fair to keep a cure to yourself, if you really have one.”

Zed said, “You know you’re right. I will — I’ll write to the President. I can’t keep this to myself. You’re completely right Yod. I’ll do it.”

~~~

Things developed quickly as the BirdFlip Coronavirus spread quickly. Faustus had to attend the Pandemic Advisory meeting twice a week with President Crump; he didn’t like Crump much, but he did his best to serve him even so.

Strangely enough, though Faustus could see no sign of Gill Bates’ hand in the events, Gill Bates’ agenda was
~~~

immediately in full swing, as though everybody had been told what to do, or as though some mysterious overbearing force was directing them all in the same direction — the Mayor of DC had already signed an order putting in place emergency health measures and the Health And Homeland And Security Emergency Agency Management Legislature Enacting State Secrets (known as HAHA-SEAMLESS) had been put in charge and here they were, planning for their first lockdown, which was going to take place in the middle of March.

It was during one of those meetings with the President that Faustus had the perfect opportunity to speak in Crump's ear about Hydroxychloroquilline.

It was on one particular day when they were forced to change the time of the meeting to 4pm because Crump had a media commitment with VLPS News in the morning. Unfortunately, the traffic in DC was particularly bad that day; Faustus was the only one who made it to the meeting, apart from one or two of Crump's personal advisors, and they were left virtually on their own, as one of the advisors needed to go to the bathroom, just after Crump had sent the other one on an errand.

"So Dr Faustus, what do you think of the way that it's going? You can be candid with me, nobody's listening," said Crump.

Faustus thought for a moment, then said very diplomatically, "You're doing a great job, like no President before you."

He knew this was the kind of thing Crump liked to hear, because it was strangely enough the sort of thing Crump said about himself, ad infinitum, and Crump seemed very pleased with Faustus' comment, and that was they Faustus thought it might be the perfect time for him to drop Gill Bates' little seed into the conversation.

"Do you know, President Crump," he said, "Something I've been meaning to talk to you about; would you believe that Hydroxychloroquilline is quite safe and effective..." He couldn't believe what he was hearing: he was speaking so stiffly and unnaturally that Crump would surely realise he was lying. Or sort of lying. Or telling the truth in such a way as to make it a sort of dishonesty. In a complete mental freeze, he told his mouth to keep talking, without actually knowing what it was going to say, and his mouth continued on its own: "I don't necessarily want to suggest this myself, as I don't want to … um… alienate the big Pharma money guys, (did I say that part out loud?)"

Crump said, "You did. I get it."

Faustus, not knowing if he had completely stuffed it up or did a sterling job, took the handbrake off his mouth again with great interest, wondering what it would come out with next. His mouth said: "Yeh, I *don't* want to offend the Big Pharma guys as they've got their hearts set on a vaccine — ahem — but Hydroxychloroquilline does need to be championed by *someone* who has a bit of influence — I think it could necessarily be someone that could well and truly change the game in these early days of the virus… I mean, there must be *someone* who can champion this safe and effective treatment. (I can't believe I said that either.)"

Crump said, "Well, no other President has had to deal with what I've had to deal with, Dr Faustus — even the 1918 pandemic was not such a bad pandemic as this one is, no other pandemic ever affected so many countries — no one else has had to deal with what I've had to deal with in pandemics."

Despite being generally out of practice and not having been exercised for some time, Faustus' conscience suddenly and unexpectedly activated and pricked him, momentarily overcoming his very wise and rational decision to roll over completely and do whatever Gill Bates wanted. Suddenly his mouth had switched riders, if indeed a mouth can be compared to a horse, and his conscience was riding it, an experience he was not accustomed to. He said to Crump, "Well, the proof, admittedly, is a *little* poor on the ground. That's what certain experts say, anyhow... I don't know about Hydroxychloroquilline, really, it might not be any good..."

Crump fixed him with his gaze and the President patted Faustus' hand (something Faustus really hated, especially during a pandemic) — did he feel a bit sorry for him? Faustus found that he resented that too. And the President said, "My Presidency is going to go down in history, Faustus, because I am the greatest President in history, precisely because of this pandemic, there has never been a President like me, and Crump is the only Crump who could ever make the best decisions for this country in this situation, decisions that no other President in history has had to make, and I *will* recommend Hydroxychloroquilline, as no one else in history has, and not only recommend it, but I will be buying millions of doses and stockpiling them in Washington DC. Do you know, nobody knows more about

Hydroxychloroquilline than me, and nobody knows more about the media than I do, I understand the media, and I understand social media, more than anybody, based on my results, right?"

"Oh, good," said Faustus, rather puzzled about how well this interchange had gone. Or badly. He wasn't really sure if it was a good outcome or a bad one, actually; but he could see that Gill Bates was going to ascribe the positive outcome to *his* efforts, which seemed to have down-side as far as he could see.

Crump added helpfully, "Do you I *had already* heard that Hydroxychloroquilline is a useful drug for treating BirdFlip... There was a video on Tic-Tac-Toe, by this Jewish Doctor in a Hasidic community in upstate New York; he says it has saved lots of lives. And you know, Faustus, I have a friend who's a Doctor, a very good doctor, Scott Mercator, and would you believe he *also* recommended Hydroxychloroquilline, just like you did. I think I'll bring him in on the team, what do you think? Good work George. Excellent work." And Crump patted Faustus on the back. And the others came back into the room, then, and Crump said, "You're on the track here, men, on the track to greatness with President Crump, let's pan this plandemic[33], I mean, plan this pandemic." And Crump patted Faustus on the back (another thing he really hated) and then they put their heads together, and that was even *something else* that Faustus really loathed (he was always worried about catching nits from someone).

And so the planning for the imminent lockdowns continued.

~~~

When the lockdown in DC began, in mid-March, Madeley was scared. Her Dad was still going to work, because his job driving Mr Faustus around was considered very important, and they had closed big venues and the restaurants had to have social distancing, but she had to go to school.

Her mother Linda said, "You really don't want to go to school, do you?"

Madeley said, "I'm afraid I'm going to catch the BirdFlip coronavirus."

Linda said, "Do you know, Madeley, you don't have to be afraid. It hasn't even reached Laurel yet, you have nothing to worry about."

[33] I mean, that's just ridiculous. Plandemic isn't even a word.
~~~

Madeley said, "I don't want to die. And what if there's not enough toilet paper?"

Linda said, "Have you looked in your Dad's basement lately? What's in there?"

Madeley said hopefully, "Toilet paper?"

Linda said, "No, on the shelf near the heater."

Madeley said, "What? All those old newspapers?"

Linda nodded.

Madeley said, "What?"

Linda raised an eyebrow.

Madeley covered her mouth and said, "Oh! No."

Linda nodded.

Madeley said, "I'm not wiping my bum with newspaper!"

Linda said, "Well, I - I think that thing where everyone is buying up toilet paper — I think it's just a fad. I can't see that the BirdFlip Coronavirus can possibly impact on the number of rolls of toilet paper that would be made. After all, they're made out of trees, and that's an outdoor job. How would one woodsman possibly catch BirdFlip from another woodsman? And even the paper mill — the place they *make* wood into toilet paper. Well, it's probably all robotised today, there's probably not even anyone working at the toilet paper factory these days. And they can ship it and drive it, without anyone ever touching it. I honestly don't think there will be a shortage of toilet paper."

Frank said, "I think it's the people who are particularly anal who are buying the toilet paper[34]."

Linda said, "Frank. You're speaking in front of our daughter."

Frank repeated, "Particularly anal? Get it? Ah, never mind."

Madeley said, "What does anal mean?"

Frank said, "Oh no, now I have to explain it."

Linda said, "Your fault. You caused the problem. You deal with it."

And Frank swore, sighed and began to explain to his daughter the nuances of anal and anally retentive.

And Linda thought to herself, "Well done, Frank. Nothing like a bit of gratuitous profanity to take Madeley's mind off all the doom and gloom." And she went in to the kitchen and made herself a gin and tonic, and looked out the kitchen window at her husband explaining what "anally

---

[34] Strangely enough a study published in Pmoss Stone discovered that people were more likely to hoard or stockpile if they were especially frightened by BirdFlip, if they were more emotional, fearful and anxious, and if they were high in conscientiousness, prudent, perfectionist, organised and controlling. Who would have thought it?

retentive" meant to their daughter, and thanked God that he had sent her such a man.

CHAPTER 8

The WooHoo Flu.

The free press, which was so free it pounced on every single pronouncement of Danill Crump, the Forty-Fifth President of the United States, with an avid lust to contradict, disprove and ridicule everything he said, indeed, the free press loved nothing so much as to make Danill Crump look like a fool, again and again. To say they hated him was the understatement of the century: to them, Danill Crump was the deplorable of deplorables.

Thinking about this, Danill Crump remembered the moment Hilaire Clintock had lost the 2016 election with great fondness: it was that speech when she had said that "half" of the supporters of Crump were a "racist, sexist, xenophobic, Islamophobic, homophobic, bunch of deplorables," a comment she later apologised for, saying, "What I said was half" which sounded a bit like she only said half of what she had wanted to say, but the people only heard one thing from that sentence: the word deplorables, a word that had stuck in people's minds, a word that had won him the election.

He had worked it out: with this single word, she had mobilised all the swinging voters for him; every single man and woman who had even mildly entertained the idea of voting for Crump was insulted and mortified, and every single one of them from that moment saw Clintock as an elitist who looked down on the common people as deplorable, dreadful, common people, they saw her from that moment on as a holier-than-thou self-righteous superior intellectual rich selfish snob, which is exactly what she was.

And whatever you might think of him, Danill had the gift of reaching the common people. They'd had enough of hypocritical self-serving politicians who lied with their every second breathe. Danill, with his habit of mouthing off, boasting, speaking the unadorned truth that no polite person would mention, knew that this was how he appealed to the masses. He thought of himself as a more thoughtful person than his blunt, brusque public persona might suggest.

That particular morning he was doing an interview with NBD. And especially for today, Crump had coined a new phrase to use in this interview: the "China Virus". He called it that because the BirdFlip Virus came from China; no other reason. But he also called it the "WooHoo Flu", a phrase he had also coined himself. He was proud of his linguistic ability; he was the most inventive President ever, indeed, throughout his life, his two greatest assets were his mental stability and being really, really smart. Hey, he should put that phrase out on Twit, the social media platform he absolutely loved.

~~~

Later that day, Faustus was sitting there in the hall watching the interviewer from NBD asking the President, "Mr President, some of the European countries are asked for China's hosting of the Olympics in 2022 to be cancelled because they've spread the virus around the world. What do you think of that? Do you think they should be hosting the Olympics?"

Danill Crump, the forty-fifth President of the United States, answered, "I just made an agreement with China, where they're going to be putting in three hundred billion towards the product, the vaccines, when you add that to the forty or fifty billion that Big Pharma is putting in, well I just want to see how China goes with this transaction. I want to see if they keep their word — are they holding up their end of the bargain, their end of the agreement? We're holding a lot of discussions, but I'm unhappy with them, and I spoke to them, they could have kept the Birdflip Coronavirus in China, they didn't tell the rest of the world what was happening, they let the flights continue to the rest of the
~~~

planet, so, no, no, I'm very unhappy with them, and if they were a child I would certainly spank their bottoms. Second question?"

The second interviewer was that whiny woman from America's biggest broadcaster, CNB, and she said, "Mister President, I'd like to address a question to Doctor Faustus. Could you tell us what you think of the idea that the virus came out of a laboratory in China? You're a scientist, aren't you, Doctor, and I believe you know a lot about viruses?"

Danill Crump's orange toupé flipped up and down, and Doctor Faustus took that as a sign that he should answer. "Now first of all, I don't think we should call it the WooHoo Flu — that could come across a bit racist. Anyhow, there has been a study," he said, "I have a study, I don't know who the authors are, but a bunch of qualified microbiologist virologist mathematical scientifickal geniuses have been looking at the BirdFlip Coronavirus and the — ah — the genetic sequences that have evolved in the *Red-footed Boobies*, the *Red-footed Boobies,* let me emphasize that point, and the point I'm trying to make is, it's completely consistent with a jump from a bird species, penguins, pangolins, pigeons, Red-Footed Boobies — or any other convenient animal really — to a human being, and I must emphasize, from a *natural* animal to a *natural* human being. The study I'm talking about should be available soon — or it might be available already, who knows? — and as I say I can't remember the authors' names — but we will make that available to you — just email my office."

The whiny reporter — was her name Jan, or Jee-anne, or something — called out to him, "Who wrote that study again sir? We want to look it up. We think you probably know better than us, Dr Faustus, but it doesn't hurt to fact-check, does it?"

Dr Faustus said, "Oh, gee, Anne, you don't have to fact check *me*. I am the... Ahem. This is Science, Jee-anne. Look, I... can't remember their names off-hand — somebody somebody and somebody else and the other one, et al — but email my office, . I'll get them to send it to you." And he whispered to Petronia, "Get ready to send out Proximal Origin to anyone who asks[35]."

Another reporter asked him about the lockdowns: "Just asking you, sir, about the protests — people are saying they want the economy reopened. Doesn't that concern you at least a small, itty-bitty, amount? Are you worried as a health

---

[35] by Jerry Blacksmith, Kristen Solo, Barry A Gog, Shamrock Holmes, Frostey Kristoff, et al. "**The proximal origin of BirdFlip-CoV-2**" *Denature Epidemiology Magazine* **26**, 430–437 (2020). https://doi.org/10.1038/dem41591-020-0820-9

expert when you see that folks are stuck at home, moping around, not exercising, not seeing their Doctors 'cause they are afraid of catching BirdFlip, maybe not even seeing the Doctor when they have the symptoms of cancer or heart disease or liver problems or extreme hypochondria caused by too much time alone, getting depressed and suicidal at home and possibly even drinking too much alcohol, to the point where the person might begin to think that they are a suicidal alcoholic who can't get rid of certain thoughts that go around in their head all the time, round and round and round like funny little twisty whizzy things, Catherine wheels, or spinners or whizzy-dizzies, buzzing and bizzing to and fro like some kind of mosquito or dark Lovecraftian winged insect inside one's head and never letting up, Oh God, it's dreadful being on my own during the lockdowns! Auuughhh!" And he ran out of the building and nobody ever saw him after that.

But the one of the other reporters, being a consummate professional, took the baton and said, "And are you worried when people congregate in large groups? Are you worried if that sort of bad behaviour is encouraged?"

Faustus said, "Well, I mean, I'm looking at all this from a public health standpoint, I mean, let me emphasize, I understand that people must be frustrated with all the lockdowns and the social distancing and the fear and social control we're exerting — I understand that — but I have a specific role here and my role in the task force is to make recommendations that are designed to protect and ensure the health and safety of the American people. And I hope that everybody understands that, I mean, that we're not consciously trying to drive the people of America insane with all these public health measures, and *if* that is a byproduct of them, and if these public health measures *do* happen to cause slightly more harm than good or even a lot more, well I would challenge you to prove that with a double blind placebo controlled trial. And hopefully what we're doing will put an end to all of this. Conversation. This conversation. Is over. Thank you."

~~~

Frank drove Faustus home that afternoon. Petronia was not with him, which was a little unusual.

They were stuck at a set of traffic lights, waiting for them to change.

Frank decided to ask him, then. He prayed first, something he didn't do often while on the job unless they were in a bad fix with the traffic or couldn't find parking
~~~

somewhere, but this time, he really, really prayed, silently and desperately he asked for help, "Lord, please, please, please, I need your help, Amen, please let him say yes."

And then, when he felt a sense of peace, finally, Frank spoke up, "Ah, Doctor Faustus? I know we don't usually talk, but I have a question to ask you."

Faustus said, "Yes, ahh — ?"

Frank said, "Frank. That's my name — Frank. Remember; 'to be Frank?'"

Faustus said, "Ah, yes. To be Frank, yes I do!"

And Frank laughed more out of obligation than humour, for this was a joke he had only heard about a million billion times, and then, when he felt he had laughed enough to be polite to Faustus without beginning to sound like a barking mad hyena, he said, "Doctor Faustus, my wife works mornings at the bakery."

Faustus said, "She does, does she? You know Frank, bakeries don't interest me much."

Frank said, "Yes, but you do enjoy Linda pastries, when I bring them in, don't you?"

Faustus said, "Oh, I thought Petronia got those for me?"

Waiting for Faustus to say something more, Frank waited, but he didn't, so Frank said, "Dr Faustus, I was just wondering if I could bring my daughter Madeley into work?"

Faustus said, "Madeley? You have a daughter, do you?"

Frank said, "Yes, Madeley is her name. And you see, because my wife works as a baker in the mornings, she can't be home to look after Madeley, if I have to go to work, and we do have her grandmother who normally babysits her from about 7 until school time, but right now Madeley is not going to school."

Faustus said, "She's not going to school? Is she ill?"

Frank said, "No, sir. The lockdowns. The schools are closed, remember? That's why Madeley has to stay home. But the thing is, I don't think her grandmother can cope with looking after her all the morning until Linda gets home, which is usually about two, two thirty. So if I could bring Madeley with me, well it would solve a few problems for us; I mean, until the lockdowns are over, sir. Dr Faustus."

For a moment, it was as though Faustus was talking to Gill Bates again: his brain simply froze up, as though some of the gears had stuck. This was a totally foreign conversation to him; it was as though he was suddenly living on an alien planet or had been thrust into an alien dimension and one of the aliens was talking to him in English and yet he couldn't understand a single word that the alien was saying; yes, he examined his memory of the words: Frank was indeed speaking in English, but there seemed to be a series of completely alien presuppositions and assumptions with which Dr Faustus was completely unfamiliar.

Faustus said, "Just explain all that again, please Frank. I'm not sure I understand."

Frank was suddenly thrust into another alien dimension as well: Faustus, whom he had always respected as a highly intelligent person, suddenly looked to Frank like a... well... like a proper Red-Footed Booby, an unintelligent boob. Faustus had clearly not comprehended a single word Frank had said. Was the good Doctor completely stupid? Why couldn't he understand? He looked at the man with an open mouth, wondering at the fact that the world was ruled by people like him, people who everybody respected but who couldn't even understand the simplest of needs, and Frank's tongue was completely tied and he couldn't say a thing.

Faustus said suddenly, "Ah, don't sit there with an open mouth, Frank, keep your eye on the road." And Frank realised the lights had changed, and all the cars behind them were beeping their horns at him.

"Ah — sorry," he said, and started up the car. "It was just — I don't understand what you don't understand, sir, about what I just said."

Dr Faustus said, "Ahhh — let's start with — why don't you hire a babysitter?"

Frank said, "Well, sir, there's the mortgage, and the college fees that we're saving for Madeley, and the price of food which seems to have just sky-rocketed, and the price of gas, and the loan we took out to build an extra room on the house Linda was pregnant and we thought Madeley would have a little brother, and the car loan, and don't forget my wife's mother who had cancer last year and we're still paying off the debt... Do I need to go on?"

Dr Faustus said, "Well, what about child care?"

Frank said, "Sir, I don't want to insult your intelligence by telling you that child care is astronomically more expensive than a babysitter. In any case, I believe the child care centers are all closed because of the lockdowns. Do we even know how long the schools will be closed for?"

Dr Faustus said, "Oh, not very long. Probably just until the end of the school term, that's all."

Frank said under his breath, "That's a long time," then said, "Well, sir, there's no way we could afford a babysitter until then, and furthermore my wife's mother — well she's not a well woman — and although Madeley is a good girl — she really is — she's an angel and very easy to manage — I just know she would wear out her grandmother, not just because she would even do anything to wear her out, she'll probably just sit there reading books and drawing pictures, but because her grandmother is so eager to please the girl, she would be going out of her way to be nice to her, and she just doesn't have the energy any more. You know?"

Dr Faustus said, "I know," thinking of himself and how much energy this conversation was taking out of him. This man was a psychic vampire.

Frank said, "Well, what do you think?"

Dr Faustus snapped, "What do I think about what?"

Frank said, "What do you think about Madeley staying with me if I'm working for you in the morning?"

Dr Faustus said, "I really don't know, Frank. It's highly irregular. Can't your wife look after her?"

Frank said, "She's not working in a non-essential business, sir. She works in a bakery, and they have to stay open. It would not be long. It would just be until the end of the lockdowns. You *yourself* said they would not last very long." And Frank thanked the Lord that Faustus had been given that phrase to say, that the lockdowns would 'not last very long.' It was a blessed phrase.

Dr Faustus said, "Not very long. Well I suppose you've got me there, haven't you, Frank? I did say the lockdowns will not last very long..." There was a long pause, and finally Dr Faustus said, "Alright. Alright, Frank, bring your daughter along. We'll see. You'll have to keep her in the front with you. I suppose that would be covered under the provisions for caring for a family member or pet."

Frank said, "Thank you sir. Madeley's a good girl, she would be less trouble than any pet."

And Dr Faustus showed a little glimmer of humanity, then, because he smiled at Frank and said, "Well, she's your pet, I can see that"

Frank said, "She is sir, and the twinkle of my eye."

~~~

Frank dropped him off at his home office that morning: to be fair, Faustus himself wasn't doing a lot at work in Bethesda, either, at the moment; he was obeying the lockdowns and mostly staying at home; although of course his work was defined as an essential service. It wouldn't be as
~~~

onerous as he thought it would, babysitting the little girl, he told himself.

He glanced at the news on his computer. Crump was all over the news, as usual, talking about Hydroxychloroquilline, and how marvellous it was, and how marvellous Crump was. He wondered what Gill Bates thought about this. It was almost as if the billionaire's plan had back-fired. He had created a monster.

Someone had sent Faustus a website, too, via email — he opened it up. The site was called, "hcqmetastudy.com," it was a list of all the studies into the effectiveness of Hydroxychloroquilline for the BirdFlip virus. Good grief, some one had gone to a lot of effort here: every single study looking at the efficacy of Hydroxychloroquilline into any virus whatsoever was listed here, as well as some earlier studies into Chloroquine and even Quinine. Who would even bother? This person who had authored this website was *anonymous*, for goodness' sake. What were they afraid of?

He quickly closed it and realised that he was finding it easier and easier to get off task and end up being sucked down into some internet whirlpool of dark ideas and strange thoughts and weird video clips and all the rest, with each passing day of the lockdowns. He'd have to watch this. He closed the "hcqmetastudy.com" site and resolved never to look at it ever again.

For now, they were holding many of their meetings on Zooz, a new teleconferencing platform that had taken off during the pandemic.

Now, he just had to go over all that stuff Petronia had sent him about the new vaccines that they were looking into...

The big problem was the public relations. All of these things — they were all experimental. Here we are, faced with a genetically engineered virus — that was a thought he rarely even let himself have — a virus, created in the lab to be extra transmissible and deadly; who knows what 'features' they had put into it, Bar-tailed Godwit, and then the Chinese. And all we have to fight it is Hydroxychloroquilline, which Gill Bates either thinks is completely useless, or wants squashed to get the profits from his *highly* experimental vaccines, either one could be true, and then we have the other things, monoclonal antibodaddies or whatever they're called, and all of these they're expecting to develop within the year, and how can it be done? But the public relations of it: that's the rub. We have to convince the public to take these experimental vaccines, and any fool who knows even a small amount about pharmaceutical trials knows that it takes fourteen and a half years to get FDA approval; well, hold on a sec, he said to himself, think rationally, George; you know, they get drugs approved in three or four years these days, what with running all the animal and human phase one, two and three trials concurrently, and we have control over the FDA. Still, in less than one year. There must be a lot of people out there who know that's not long enough. How do we convince them?

It's going to be rushed. That's what it is. It's really going to be rushed, and somehow we have to convince the general public that they can make a safe and effective vaccine —- an experimental mRNA vaccine — in less than a year.

And the other problem is, can they really do it? Is Gill Bates right, is this the future, or is it a giant bleep-storm waiting to blow up in his face, covering Faustus' face in manure, just blowing up like an exploding sewerage farm, right in front of Faustus, blowing faeces everywhere, with a wet kind of explosive sound, Kablerphloom, followed by a damp squishy sound as the number twos landed everywhere. And at this point he meandered off into a dream about a giant sewerage pipe, covering him in sewerage, and he was afraid, because the waste was full of mRNA and lipid nanoparticles that had come alive and were crawling on his skin trying to get through any available orifice, and if he breathed it in or got it in his eyes, he'd be infected with it, because Gill Bates had got it wrong, the mRNA was just as bad as the virus, only worse, it was way worse, it was seeping in through the sewerage on his skin and he was having some sort of reaction, was it a heart attack? He was suffering a seizure, all his muscles were spasming, and his heart was bounding out of his chest, thump, thump, thump.

He woke up, with Gloriana shaking him. "Darling, wake up. You were having a nightmare."

After taking his pulse and checking that he wasn't having a heart attack, Gloriana repeated, "It's just a nightmare."

Faustus said, "It is, it's a public relations nightmare, Gloriana. It's the worst nightmare of my entire career. I don't know how I'm gonna get through it."

"You will," she said. "You certainly will. That's what we've always said, George, you've got staying power. You're like an institution on your own: a scientific institution; you are a rock, the rock on which the NHIJ is built."

Faustus, still half asleep, said, "I am the Science."

Gloriana said, "Well, darling, I wouldn't go that far, but if it helps you to believe that, then believe it."

~~~

When Frank arrived home, his mother-in-law had already made dinner, a splendid pork roast, and Madeley was sitting at the table all ready to eat. Linda was still at work that day, because someone was sick with BirdFlip, so his wife had been asked to do a double shift.

Frank sighed and said, "Mary, you didn't have to do that you know. Linda will be home soon — we can have our dinner a little later than usual."

Mary was stubborn and kind, and spoke with an Irish lilt, "Now, Frank, you know perfectly well that to cook dinner your wife will be too bone-tired and far too weary by the time she gets home, so who'll be cooking, then? Will you? I think that you're bone-weary too, son, so just sit down and eat and don't look a gift horse in the mouth."

Frank sat down and shut up. He knew when he had met his match.

While the three of them were eating the precious, lovely, sumptuous meal completely silently, Linda came home, and Frank got up and embraced her gratefully. After the usual endearments, Frank said, "Faustus said yes."
~~~

Linda said, "Oh, I'm so glad. Mother, you're going to have a bit of a rest: Faustus has said that Maddie can come to work in the car with Frank and spend the morning with him."

Mary said, "Oh, but you know our little girl is one I don't mind taking care of, any time you like, Frank, she is after all my own flesh and blood."

Frank said, "Be that as it may, we don't want to wear you out, Mary. You've been ill, and we're just grateful to the Lord that we still have you with us."

Mary said, "Oh, Frank, it is that you always know the good things to say." He bent down and gave her a gentle kiss on the aged forehead, and the four of them finished the meal together, talking about nothing, basking in the gentle light of the evening.

~~~

Meanwhile, Faustus was on a Zoom call with President Danill Crump, Clarence Collins director of the NHIJ, Dr Aleric Hazard, the Health and Human Services Secretary, Dr Redmond Redmeadows, Director Of The CDE, The Center For Disease Elimination, and Dr Nancy Balm, the Senior Director Of CDE's National Center For Immunization And Respiratory Diseases.
~~~

President Danill Crump was about to announce something; Faustus knew it — he was getting used to the President's moods, and the peculiar smirk he had on his face right now was the one he wore when he was about to announce something that showed how very clever he was, so much cleverer than anyone else.

Crump immediately said, "Hello everyone, Dr Faustus, Nancy, Aleric, Redmond. I am just about to announce something, and it is something that shows how very clever I am, so much cleverer than anyone else." Faustus nodded to himself: exactly right. Crump continued, "I have come up with the name for our vaccine drive: a name that came to me yesterday while I was pondering the many great successes I have achieved in my Presidency. And I thought to myself: you want to create a new vaccine, a new, experimental medication, the mRNA vaccines, a new technology, in record time. I was thinking about notable achievements — things that mankind has accomplished — and an immortal phrase came to me: 'Space: The final frontier. These are the voyages of the Starship, Enterprise. Its 5 year mission: to explore strange new worlds, to seek out new life and new civilizations, to boldly go where no man has gone before.' And I thought, that's what you guys are trying to do with these vaccines, isn't it? And I thought of a name. Operation Starship Enterprise. You see, the Starship Enterprise goes at Warp Speed. That's really fast. Faster than anyone has ever gone before. Faster than the speed of light. And that's exactly what you're trying to do. Operation Starship Enterprise."

"Hmm," everyone on the Zoom call said, "That's a good name." "Really good." "Great." "Great work Mr President." Of course, Faustus knew that they were all thinking the same thing he was: what a stupid name. A stupid, stupid name.

Then Crump said, "Or… and here's my other choice. Operation Light Speed."

For some reason, Faustus stomach dropped. It really was a good name; but he really didn't want to admit it. He conceded, "That's alright," and the others all said, "That's not too bad," "That's okay," "Not too bad," and Crump said, "What, you don't sound so excited? So you all like the first one, Operation Starship Enterprise?"

"No, no!" they all cried out. "No, we like the *second* one." "Operation Light Speed." "It's good." "We like the *second* one, sir."

And Crump said, "Well why didn't you say so? You were all saying about the first one, great, that's a good name, like, great work Mr President, and then for Operation Light Speed, it's like, oh, that's alright, not too bad, okay, not bad, like, far more conservative, as though you didn't like it."

Clarence Collins said, "Well, sir, you see I… think it's a cultural thing: we're scientists. When we don't like something we say it's great, but internally we are actually thinking how — ahem — useless it is. When we like something, we hedge around it, because after all, every scientific statement must be qualified and be made carefully to make sure it is factual — it's a habit of thought, Mister President."

Faustus was astounded — Collins was magnificent, really — Faustus simply didn't know how the man managed to tell the truth to the President in such a tactful and gentle way that the rambunctious man wasn't offended.

Then President Crump said, "Well, I'm very offended that you wouldn't tell me in the first place that you didn't like Operation Starship Enterprise. I thought it was good, and I rely on you people to tell me the truth. The simple, unadorned truth. It is very difficult for a straight speaking man like me — and do you know I don't think there's ever been a President who is so straightforward as I am in American history — "

Then Dr Redmond Redmeadows said, “Sir, what about Abraham Lincoln?”

Then President Crump gave the first sign that there might be a tiny atom of humility somewhere in his bombastic soul: he said, “You’re right. Abraham Lincoln. Abes. He was very straightforward, very straight talking. I am just as straight talking as Abe. But honestly, tip-toeing around you people when you’re trying to explain what you think and hedging it about all the time with conditions and assumptions and scientific mumbo-jumbo. All I want is the clear and simple truth.”

Nancy Balm saved the day by saying, “Yes, President, and it is plainly and simply true that Operation Light Speed is a brilliant name for what we are trying to do with these vaccines. And it will go down in history as one of your greatest achievements — the accomplishment of your Presidency — equal in many peoples’ eyes to Abraham Lincoln’s victory over the South in the Civil War. Yes, sir, you have coined a brilliant phrase, that will be remembered forever.”

President Crump said, “Thank you Nancy,” and he said to his offsider, some aide or other, “Give that woman a raise.” The offsider laughed, and Crump said, “No, I’m serious. Give her a raise. She's not making enough as Senior Director of the Vaccine Section — Nancy, what are you on? One hundred thousand? Two hundred thousand? You've got spare money in the coffers, 'cause I'm only charging a dollar a year, give some of it to Nancy. Add twenty percent onto whatever she's earning right now."

"But, sir," the offsider said, "If we give her a raise then we have to give a raise to everyone working at that level in the public service."

Crump said, "Well, I'm President. Can't I give her a raise? Work out a way. Give her an annuity for being on this committee or something."

"Well, we'd have to give everyone here an annuity," the offsider said.

Crump said, "Then give everyone an annuity. Everyone on this committee gets an annuity. Can't I do that? I am President, I can do anything. Come on, Bob, there must be a way."

Nancy said, "Sir, much as I'd like to have a raise, we have business to talk about."

Crump said, "Do it," and the man rushed out with a wrinkled brow and a very concerned and troubled look on his face.

"Now," said Crump, "I've had an idea — an excellent idea — about how we can put this vaccine across to the public tomorrow, George."

Faustus said, "How is that, Mr President?"

Crump said, "Good cop, bad cop. You know, with everything you've been telling me about these vaccines, one year, it's not very long, is it? I mean, to develop a vaccine? An experimental mRNA vaccine? It's not very long?"

Faustus had to admit, "No, it's not very long. Seven years, maybe up to fourteen years, for the clinical trials. But good cop, bad cop? What does that mean?"

The others were looking puzzled as well.

Crump said, "Well, like this: you say, Oh, Mister President, it's going to take a year to develop the vaccine, then I say, oh, that's far too long, couldn't we get it done in a week? Then you say, oh no, sir, we're being cautious. You see, in a business deal, you have to manage expectations. If everyone's hearing me say, oh, get it done in a week, two weeks, then you're saying, oh, a year, well, then, everyone will think a year is really conservative and careful." The others were stunned — Faustus had to admit it really was clever psychology. "When it's not," Crump said.

Faustus said, "What do you mean — it's not clever psychology?"

Crump said, "No, no, it's clever psychology. I'm the most clever psychologist there's ever been, as a President, but no, Faustus, I mean, it's not really careful and conservative, is it, Doctor? One year is not conservative and careful. Five years is still rushing it. Seven, maybe. Maybe not."

Faustus said, "You're right, Mr President." And for once, he was completely stumped for words.

This had been the very problem he'd been turning over in his mind for days; how to get the general public to accept highly experimental medications, when the precautionary principle dictates that one should make every effort to test a new medicine, to make sure that it doesn't hurt or maim or even kill the patients; and that process of FDA approval was supposed to take fourteen and a half years. They were going to do it in less than one; that's what VacCureus and Pfutticup and Moodyearna were telling him.

A potential public relations problem that could completely dwarf every other problem he had ever encountered in his entire career; and it looked as though Crump had solved it for them.

~~~
~~~

So it was that early on the following morning, Faustus was preparing himself for a press conference he would be giving on Operation Light Speed; Danill Crump was going to be there, more's the pity, for the more he knew him the more Faustus realised the man was a booby, but a powerful booby is a dangerous booby, as he often liked to say to Hugo; and here we are in the middle of the Red-Footed Booby virus — and they would laugh, because he wasn't talking about the virus as the virus.

Dr Aleric Hazard would be there, today, too, the HHSS, Dr Redmond Redmeadows, Director Of The CDE, and Dr Nancy Balm, the Senior Director Of CDE's National Center For Immunization And Respiratory Diseases, Meme Qualmsley and Lenny Schlenny, both Health Bureaucrats whose roles Faustus was a little fuzzy about.

It was a large press conference and most of the press would be there.

Faustus stood in front of the mirror and looked at himself. He looked pasty and worn, and his eyes seemed to him to lack something, spirit or something, and his hair looked dishevelled, and his smile was fake, and when he didn't smile, he looked like a store mannikin of himself, soulless and empty inside, just a shell, an empty shell.

"I am the Science, I am the Science," he said to himself. He thought of Petronia — how she had started him off saying this phrase — and how much he was missing her *presence* during the pandemic — BirdFlip was making things so difficult for him — not having Petronia there in person was a real trial — of course, at least he could still talk to her in zoom but it just wasn't the same.

"I am the Science, I am the Science," he said, and he didn't feel anything — he wondered if the phrase was wearing off — he wondered if it was losing its *Mojo*, its *Cojones*[36]. Faustus suddenly had an overwhelming feeling of existential dread; what would he do if he couldn't speak in public, if his courage was gone? What would he do if his confidence was busted? His life would be over. How could he do it?

He couldn't do it. He would call in sick. He would tell them all he had the BirdFlip. That's what he would do. He just couldn't do it today. He didn't have the energy. He didn't have the confidence. He didn't have the *Cojones*[37], no, he definitely didn't.

---

[36] Spanish, meaning balls.

[37] I told you already! Weren't you listening*? Spanish, meaning balls, i.e. testicles, i.e. courage and confidence to take on anything. Yes, that's *balls.* *Meaning, weren't you reading?

At that moment Gloriana said, “Aren’t you ready yet? Your chauffeur is here, darling. Get dressed! You can’t leave him waiting like you did last time.” He heard the curtain on the entrance hall window slide back. “That’s funny. There’s a little girl in the passenger seat. Who *is* that?”

Faustus said, “Oh, that’s whatsername, ah, whatsisname’s daughter. Whatsisname? Fred?”

Gloriana said, “For God’s sake, George, you can’t even remember the name of your driver. Are you sure you are not going senile?”

“Definitely,” said Faustus. “I’m definitely going senile. No doubt. Believe me, I’m a doctor.”

Gloriana said, “Well don’t forget to put your clothes on, then.”

Faustus said, “Alright, I’m on it.” He already had his trousers on, and he quickly buttoned his shirt and put on a tie. He hadn’t shaved: he preferred the wardrobe person to do that; they were much less likely to cut him than he was.

He walked out through the corridor and Gloriana clapped. “Well done, husband,” she said, “Record time.”

Faustus kissed her on the lips. “Aren’t you going to work today, Gloriana?”

Gloriana said, “Non-essential. The hospital said to stay home; all my administrative tasks can be done at home, and the research tasks can *definitely* be done at home.”

Faustus said, “Alright. I’ll see you this afternoon. You know, I don’t mind these lockdowns; I get to see a lot more of you.”

Gloriana said, “Frank.”

Faustus said, “What?”

Gloriana said, “To be frank.”

Faustus said, “To be frank you don’t like seeing more of me?”

She said, “No, silly. Your driver’s name. Frank.”

Faustus said, “Ohhh. Frank, that’s right. And his daughter’s name’s Madeleine.”

“No,” said Gloriana, “No, no, no; I think it’s Madeley? Perhaps you’d better check with Petronia?”

Faustus said, “Ok.” And he quickly dialed Petronia on his mobile, and after a short pause while she checked the personnel files on her phone, she told him, “Madeley is Frank’s daughter’s name.”

Faustus said, “Thank you. Alright. Well here we go.”

~~~~
~~~~

Frank was waiting in the SUV, in the semicircular driveway of Faustus' mansion. Madeley was sitting on the passenger seat next to him, with her headphones on, listening to an audiobook on her Walmart $99 tablet; either the Hobbit or the Lord of the Rings. She liked Anne McCaffrey as well, and was a big fan of the fantasy genre in general.

It was a cold, grey morning, and a gentle drizzling rain was falling over the green birches and willow trees, and the alders, running down the roof tiles of the mansions in small rivulets, and falling through the empty, bare branches of an oak tree that hadn't yet sprouted in someone's yard; what a beautiful suburb. He suddenly realised that having money actually meant you could live in a beautiful place like this. He wondered if the people in these houses appreciated how beautiful it was here, how elegant their houses and their furniture and the view out of their windows and even the fittings on their bathroom taps, which would be so much more elegant and refined than *their* bathroom taps, which were cheap and generic; even so, he and Linda had made a life for themselves, they had carved out their own place in this world and they had a home to be grateful for and a beautiful daughter — Madeley — and such a nice backyard, too, with the hammock hanging between the oak tree and the maple. And they had family, and they knew that they cared for each other. If all the money and privilege and beautiful things disappeared, would these people's families still be there for them?

Frank knew what he had to be grateful for: if his life had've been easy, maybe he wouldn't have known that his wife loved him; he wouldn't really have known. Linda had stayed by him through thick and thin. She had stayed by him after Afghanistan, just after Madeley had been born, and the memories of the attack wouldn't leave him alone, and he'd been drinking too much and he'd been a right pain in the rear to his wife; he really hadn't been a good husband, then. He'd said some things to her that he couldn't forget, things that had stayed scorched on his memory, and for about four or five months he thought she was going to leave him, but he never did, and then her mother came over from Ireland and they confronted him and he ended up doing AA and he *hadn't* given up drinking, but now he kept it to one drink three times a week, and two drinks on holidays like Christmas and Thanksgiving. He knew AA said not to do that, that you had to give up entirely, but he knew he was okay, because after that he never, ever said another mean thing to his wife and really meant it like he had when he'd been drunk. And they had started to going to church, back then, and the pastor was really supportive of his efforts to keep their marriage together, and even when the job was impinging on their time together, she had stayed with him, even when she was having troubles, after they lost their unborn son, Traylen his name was going to be. They had stayed together, and he knew — he believed — they would, no matter what.

He didn't regret the difficulties they'd had; he didn't even regret the difficulties they were still having. If you never had any difficulties, how would you know anyone loved you? If you had never behaved cruelly to someone, or hurt them in some inexcusable way, or had forgotten something really important and genuinely broken their heart, only to have them forgive you, how would you ever know you were loved?

Oh, he knew people who lived in these suburbs had troubles, but while the money was still there, how did they know the people in their families really loved *them,* and not the money? He'd heard of people like this — rich people — living in mansions — who had children who were in and out of rehab. What torture it would be; having them coming back home, but not really because they loved their parents, but because they wanted the finances, the financial help, the money.

He shuddered, then, and looked at Madeley, at his daughter. What if she went on drugs, when she got older? There were plenty of temptations out there, especially at public schools these days. What if she ended up hanging around with the wrong people? Boys who exploited her, boyfriends who led her down the path into sex and drugs and wild living. She was so young and naive; would she be wise enough to tell when someone only wanted to use her? He really didn't know, but that was his job, to train her up to know the difference, to give her that discernment, that wisdom, so she *might* just be able to tell when someone was using her, and conversely, when someone really loved her.

That was why he took his daughter to church. He didn't know any better way for her to learn about real love, than by learning about Jesus. For God so loved the world that he gave his only Son...

It was impossible to explain to people about this, you had to experience it for yourself, it was not the sort of thing that someone could work out in their head, this kind of love, it was self-sacrificing love, but it always worked out better, because when you loved someone enough to sacrifice yourself for them and they loved you the same way, it was like a multiplier, it was a win-win situation. He and Linda were like this, in some ways, but it was an imperfect marriage, that's for sure. Every now and then they got a glimpse of this, like the curtain was pulled away.

He loved that Madeley was reading Lord of the Rings. That was one of his favourite books, and Linda's too. He had a copy with him in Afghanistan, that, the Lion the Witch and the Wardrobe, and the Bible. His three favourite books.

He had heard that Clarence Collins loved CS Lewis' books. Frank didn't really know the guy; he'd seen him plenty of times but he'd never had a chance to talk to him.

At that moment Faustus came out of the house. He was unshaven, and looked a bit like a mess, but Frank reckoned the make-up guys would fix him up once they got to the hall. Well, this was quite a day: Madeley would see the President. What a day.

Faustus opened the door and climbed in the back, and said, "Hello Frank. Hello Madeley. I'm Dr Faustus. Call me George."

Madeley said, "Hello Dr Faustus; George. How do you know my name?"

And Dr Faustus replied, "Well, ah, to be honest, Madeley, I had my personal assistant Petronia look it up for me. I'm a little bit terrible on people's names."

Madeley said, "I'm not bad on remembering people's names. I'll remember yours, George, I'm sure. Anyway, I haven't seen many people, anyhow, since school stopped."

Dr Faustus said, "Well I'm sorry about that, I wish we hadn't had to do that. I hope the schools will be open again soon."

Frank thought to himself slightly cynically, that Faustus meant, 'then I won't have to put up with making small talk with my chauffeur's daughter in the car before we head off to the press conference'. Frank said, "Well, then, we'd better set off, hadn't we?"

He started the engine and started driving.

Dr Faustus said, "Are you listening to something on Audible? I really like Audible."

Madeley said, "Yes I am. Lord of the Rings."

Dr Faustus said, "I really like Lord of the Rings. Where are you up to?"

Madeley said, "Well, the hobbits are just leaving the shire. The Ring-wraiths are looking for them, and they have just met Aragorn in the Prancing Pony."

Dr Faustus said, “I love that bit. When Frodo says, ‘I think a servant of the enemy would look fairer and feel fouler.’”

Madeley admitted, “Yes, I love that bit too.”

Dr Faustus said, “Would you like to meet the President today, Madeley?”

Madeley said, “Yes, I really would.”

“Well,” he said, “We’ll see if we can organise it. I can’t promise anything, but I’ll sure try.”

CHAPTER 9

Meeting Crump.

Madeley and Frank were seated in the hall, properly socially distanced at a distance of about six feet from each other and from every other guest.

Dr George Faustus began the press conference by introducing the crowd of dignitaries, then introducing the President; "President Crump, the man behind Operation Light Speed, please come up and introduce Redmond," and then sat down, in the sparse, properly distanced seating arrangement.

The President got up and walked to the podium. "Thank you, George, thank you very much. Redmond?"

Redmond Redmeadows got up. He said, "Thank you Mr President, I'm Redmond Redmeadows, and I'm the Director of CDE. I ready do want to thank everybody for coming — and everyone who's watching. I want to invite you all to approach me if there's anything that the CDE can develop, even into the FGH as you start the process of evaluating the products of your developmental process, testing them on the assembly line of humanity, as you will, and we're here, I promise, to help you, to be available to help you, to bring to fruition the — ah — fruits of your fruitful fruit-growing, because we're all counting on the countermeasures, to counter the virus encounter, and we want these in the arena very quickly, some more quickly than others, hey, Mr President?

Danill Crump said, "Yes, thank you, Redmond. Mr Shazzarmani, it's your turn."

Bel T. Shazzarmani stood up and came to the microphone. "Thank you so very much Mr President. Thanks for having me. Good day to you sir, and you, and also you, sir, and you, Ma'am, I *am* Bel T. Shazzarmani, the Chief Executine officer of VacCureus. We are a *very* advanced biotech company specialising in very clever stuff — very clever indeed, sir. We are making mRNA technology: that's messenger RNA to you plebes — and once these mRNA molecules are injected into the blood stream they weasel their way into the cell, using deceptive little lipidal nanoparticles to fool the cell into thinking, 'There's nothing there, buddy, nothing at all to worry about, buddy, I'm just a part of your body, buddy, let me in, let me in!' Normally your cells, sir, would say, 'Not by the hairs of my chinny chin chin,' but our lipid nanoparticles are the perfect disguise, you see — a disguise that the body cannot see — a kind of overcoat through which the wolfish messenger RNA may enter in to the cell without the cell even knowing what's happening. And when the mRNA gets into the cell, it floats into the endoplasmic reticulum, which is where this little thingies are I forget what they're actually called, those little thingies, Ribodromes, or Risomodes, or RiceCommodes or something[38], and those little thingies are the very clever molecular machines that the body has, that turn mRNA into proteins. Now the body is full of proteins, these proteins are the messengers of the body and fly out of the cell performing functions everywhere — the proteins tell your blood pressure to go up when you're running, or tell your bladder to release liquid when there's too much of it, and so on and so forth, marvellous, marvellous — very smart — but we have outsmarted these RiceCommodes, indeed, our mRNA floats in and the RiceCommodes make the protein *we* want it to make. And the mRNA technology brings into existence a protein that then floats around in the body — we think probably the S protein or Spike protein of the virus would be the best one to use — our scientists say it shouldn't be that toxic, not that we've tested it, it's all a bit of a rush, hahaha, but these Spike proteins that our mRNA technology fools the body into making will then *float* around like daisies on the

[38] Ribosomes you nincompoop. Are you a complete idiot?

wind — or, rather, like some sort of smoke-like emission really, on the water — a better analogy really because they're really tiny little things, like, no bigger really than particles of smoke, and these mRNA technologised proteins will in the body trigger an immune response against the virus from which the S or Spike protein comes. We hope it will be a big immune reaction but not too big because that will kill everybody. And not too small because that would be an immunoglobulin 4 response, which is a bit like hay fever, really. So we're hoping somewhere in the middle.

"So we want to make prophylactics, not condoms as such but very potent prophylactics, by which we mean, vaccines, ah, vaccines, the very thing we worship and adore, all the anti-vaxxers will be put to shame, when our glorious vaccine rides the wings of the wind, glory be to the vaccines, and furthermore we want these proteins that we deceptively fool the body into producing for use to create an immune response to cancer, or even replace missing proteins in the case when someone has a rare disease — or we might even be able to produce a tiny amount of rabies for instance to train the body to fight it, with a very low dose, again the trick is making the dose low enough that the rabies cannot reproduce or cause a truly toxic response, but high enough to produce enough of a toxic response to create immunity. For instance, in the very successful and don't you let anyone tell you otherwise phase one rabies trial that we just did we gave a half of a microgram dose, really miniscule, so small, even an electron microscope would find it hard to see.

"And speaking more broadly, we have a bunch of things going on at once, we really do. We've got a whole lot of programs in phase one clinical trials and our BirdFlip-CoV2 program with our fifth or sixth program still in phase one. The phase one trials of our BirdFlip-CoV2 mRNA vaccine will begin in late May at the latest; this way of doing things, Danill, Mister Crump, Mister President, is fast, efficient, agile, wonderful, technologically advanced, and definitely, let me say, without a doubt, incredibly *safe and effective*.

"It's amazing really, Mister President! It's plug and play, sir, plug and play, you just plug in the code for whatsoever protein you want the victim's — ah — slip of the tongue — patient's body to produce and — hey presto! — there it is. The body is producing it, in such abundance that we don't even know when it would *stop* producing it. That's the marvel — it's the things we don't yet know that are so marvellous — that's the wonder of it all — there are so many mysteries! So many marvellous mysteries we still don't have the answer to! But sir, once we have injected these mRNA vaccines into everybody on the face of the planet, we will understand everything! Every mystery will be revealed! Amen!

"Yes sir, we have the expertise and we have the facilities and we are up and running already ready to manufacture these; indeed, we have even built a fully automated robot production machine! Hahahaha! Day and night, never ceasing, never stopping, a never-ending assembly line of mRNA vaccines, it will be producing mRNA vaccines to inject into every single man, woman and child on the face of this planet, to solve all their problems, their issues, their illnesses, forever! These vaccines will treat every medical ailment known to humanity, a little jab for man, a huge leap for mankind! Yes! This is greater I tell you than the moon landing! Than the invention of the light-bulb! Greater even than the invention of fire by the first human-like hominids in the dark, prehistorical beginnings of mankind! Hahahahahahahahaaaaa! Yes, Mister President Crumpy Crump Crump, and let me emphasise to you all, we are *ready, ready, ready* to begin manufacturing at the end of

May at the very latest, Mister Crump. The very latest! End of May! The End! Of May! The END!"

President Crump said, "Gets very excited. Victims, he said, victims, that Hydroxychloroquilline is lookin good, better by the minute. Thank you. Thank you very much Mister Shazzarmani. Please, Spynill, come up, it's your turn. Yes, you, Spynill Shiverin."

Spynill Shiverin came forward, a tall, bald man wearing a yellow and black coat. He said, "Hi there. Yes, I'm Spynill Shiverin, Head of Vaccine Research Fraud and Development for Sinafil Vaccine. We've been making vaccines for over a century, and for this project we'll be using recombinating protein technology. This is the same kind of vaccine as the influenza vaccines, that's the same technology. It is very easy to apply this same technology to the BirdFlip Coronavirus, and we have already applied it to SARS, which is in fact related to the BirdFlip virus, and this was very, very promising. We're leveraging that early work so that we can get the Sinafil out there to the customers. We're thinking we can get around 5-600 million doses out there from the same manufacturing facilities where we make the influenza vaccines, and we can do all this without even affecting our flu vaccine production. We know we'll have to keep that up because influenza is a real problem every year and there's no possible reason why the flu would just disappear, even if there's a pandemic. Mr President, we're happy and willing and able and ready to work with you and NHIJ and the people who are sponsoring our research, BARDUP (that's the government's biological response to threats and chemical spills maybe I shouldn't have mentioned that 'cause it might make it look like this is a lab leak oops shouldn't have said that should I?)"

President Crump said, "When do you think you could have the vaccine? When do you think you'd be able to have it, start producing it?"

Spynill Shiverin said, "We're already producing it, but the experimental vaccines, using the protein recombinant technology, takes a bit longer, so maybe ready to put into people's arms in a year? Maybe in two years, if we're lucky and the pandemic is still going then? It's difficult to predict: it has to be both safe *and* effective, so we want to be conservative in how we do this, Sinafil really wants make sure it works before we're jabbing people in the arm with it.

President Crump said, "Okay. Thank you very much. Lenny? Please?"

Lenny Schlenny came up to the microphone and said, "Thanks for inviting us all to this summit, Mr. President. My name is Lenny Schlenny and I'm the CEO of ReGene, a company I founded with my good friend Porgy Yancamechainos thirty years ago. We primarily make things you probably haven't heard of, these are MONOCLONAL ANTIBODIES. We make them for snake venom and we make them for viruses; despite the assertions of some Chiropractors, we do not make the *same* monoclonal antibody to use for snake venom as the one we make for viruses. How this works, sir, is we find someone who has survived the deadly incursion into their bodies, and we clone their antibody responses, and then we can inject those antibodies into someone else who's been bitten or infected. So they're bitten or infected, then injected, and affected — see, it sounds like a rap. We also work with BARDUP, the government agency responsible for coordinating responses to bio-military threats; not that we're saying this virus came from a lab, we're specifically *not* saying that, please don't record this part, we are *not* saying it originated in a lab and was leaked and that's why everybody is really worried, that's *not* why BARDUP has been involved. But do you know, my group — Dr Fauci's buddies as well — were really central in a big project in the Congo basin testing our monoclonal antibody cure for the Ibezavirus. Yes, sir, it didn't make waves in the media, it was a quiet story in fact that nobody noticed, because the Ibezavirus never crossed over the Atlantic, but, Mister President, we cured the Ibezavirus. Yes we did. I swear it. And do you know we have a bundle of antibodies already in vitro petri dishes ready to bundle out into the willing arms of the population. I would estimate we have a *lot* coming out of our factories in New Jersey, hundreds of thousands, maybe a quarter million doses, all ready to go —"

Crump interrupted him, "So you'd have a vaccine ready, already?"

Lenny Schlenny said, "Ah — not exactly a vaccine, sir. Our technology —"

Crump said, "If it's not a vaccine, what good is it?"

Lenny said, "No no, not a vaccine, sir, it's a MONOCLONAL ANTIBODY. This is an entirely different thing. You see, in your body there are these tiny little things called antibodies."

Crump said, "Antibodies? Does that mean they're against the body? What do we need them for?"

Lenny said, "Well, I mean, they're not against *your* body — they help your body to fight infections —"

Crump said, "Well, what are they called *antibodies* for then?"

Lenny said, "Well, they fight other little bodies, the bodies of the virus or the snake venom. Think of viruses and venom like little enemy bodies floating around in your blood, sir, and the antibodies as soldiers sent out by your immune system to fight them."

Crump said, "If they're enemy bodies, doesn't that mean they're dead? Why do we have to fight them if they're dead?"

Lenny said, "Well, they're not dead. They're alive, enemy bodies that are alive, so your body has to fight them."

Crump asked, "But I thought someone said viruses are not alive?"

Lenny said, "Well, technically you're right, viruses are not alive, but these are live viruses that we're talking about."

Crump said, "This sounds like a lot of nonsense, Lenny. So they are the bodies of live viruses that are not alive, and our immune system has to fight them by sending out little antibodies that help our bodies, and what you're putting in — this monocolloidal antibodies treatment — are antibodies from outside our bodies, to fight the enemies — which are really enemy bodies, that are not dead — and they help your body just like a vaccine but are not a vaccine?"

Lenny said, "Er... yes. Exactly."

President Crump said, "I see." He gathered himself, then asked, "So when would your vaccine be ready?"

Lenny Schlenny said, "They're not vaccines, sir, excuse me, but if you want to call them vaccines, Mister President, go ahead, we'll agree that they can be called vaccines, just for today. Now as to when they're gonna be ready, that really depends on the FDA approval process, sir. We really depend on them not dragging their feet — they're reached out to us — but we're ready to work with them sir, but you know how they are. We want to get this stuff into people's blood as soon as possible."

Crump said, "So that process to make your 'vaccine'" (Crump indicated quote marks around the word) " — would it be quicker to reach fruition than Spynill Shiverin's vaccines?"

Lenny Schlenny scowled at Spynill Shiverin, then said, "Yeah. Yeah. Much quicker than his. Much much quicker."

Crump said, "Would you explain why yours would be quicker than his?"

Lenny Schlenny said, “Well, ours are just, you know, passive vaccines let’s call them. You put them in somebody’s arm and the MONOCLONAL ANTIBODIES will protect them even if they’ve never been infected before, and will also protect them if they’re already infected. So get injected, whether you’re infected or not infected, that’s what I say. We’ve got the processes sped up these days: we don’t worry about doing our trials the long way: we like to everything quickly and concurrently, which means we can get it going real quick, sir. Real quick; so we’re really excited to work with you on this, Mr President.”

Crump said, “So it’s kindof a combination of a vaccine and something else that makes you better in some way that I don’t understand?”

Lenny Schlenny said really slowly, like an adult speaking to a toddler or an idiot, “Well, think of it this way, sir, you take a vaccine and your body makes the antibodies which fight the virus. You take our treatment, which is antibodies, and you’ve already got the antibodies. Your body doesn’t have to make them, so our process is quicker. Do you understand?”

Danill Crump said, “Yes, yes, I get it now.”

Lenny Schlenny added, "Our process is not only safer, and quicker, it's truly miraculous how effective it is — using these MONOCLONAL ANTIBODIES we can save many, many lives, sir."

Danill Crump said, "Thank you Lenny."

Lenny Schlenny responded, "That's alright sir. And I want to see everybody succeed. I don't want this to be an either/or type of thing — a pandemic like this can lift us all up — it can be a win/win for every company that wants to exploit the unprecedented opportunity that sickness and death brings to us. Sometimes, you know, we pharmaceutical companies... get it a bit wrong. You know, we do... a little more harm than good, sir. We have suffered losses in our shares at times because of this, real harm, real harm to our profits instead of good. But we're going to win here, we're onto a win, and that means more good than harm: in other words profits, money in our pockets, money out of yours, never mind about what happens to the patients. Today is what's important, Mister President: we can deal with the financial fallout later, once they work out what's gone wrong with all the experimental stuff and how many people it's killed[39]."

Crump said, "Lenny, I'm not sure you meant to say that last bit out loud. Anyhow, thank you Lenny, show your appreciation everybody, thank you. Stevana, it's your turn buddy."

Stevana Banacello came up to the microphone and said, "Thanks Mr President, for having us here. I'm Stevana Banacello the CEO of Modyearna. We're really chuffed, sir, to be working with the Government and the lettered agencies, and do you tell I have to tell you, we had the basics of a vaccine ready within a day of getting the virus sequence from the Chinese, and we've already sent in only 42 days later, our trial vaccine to Dr Faustus' team at the NHIJ. All we're waiting on now is FDA approval, and once that roadblock is passed, we'll be on the highway to injecting everybody with our experimental mRNA injection. Yes, sir, it's mRNA — messenger rNA — it's an informational molecule that carries the computer code to tell the cell to be promoting a protein, a little piece of molecular messaging to the body that causes it be become immune to the virus. We

[39] Ironically Lenny's product seemed to actually do more good than harm, in the long run; in retrospect the MONOCLONAL ANTIBODIES were apparently a successful therapy when used in the fight against the BirdFlip Coronavirus.

too are working with the governments in US, Germany, Australia, and other places, to make treatments for respiratory diseases. We are currently working with the Department Of Defense, with BARDUP, who are the ones tasked with fighting engineered viruses. Of course the fact that DOD and BARDUP are involved does not mean I'm admitting *publicly* that this BirdFlip virus is an engineered one; we worked with them on MERS the camel virus a while ago, and that's also a Coronavirus, and Dr. Faustus's group of scientists was very helpful back then as well.

"And that's why we can move really fast, from a couple of emails and teleconference calls, to getting an injection optimised for putting into people's arms. We're working on the phase two injection already, so as soon as the NHIJ has finished working on the phase one one, we'll be able to start testing the phase two too."

Crump said, "So is that one a phase twenty two or a phase two point two?"

"No, no," said Stevana, "Phase two — too, T, O, O."

Crump said, "So the T. O. O. version — what does the T O O stand for? Is that some military term?"

Stevana tried not to roll his eyes, which paradoxically had the effect of making it more obvious that he was rolling his eyes (at the President, for God's sake, how could he roll his eyes at the President!) and he said, "Yes, it's a military term. It means in addition to that which has come before. Too. T.O.O. We also use another term meaning the same thing, also, A.L.S.O."

Crump said, "Also. I haven't heard either of those before. T.O.O. and A.L.S.O. I'll get the Generals to tell me about it."

Stevana said, "So we will have our mRNA vaccines ready very soon."

Crump said, "So what's your timeframe on that?"

Stevana replied, "Well, as soon as we get the go ahead from the NIH — as soon as that road block is removed — then we'll get the phase one on the road. Once we have some human data, we'll be able to work out the therapeutic dose in order to start the injections straight away."

Crump said, "The therapeutic dose. What does that mean?"

Stevana said, "Well the therapeutic dose is the dose that's therapeutic — that means, the right dose — you know, Mister President, if the dose is too low, it won't do anything, if it's too high, you may have adverse events. Not many, a few deaths and heart attacks here and there, maybe the odd episode of myo/pericarditis, nothing to worry about. It will be safe and effective *at the therapeutic dose.*

Danill Crump: "So what are we talking here? One month? Two months? Six months? How long till you have a vaccine? Two months?

Stevana said, "Yes that's right. That's for phase two."

Faustus corrected him, "You won't have a vaccine yet, Mister President. You'll have to get it tested first. That's just phase two — that means, trying it out on a few people to make sure it doesn't kill them straightaway."

Stevana said, "Exactly. That's for phase two."

Crump said, "So that's not T.O.O., it's the number two, right? So how long would it take, before we have a vaccine ready?"

Stevana replied, "Well, once phase two is done, not T.O.O, the number two, it's like, two or three months after that, that we can start the phase three trials."

Crump said, "So you're saying within a couple — "

Faustus said, "Well, ten to twelve months. A year, like I've been saying all along Mister President."

Meme Qualmsley butted in, "So altogether, you're talking a year and a half?"

George Faustus said, “A year to eighteen months, Mister President.”

Crump said, “But... Lenny Schlenny’s talking about two months.”

Lenny Schlenny said, “Yeh — like — we’d be there by June, Mister President, in phase *one* trials.”

Crump said, “In two months, thereabouts?”

Lenny Schlenny said, “Yeh, two months.”

Crump said, “I mean, I prefer the sound of a coupla months. Let's be frank.”

Aleric Hazard put his hat in the ring then, “But Lenny Schlenny, when you say June, you mean, June to start phase one, right? You won’t have a completed vaccine then. You’ll have something ready for testing in phase one?

Lenny Schlenny, “Yeah, yeah, alright, I admit it, it’ll only be ready for testing in phase one, alright? There’s no need to embarrass me in front of everyone here. That’s phase one — alright — I admit it — phase one everybody — that’s what it is — do you want me to spell it out? P.H.A.S.E.O.N.E., phase one, yeh, just embarrass me in front of my colleagues here Aleric, I wanted to say we’d be the first cab off the rank, but alright, it’s only phase one. In two months, that’s it, in two months a phase one would be ready, alright Aleric? I admit it, Man, you sure are a sour sack of sh — "

Danill Crump said, "Ready to use. A vaccine ready to use."

Lenny Schlenny said, "Yeah, finished, completed, kaput."

Crump still hadn't quite caught up with the conversation; he said, "When — ready to use — when do you think it would be ready to use?"

Spynill Shiverin said, "On the public? Not on laboratory rats or penguins or whatever they're using these days?"

Bel T. Shazzarmani said, "Well, in my humble opinion —"

Crump said, "What you're saying — I think — is it wouldn't be usable till next season? That's a long time."

Bel T. Shazzarmani said, "Well, assuming that it's *safe and effective,* as Spynill said, well the question is, how long will it take the FDA to remove the roadblocks in our way — to make every mountain low and raise up every valley for the coming of the vaccine. I often feel like a voice crying in the wilderness, Mister President, 'make way for the coming of the vaccine!' We need to make ready the road of the vaccine with some sort of fast track plan to accomodate our need to get it through phase one to phase two and three."

Crump said, "You want it fast-tracked. Operation Light Speed. You want to go at Light Speed."

Bel T. Shazzarmani said, "Even faster than Light Speed, at Warp Speed Mister President."

President Crump said, 'What, Warp Speed is faster than Light Speed? I didn't know that. Well, you learn something new every day. How about that. Warp Speed is faster than Light Speed! There you go — you think nothing's a mystery any more and then you learn something new. Waddayou say about that, Lenny?"

Lenny Schlenny said, "Well... Look, I'm getting — like — vibes of cautiousness from the good Doctor Faustus, sir, he's giving off a kinda atmosphere of 'let's be cautious about this' — 'let's not rush into it' — and that's what I like to hear, Mister President. He's on the conservative side of these things — he's not pushing us into some kinda 'oh let's vaccinate everybody with an experimental medication and nobody knows if it works or not or if it's gonna kill people' Dr Faustus is, like, sayin, look before you jump. Two months is not long enough. Let's wait a year or a year and a half, until we know if these products work or not. You know, be alert, be wary, haste makes waste, better be safe than sorry, measure thrice and cut wise, proceed with caution, prevention is better than cure, he who avoid risks avoids tusks, an old proverb we say when we're pig hunting."

Crump said, "Pig hunting? But I thought you were Jewish?"

Lenny Schlenny said, "I like bakin' pies."

Crump said, "Bacon pies? But that's not kosher is it?"

Lenny said, "Bakin'. That's, B A K I N G, Bakin'. I like Bakin' bacon pies, too, actually. But you know, sir, you don't want to be makin' the disease worse: you don't want to rush out and inject everybody and find out that you're makin' ninety percent of 'em worse, Mister Crump. As they say, caution is the better portion."

President Crump said, "I like the sound of that. That sounds good. Caution is the better portion."

Lenny Schlenny said, "And you see, that's why *ours* is the best bet — I don't want to make these other chumps look stoopid, but the thing is —- we already tested it on the Ibizavirus, and we know that it would have worked for MERS if we had any patients to try it on. See *ours* is the one that would work, sooner than these chumps pushing their mRNA poison, Mr President. Trust me. Don't trust them."

Spynill Shiverin, Bel T. Shazzarmani and Stevana Banacello suddenly erupted into shouting, "Them's fightin' words Lenny Schlenny!" "Come here and say that in my face you chump!" "Let's step outside and settle this like men!"

President Crump said, "Okay, okay, guys, settle down, there's no need to get excited. We're not making the final decision today. Settle down."

Lenny Schlenny said, "But let's not gild the lily — that's the way it is — them's the facts, Jack."

President Crump said, "Thank you Lenny, I'm sure we will all agree with you. Bobajob, what's your take on this?"

Bobajob said, "Yeah, thanks Mr President, thanks for inviting us. I'm going to change gears, guys, we're going to a higher level of the game plan."

"Great," said Crump. "That's sounding great — go ahead, Bobajob."

Bobajob said, "Testament Pharmaceutical Sciences has worked with a lot of the people who are present at this meeting. And first, let me thank you Dr Faustus, for everything you've done, particularly in the HOOV program, to eliminate the dreaded HOOV virus. It's a great thing, that we can now treat this virus when we couldn't treat it before, and it's just amazing everything that's been achieved. Don't you think, Mr President?"

Crump said, "I do, I agree completely Bobajob. Great stuff. We started this as soon as I heard about it — so everyone's saying HOOV could be dead in the water in 9 years. Or maybe 10 years, what do you think, Dr Bobajob?"

Bobajob said, "I think we can defeat it in the US of A, President Crump, and maybe Europe and England as well. We've made great strides in treating this virus, and we're doing really well; and a similar approach to BirdFlip-CoV2 is what we're looking at. We have a great medicine — an anti-viral called Rundeathisnear, which has had proper pharmaceutical trials; yes, we may have run the first parts concurrently as we like to do, but you know, we've had a proper development timeline, of eight years, plus the initial animal trials, altogether this antiviral *is* safe and effective for SARS, MERS, the Ruddy Shelduck Virus, the Tibetan Snowcock Virus, and even the Knob-Billed Duck Virus. This has been a long experiential journey for us in which we have massaged our expectations again and again, but what we do know is that in-vitro —"

Crump said, "That means in the test tube, yes?"

Bobajob said, “Yes exactly — in the test tube, although it’s more of a Petri dish in practice, Rundeathisnear kills the BirdFlip Coronavirus. Mind you, it kills just about everything else including human liver, kidney and lung cells, but that is something we don’t like to mention — because the truth is, if someone *can* actually survive a course of Rundeathisnear, they will be truly immune to the BirdFlip virus as well, I can guarantee it.”

Crump said, “So this medicine — Rundeathisnear — it’s ready to use now? And you’re saying it kills the BirdFlip Coronavirus?”

Bobajob said, “That and everything else.”

Crump commented, “So that’s great — you can know by Friday whether it works or not?”

Bobajob said, “Well, we still have to do some randomised double-blind placebo controlled clinical trials, and in fact, would you believe, we already have some double-blind trials going on right now in a Uyghur — er — community in China. We’ve already got a bunch of Uyghurs involved in it, over 500 have been enrolled in the trial. What do you think of that?”

Crump said, “So over 500 of the Uyghurs have enrolled in the study?”

Bobajob said, "Well, they've *been* enrolled in the study. Yes..."

Crump said, "Any results yet?"

Bobajob said, "Well, unfortunately they're double-blinded randomised placebo controlled trials, which is great, but we can't unblind the trial, so we won't know until the trials are finished. Should know in about one month. Then we've been working with the NAIAD and the NHIJ and Tony to test it in China, and in the United States we're going to do a trial of a test for the BirdFlip virus as well. And we've got some more trials happening of Rundeathisnear as well."

Crump said, "Great — that's great. So you're doing some trials in the United States?"

Bobajob said, "Yeh, in Utah. And we're working on a few other trials with Dr Faustus here. Aren't we Tony? He's my bro."

Faustus disliked familiarisms like 'bro,' however Bobajob's work was really valuable in terms of grants, and so he put up with it. Faustus said, "We've got some other trials happening in Oklahoma as well."

Crump said, "Wonderful. Well, thank you all for coming."

The cameras switched off, and Faustus remembered, and he quickly said to Crump before the secret service whisked him away, "Will you come and meet my driver's daughter, Mr President? Her name's Madeley and she really wanted to meet you. Her father's Frank."

Crump nodded a query to one of the secret service guys, who said, "It's not scheduled — but we have the time. Where is she?"

Faustus said, "Just sitting at the back of the hall, Mister President, with her father."

Crump said, "Can we do it on the way out?"

"Sure," said the secret service guy. "Where is she seated?"

"Just there, a few feet from the entrance," said Doctor Faustus. "That's her Dad next to her, with the black coat and the NHIJ tie."

"Alright," said the secret service guy. "Ah, just send Olivia over there to talk to them, and then we'll take him past and speak to her and her father on the way out."

Olivia was a woman standing at the door at the back of the hall. She went over to talk to Frank and Madeley.

~~~
~~~

Frank looked up from his mobile phone — an attractive woman in a black suit jacket and pants, wearing a pale blue shirt, was standing next to him — she had just said something. "Hello, are you Doctor Faustus' driver?"

"Yes," said Frank.

Olivia said, "I'm personal assistant to President Crump; my name is Olivia. The President is coming to meet your daughter on the way through. Please stand to show your respect and the President will shake your hands and speak to you."

"Oh!" said Madeley, "I'm going to meet the President! I'm going to meet the President!"

Olivia spoke into her lapel mic, "They're ready."

~~~

The secret service guy heard Olivia and said, "Okay. Are you ready to go Mister President?"

Crump said, "Sure, Jim. Let's do it."

And the secret service security machine went into action; the coordination was incredible, with men were talking into their lapel mics, listening on their earpieces, the car came around out the front, and they moved into action.

~~~

The President marched off the stage and through the centre aisle, between the chairs arrayed on either side. When they reached Madeley and Frank, the President stopped and said, "Madeley? I'm very pleased to meet you."

Madeley said politely, "Very pleased to meet you too, sir. Do you like being President?"

The President said, "Yes and no, Madeley, yes and no. But I keep doing it 'cause it's my duty."

Madeley said, "Oh, that's good. That's what my Dad says, that we all need to do our duty."

The President said, "Oh — is that your Dad here?"

And Madeley said, "Yes. His name's Frank."

Mr Crump said, "Frank. Very pleased to meet you."

"Thanks," said Frank. "I think you're doing a good job."

Crump said, "I'm doing my best."

Frank said, "Well, I think you're the best President ever."

Mr Crump said, "Well, thank you, so do I."

Madeley said, "So do I."

Crump said, "Well, George Washington might have been better than me, but don't tell anyone I said that. I have a reputation to uphold. And honest Abe. Just don't tell anyone — everyone thinks I always boast, so I don't want to disappoint them, Madeley. It was nice to meet you."

Madeley said, "It was nice to meet you too, Mr President."

~~~

So it was that ten or fifteen minutes later, Faustus was sitting in the back of the SUV, being driven back home by Frank, and Madeley was in the front.

Frank and Madeley were unusually quiet on the way to his home, so Dr Faustus asked her what the President had said to her.

Both Faustus and Frank laughed when Madeley gave her answer, because she imitated Crump's voice rather well indeed: "I asked him if he likes being President and he said, 'yes and no, but I keep doing it 'cause it's my duty.'"

"Then she asked me if this was my Dad and I said, yes, and Dad told him he was doing a good job, and he answered 'I'm doing my best,' and then we both told him we thought he was the best President ever, and Mr Crump said, George Washington and honest Abe might have been better but he had a reputation to uphold for always boasting, and he didn't want to disappoint everybody."
~~~

Faustus said, "Wow. You got him in a rare moment of humility. That's amazing. He must have taken his off his public persona for a moment with you, Madeley, which is quite amazing, really."

When they arrived at Faustus' mansion, and as he got out of the car, Madeley said, "You have a very big house." Frank said, "Shhh, Madeley."

Faustus, a little embarrassed, said, "It's alright, Frank. Madeley, it never seems particularly huge to me; sometimes I feel like we don't have enough room for everything, and we keep having to throw stuff out. After our children left home, we had a lot of rooms that didn't have much in them. But, you know, now one's a library, we've made the others into guest rooms for our daughters to stay in when they come over, and so on and so forth. It is a little large just for the two of us."

Then they said goodbye, and Faustus went in.

On the way home, Madeley said, "Why did you shush me when I told Mr Faustus' house was big?"

Frank said, "Well, it's not the type of thing polite people notice, Madeley; that someone's house is bigger than yours."

Madeley said, "Why not?"

Frank thought about it for a second. “I’m not really sure, Madeley.” He laughed. “I don’t know. And I don’t even know if I should have shushed you at all. Why don’t people want to notice those things? I really, really don’t know.”

And so they drove home, and Madeley told her mother all about their day, meeting President Crump and talking with Dr Faustus about it afterwards. And so it was that Madeley slept very, very well that night, looking out of her window at the clear April sky, for everything was well with the world.

~~~

While Madeley was sleeping, Faustus was looking at his emails and his phone rang.

He answered it.

The name showed up: it was Gill Bates.

“Hi Dr Faustus. It’s Gill here.”

“Yes, Mister Bates, I know, I had Petronia put your mobile number into my phone contacts. To be honest, I don’t have a clue how to do that.”

Gill’s picture appeared on the phone, it was some sort of video call.

Gill snapped, “Turn your video on, George.”
~~~

George fumbled around on his phone; he didn't know how to.

Gill said, "It's the little icon of a video at the bottom with a line through it. Press that."

Gill didn't look too pleased. "You may guess from my tone of voice that I don't sound very pleased. Well, one of my personal assistants at the Foundation has the job of looking at the studies, seeing what's out there in the pipeline, and noticed that the NAIAD is doing a study into Hydroxychloroquilline."

"Yes, it's supposed to be the biggest clinical trial yet into Hydroxychloroquilline and that antibiotic, I forget what it's name was. The scientists are looking into whether it's effective for the BirdFlip virus, sir," said Dr Faustus.

Gill said, "Well I'm not going to tell you to squash it, that would be unethical, but imagine how I feel about this, Dr Faustus, when we've got these vaccines being trialed at the moment and I don't want some pathetic little anti-malarial drug getting in the way. Can you squash it?"

Dr Faustus said, "Well, sir, that would be very unethical for me to agree to do that. You know, these studies need to be done. We need to know how these drugs can work to treat the BirdFlip, don't we?"

Gill said, “It doesn’t work. You yourself know that BirdFlip was made in the lab by the most dastardly virologists in the whole world, with ties to the military. How could a common little generic anti-malarial drug defeat a virus made in the lab that is going to kill hundreds of millions of people? Tell me that, Faustus? How?”

Dr Faustus said, “I don’t know. Who has ties to the military? Does Peter Dackazacka have ties to the military, sir?”

Gill said, “No, I’m talking about ZhengLeng Penguin.”

Dr Faustus said, “Does ZhengLeng Penguin have ties to the military, Mister Bates?”

Gill said, “What? Of course she does. All the Chinese labs do. All the Chinese businesses do, ever since they brought in the ‘dual use’ policy in 2015, George. They had a military guy on staff, some kind of medical military guy or something, I forget his name; ZhouLou Kaka. There’s someone else, too, on the managing committee, who has authority.”

Dr Faustus looked on the English language website for the WooHoo lab. He couldn’t find the guy listed there. He said, “His name’s not on the website.”

Gill said, “No, that’s because he was one of the first to die with the virus.”

Dr Faustus looked some more, “There’s nothing here about him at all in the archived posts.”

Gill said, “Well they deleted everything, George. Didn’t you realise that? Back in September, they deleted all the data and everything about the birds they had taken the viruses from, the genomes they were sharing, everything. They probably deleted ZhouLou Kaka’s name as well at the same time.”

Dr Faustus said, “I - I see.” He didn’t, though, he really *didn’t* see what Mr Bates was getting at.

Gill said, “Well, I’m telling you, Dr Faustus, that we shouldn’t be wasting time on generic medicines, when we have these mRNA vaccines coming out. Look, I’ve put a lot of the money into BioZTechno, the company that is going to be manufacturing the vaccines.”

Dr Faustus said, “I see?”

Gill said, “Well if that study is squashed, it would be a good thing, wouldn’t it? What a waste of public money. Hydroxychloroquilline doesn’t work, George.” And he closed the call.

~~~
~~~

The schools stayed closed over the next few weeks in Washington DC, and the authorities eventually decided to end the term early, and keep the schools closed until the end of term. In the meantime, Crump was trumpeting his "Operation Light Speed" vaccine program and the media were calling him irresponsible.

> Crump Presses to Speed up BirdFlip Vaccine Development, Despite Widespread Safety Concerns
>
> *The President wants a widely available BirdFlip vaccine before the end of the year, even though his public health experts are telling him it will take at least a year to a year and a half.*
>
> WASHINGTON — The news from the Capitol is that President Crump is pushing his health officials to develop the BirdFlip vaccine program at "Warp Speed, like the Starship Enterprise," apparently, and that he wants a vaccine out "tomorrow, if not yesterday." The health officials are very skeptical about speeding up the vaccines because they are very worried about health and safety, very worried indeed. They are saying that eight or nine months is too short a development timeline, and that a year to eighteen months is much much better.

It all came to a head a few weeks later when Crump said in the media that "they have 2 million doses of vaccine already available," and then fired the chairman of Bardup for not recommending treatment with

Hydroxychloraquilline, and so Dr Faustus decided he had to do something about the President's irresponsible behaviour.

Faustus called a press conference, and this is what he said to the media: "You know, honestly, Coronaviruses like the BirdFlip, they are very quick to evolve. Just when you've got immunity, the virus mutates and suddenly you can catch it again; that's the problem with Coronaviruses. How do you solve a problem like the BirdFlip? It's a flibbertigibbet! A will-o'-the wisp! A clown! How do you catch a cloud and pin it down[40]? This riddle-like quality of the BirdFlip virus means that any vaccine is only going to be effective for six months if you're lucky, the protection is not going to last."

After this press conference, Faustus came home exhausted. It was a cold night for early June. Gloriana was working in her office. He went into the lounge room and sat down in front of the fire. She came in a little later and sat down next to him, and handed him a Scotch whisky.

"George, you look exhausted," she said.

He said, "This little tussle with Crump is getting to me, Gloriana. Do you know, when we did that first press conference on vaccines, he came up with the idea of good

[40] Doctor Faustus (or his speechwriter) seems to have inadvertently quoted the Rogers and Hammerstein song, "How do you solve a problem like Maria" in this passage of his speech.

cop, bad cop, but it's really getting out of hand. I don't know; it's just not scientific, any of it. I got into this to do science. Now I'm doing politics."

Gloriana gave a sort of cough, which he realised was a laugh.

He said, "I don't know why you're laughing at me. I don't think it's funny. I don't think it's funny at all."

Gloriana said, "Look at you — everything that you do, George, is politics. And that's okay — it's a minefield — somehow you've got to make every next step without stepping on a mine. I don't know how you do it, but you do. You have staying power. You survived the HOOV epidemic and you'll outlast this one. You're a rock, Faustus, an immovable rock, and you haven't met the irresistible force yet."

"Well, yes I have," he said. "When we met eyes over that hospital bed where lay the patient dying of pneumonia, you bowled me over."

Gloriana said, "Haha, when you asked me out on that date, I thought it was all about the science."

"I *am* the Science," he said.

Gloriana said, "You are — in this sense — what you decide is proper science is what gets funded. You have the power to decide what is science and what isn't. In a certain way, it's like the electron: you can't measure its position without stopping it, and then, it's gone — if you don't look at something, if you don't study something, it never even becomes a fact. That's the power of observation — does a tree fall in the forest? etcetera."

George said, "Gill Bates said he wants the Hydroxychloroquilline study squashed."

Gloriana said, "What? That's exactly what he said? I can't believe that. He's very careful not to make unequivocal statements like that."

George said, "Not in so many words. He said it doesn't work anyway and we shouldn't be spending time on it."

Gloriana said, "Well, you know, government resources are precious. He's very invested in the vaccines, though, isn't he? Do you think the FDA will give the mRNA vaccines emergency use approval if your study shows that Hydroxychloroquilline is a safe and effective treatment?"

George shook his head. "Well, any safe and effective generic treatment could cast doubt on the emergency use approvals; you know, I don't know that the FDA really cares, I mean, everyone on the approvals board are all very pro-Pfutticup and Modyearna, really, very pro the pharmaceutical companies in every way, and you know, how can they be expected make money out of cheap generic medications, that are out of patent? If Hydroxychloroquilline is looking good, that could be bad, Gloriana, for the whole pandemic; I'm sure Gill Bates is right: ultimately the vaccines will be vastly more efficient at stopping the virus than any mere anti-malaria medication that's essentially a hundred years, even if this iteration is more recent. Don't you think? Do you think he's right?"

Gloriana said, "That mRNA technology is very important, George. It could make many treatments much more cheap and effective. And pharmaceutical companies do have to make money; that's the conundrum — how can they make money out of a cheap, generic medication like Hydroxychloroquilline, that's out of patent? I think the duration of the patents is just too short. And this research is really important."

George said, "You don't mean the research into Hydroxychloroquilline, do you?"

Gloriana replied, "No, I mean the research into the mRNA vaccines is really important. It's such an exciting new platform for the delivery of drugs — you know, you're making the cells of the body make the drug for you."

George shook his head. "But... what about the safety of the mRNA vaccines?" he said. "I mean, have they solved all those problems they had with inflammation? It's no use rushing it if it's not going to work."

Gloriana said, "It will work, George — have a bit of faith in Science. This is the direction it's heading in. This technology is where it's at, that's what everyone is saying. It will work."

George said rather impressively, "I *am* the Science."

Gloriana said, "Let's have pizza tonight, George."

~~~
~~~

CHAPTER 10

Qualms.

The next day, the whole morning was taken up in emails and Zoom calls that seemed to go around in endless circles. Faustus went for his usual walk at midday, with his mask on, for masks were mandated now in DC, and ended up thinking it all through.

God knows, they'd had their fair share of experimental vaccine disasters, all because things were being pushed through too fast. But you had to do that in a pandemic, didn't you? I mean soon enough the whole thing's over, everyone's either immune or dead, and then the opportunity to test the new medication is lost.

But think about it — some of these medications could end up being real public relations disasters.

Faustus shook his head; there was the Zippa virus DMTPRQ vaccine that caused microcephaly in newborn babies in some South American country about five or six years ago; he forgot which country it was in. Faustus had successfully framed the story to blame the virus itself for the microcephaly cases, and had in the process managed to gain a huge increase in funding for research into Zippa virus vaccines, but it could have so easily gone wrong, couldn't it?

For a while it was all sitting on a knife edge; it could have gone either way, but it's all about optics, isn't it? It's all about optics. It's all about how you frame things; Gloriana was right. If you don't study something, it doesn't really exist. If no one hears the tree fall in the forest, did it actually fall?

Then there was the pharmaceutical trial of Dungvaxio, a vaccine against some fever or other in the Phillipines, and the Bates foundation and the NAIAD had underwritten it for Sinafil, a big pharmaceutical company.

The whole thing was a huge disaster. Faustus didn't even like to think about it; the whole episode was like a wound on his psyche. They sure didn't get out of that one unscathed. It was like a warning to him, shouting across the years, don't get involved with experimental vaccines!

But vaccines are a good thing. The thing is, they are the whole foundation of modern medicine. Why get immunity from having the disease, when you can have complete immunity provided in a two second injection? It's one of the wonders of modern medicine. But Sinafil began a huge vaccination campaign in the Philippines, before the clinical trials of Dungvaxio were even finished. And that's when the problems began: children began dying. Well, an interfering medico started looking into it, and it turned out that if the kids caught the disease *after* having taken the vaccine, it caused fluid to leak from the blood internally; it was a horrible way to die. This Doctor started writing articles for medical journals and making online videos, and all this, but Sinafil contradicted him in the journals and said he was full of it, basically — they said the government had approved the vaccine because it was safe and effective and woe-betide anyone who contradicted him.

Faustus didn't think the medication was to blame, but the government began gathering data, and you know how that goes: if you don't study something, it doesn't really exist. They found that 600 children had died from the vaccine. It was a public relations disaster. Autopsies were done on the kids who had died, and the government eventually indicted the health minister and a bunch of Sinafil people as well for reckless imprudence resulting in homicide.

Bad optics all round. Now *that* was bad for science; if you have bad optics, it affects the government's willingness to fund the scientific endeavour. Science relies on funding. When things like this happen, people stop trusting pharmaceutical products, and that affects their bottom line, and *that* affects funding.

Well, that's what it came down to: optics. If these new mRNA vaccines ended up not being safe and effective, it could damage the scientific endeavour for years to come, maybe forever. That Crump — pushing to have the vaccines ready as soon as possible — it could really cause problems down the track. God knows, Faustus didn't even think one and a half years would be long enough. He remembered when he was in medical school — he was taught that it should take fourteen years.

But even if they did everything *right,* it could still go wrong. If they intentionally rushed something that was already being rushed, it could go *badly* wrong.

Faustus was rounding the bend, now, at the park; he was heading back home now.

And then there was the Nuremberg Code. The code of Medical Ethics that dated from World War II. The code that said at the start, "The voluntary consent of the human subject is absolutely essential." Now, Faustus actually had remembered the first paragraph of this code, word for word, when he was at university: they had made them remember it back then and regurgitate it in the exam.

He still had it in his mind.

It went on:

"This means that the person involved should have legal capacity to give consent; should be so situated as to be able to exercise free power of choice, without the intervention of any element of force, fraud, deceit, duress, over-reaching, or other ulterior form of constraint or coercion; and should have sufficient knowledge and comprehension of the elements of the subject matter involved, as to enable him to make an understanding and enlightened decision. This latter element requires that, before the acceptance of an affirmative decision by the experimental subject, there should be made known to him the nature, duration, and purpose of the experiment; the method and means by which it is to be conducted; all inconveniences and hazards reasonably to be expected; and the effects upon his health or person, which may possibly come from his participation in the experiment. The duty and responsibility for ascertaining the quality of the consent rests upon each individual who initiates, directs or engages in the experiment. It is a personal duty and responsibility which may not be delegated to another with impunity."

Suddenly, when he thought about it, Faustus had many more qualms.

They were calling these mRNA medicines 'vaccines' and they were anything but — they were a completely new medication. What it was intended to do was completely different to any other vaccine. A normal vaccine would just put a little bit of 'dead' virus or pathogen into the blood stream, and then be recognised by the immune system as foreign, and the body would attack it, and in so doing learn how to destroy the real thing when it came along.

The mRNA was a whole different, new process.

The mRNA was injected and what was supposed to happen is it would travel into a person's cells, and when it got there, it would *hopefully* be taken up by the ribosomes, inside the cell, which is the little machine where the cells make proteins; it's a highly technical process, and it's quite amazing how it came about by evolution, this manufacturing centre of the cell. In the ribosome, the foreign mRNA would be translated into a protein. This protein would then shuffled along to another part of the cell and be given legs, so to speak, in the Golgi apparatus, which would add some bits to enable the protein to be transported out of the cell.

Now at some point in this process the body's immune system would presumably recognise this new protein being made by the cells was a *foreign* protein and attack it, and then the immune system would thereafter attack the virus if it came along as well.

Yes, this is the amazing thing about the body, really, it is incredible that this could evolve by itself; I mean the whole thing is really an information code transmission process — when you think about the cell — the way it works normally (not with foreign RNA, but DNA) is quite extraordinary.

The DNA somehow gets a signal from a hormone or some transcription factor or promoter or signalling protein somewhere in the body — Faustus didn't fully understand this bit — but this signal, wherever it comes from, tells the DNA that a new protein is needed somewhere to do some job or other — as far as Faustus understood it — and the DNA would unzip off half of the double strand and make a copy of that inside the cell nucleus, copied into RNA, which would then be brought to the Ribosomes, and the whole process continues there with the RNA being made into a protein and the protein transported to where it's needed in the body.

It was quite amazing that evolution ended up creating this whole process — when you think about it, it was like having a giant bowl of alphabet soup, picking out the letters one by one, and ending up with a novel in the English language — Clarence Collins seemed to think it made sense that this process could happen by blind chance (although Clarence thought it was God who did it — throwing the dice of the universe so to speak and ending up with an extremely unlikely outcome, i.e. life) — Faustus didn't really understand it, but he knew evolutionary biologists like Kristen as well that did know it inside out, and they seemed to think that this whole process of evolution coming by complete chance to create DNA and RNA, which were basically codes, computer codes, they thought it made a lot of sense, so who was he to argue with the experts?

Yeh — computer code. That's exactly what is was like. DNA is like the operating system, and the RNA — well that's where the analogy breaks down already, at least for Faustus, because he didn't know much about how computers work, actually.

But he remembered the scientists from the Pharma companies had said they were going to put the mRNA code in to make the whole spike protein from the virus. So that Spike protein would then be shuffled out of the cell, and the body's immune system would see it there and attack it, and then hey presto! You've got immunity to the virus.

It all sounds marvellous, they say, "We know what we're doing," but he'd heard these assurances before. Oh, yeah, you know what you're doing, well that's exactly what they said with Dungvaxio. "Don't worry, we don't have to finish the clinical trials, we know enough about it already to get started. This is such a terrible disease, we've got to nip it in the bud before it spreads. Yeh, we know what we're doing." Right.

It just takes for one little bring of essential knowledge to be unknown, sometimes, for the whole edifice to come tumbling down. It's like one brick is missing; if that happens to be the cornerstone of the building, the rest is unstable, and Dungvaxio was exactly like that. They just didn't know — how were they to know? — that when the kids who had been vaccinated caught the virus afterwards they would be much, much sicker than those who'd caught it the first time — and this was because the second time you caught that disease it *was* worse— he forgot the name of that stupid disease — it would be way worse than the first, and they had just replicated this quality of the disease with their vaccine.

Now the World Health people only recommended kids who had already caught the disease *once* take the vaccine — that seemed to work — but what use was that?

It was all a disaster, just because one little piece of information was missing.

What little brick of knowledge in the whole edifice of the mRNA treatment did they not know yet? He didn't know. He couldn't guess.

And he knew they didn't know either.

~~~

Gloriana was working from home, of course, because of the lockdowns, and Faustus walked in. She said, "Don't come any closer, you've been outside, you might have the virus."

He said, "It's very unlikely, darling, I don't think I went within twenty metres of another person on my walk, unless it was someone driving past in a car."

She said, "Alright. No one sneezed or coughed on you from a car, then?"

He said, "No, no one sneezed on me. I just wanted to run some things by you, though, Gloriana."

She said, "Ethics?"

He nodded.

She dropped what she was doing and listened as he told her about his qualms.
~~~

At the end of it Gloriana said, "Now, Dr Faustus, you are looking at this the whole wrong way. Think of it like the moon landing. Did those astronauts, and NASA, get to the moon by being afraid to do it, in case they failed? It was a really unsafe enterprise, George, and they didn't get there by being afraid. They took the bull by the horns — so to speak — and they went forwards — and they thought of the joy they would have at the end, when they had explored the surface of the moon — they didn't say, 'Well, what if we don't come home?'

"This is Science, George, Science, and it must go forward, always forward. It is not the faint-hearted that do the great works of exploration and discovery. It is not the people who say to themselves, 'What might go wrong?' who are the ones that do the great deeds, but the ones who say, 'What might go right?' and who affirm to themselves that they *can* do it, that it *is* possible, that it *can* be done. No one achieves anything without taking risks.

"And when you look at it from the right point of view, George, you'll see that this *is* exploration — Gill Bates is right — the mRNA is a whole new technology — and this pandemic must be seen as an *opportunity* rather than a challenge or even a disaster — an opportunity to bring this new medical platform to its fruition, George — an opportunity to advance medical science in an unprecedented way.

"We can do it, George. The company executives, Gill Bates, the NIH and the NAIAD. *You* can do it."

George said, "That's right. *I can do it.* Thank you Gloriana, I think I was just getting into a bit of a mental loop, there. I *am* the Science. Go forward not back. I *am* the *Science.*"

Gloriana said, "You *are* the *Science.* That's right, Dr Faustus, and don't you doubt it. Don't you forget it." And she paused for a moment, then said, "Do you know, we should have dinner with Gill Bates and his wife Belinda some time soon..."

"Oh, they're getting divorced," said Faustus. "Didn't you know?"

"Really?" said Gloriana. "Well, maybe just Gill Bates then... I think you need to have a long chat with him, George, about medical ethics. He has such a splendid take on these things: you see, we need to take the *long view* of medical ethics. We have to think about what's good for humanity in the time span of decades and centuries, what's good for Science with a capital S, what's good for the future generations of people. You can worry too much about informed consent and issues like that — we realise today that there has to be a bit of wiggle room — for some studies you just can't *get* consent without compromising the results — you can't always tell people about all the risks, especially when some of the risks only show up in one out of ten thousand cases. In other words, we need to have a bit of nuance with these sorts of discussions."

"Do you know," said Faustus, "I agree. You put your finger on exactly what I was worried about, Gloriana — you know, with these mRNA vaccines — they're not really *like* traditional vaccines — they're a new platform, a completely different way of engendering immunity — but the way to get them authorised and introduced to the public is that we have to reassure them that it's really just another vaccine. While on my walk, I started thinking of that as a lie, as twisting the truth, but it's not really: it's just presenting a positive point of view on these new medications. I'm pretty sure they did the same thing with the smallpox vaccine."

"Aye, and there's the rub," said Gloriana, "The Doctor knows more than the patient — that's the plain fact of the matter — and to expect the patient to even be capable of making a decision of informed consent is entirely ridiculous.

Most people don't even have any concept of actual risk, in statistical terms — and when they do they usually don't even understand the implications of the kinds of damage that can occur if they *don't* follow the expert's instructions. When you think about it, the Doctor should really have *more* say than the patient in clinical care — it's only logical. I can't even count how many times I've explicitly explained a course of action to a patient, explored the risks in great detail and made clear the possible or probable benefits, only to have them make a stupid decision because quite plainly they don't understand what I was telling them at all. No, informed consent is an idea that we've come to understand in the medical industry as requiring a lot more nuance these days."

"If we can just get those vaccines out there," Faustus said, "We can prevent transmission and end the school lockdowns. I hate to say it, but I almost think Crump is right — we need to get these new vaccines out into the arms of the populace as quickly as possible."

~~~

Crump went on television the following week, saying that the stay-at-home orders had gone on for long enough, and that the economy needed to be reopened.
~~~

That little charade at the start, where Faustus and Crump seemed to be pushing in different directions, seemed to have taken on a life of its own. Crump said, "Hydroxychloroquilline," so Faustus said, "Hydroxychloroquilline is unproven;" Crump said, "Masking is bad," so Faustus said, "Masking is good;" Crump said, "End the stay-at-home orders," so Faustus said, "Keep the stay-at-home orders going," when Crump said, "Get the schools and businesses open," So Faustus said, "Keep the schools and businesses closed."

Indeed, whenever Crump said, "Go," Faustus said "Stay;" whenever Crump said, "Jump," Faustus said, "Duck," whenever Crump said, "Run," Faustus said, "Stop."

Faustus had really come to dislike the man.

~~~~

A few days after Trump's appearance in the media casting doubt on the wisdom of the lockdowns, Frank and Madeley arrived at the mansion to pick up Dr Faustus in the SUV. They were both wearing masks.

Today they were headed to the Capitol building, because Faustus had been called to appear before a
~~~~

Congressional inquiry about school closures and the lockdowns and masking and stay-at-home orders.

"Hello, Madeley," said Dr Faustus.

"Hello, Dr Faustus," she said.

"So how are you today, young Madeley?" he said. He had come to be quite fond of his driver's daughter, who really was a sweet, friendly child.

"I'm very well," said Madeley. "Not a single sign of the BirdFlip virus."

"Good to hear," he said. "Do you know I'm going to Congress today, to speak to the Senators about our response to the BirdFlip virus."

"Really?" said Madeley. "Are the schools going to open soon? I miss my friends."

"Well," said Faustus, "No I don't think so — I'll be telling them that they should keep the schools closed a little longer. And that to expect a vaccine by the time schools come back after the summer holiday might be a little unrealistic. I'll be telling them that if they open the schools and relax the stay-at-home orders, that there's going to be an uptick in the cases, Madeley, and then I would expect the hospitals will be overwhelmed, and that's not really so good."

Madeley went very quiet then, and put her earphones on and started listening to an audiobook.

~~~

Frank was watching the traffic as he drove — it was a sunny day and you'd think more people would be out, but because of the stay-at-home orders, there was hardly anyone on the road. Half the people he saw driving in cars on their own had masks on — something Frank thought was plainly ridiculous.

Dr Faustus had insisted they wear masks, it was more for "optics" he said — Frank had noticed he used that phrase more and more these days — he noticed that Faustus looked stressed a lot of the time, too.

Frank looked at the old man in the rear view mirror. Today he looked extra stressed. "Dr Faustus, are you alright? You look tired."

"I'm alright," said Faustus, "But I do feel as though I'm pulled in a lot of directions. You know, Frank, I'm lucky to have my wife — Gloriana's really been a rock all through this — I often turn to her for advice — she's an expert in medical ethics, you know, and sometimes — sometimes I'm a little hard on myself, in these areas, I question myself too much, you know? She always helps me to step back and see
~~~

the bigger picture, see things in perspective. You know, we're not just here for ourselves, Frank, we're here to look after the future generations."

Frank nodded. "I feel the same," he said. "Very much the same." But for a moment Frank wondered if he and Faustus had the same idea of the things they'd need to do to help future generations.

For a while Frank watched the scenery as they drove along Foxhall road. It was a lovely drive, now, in late spring; the sun was shining, the trees all had their leaves and many were still in blossom even now, yellow and pink azaleas like explosions of colour, early hydrangeas blooming and even the odd red rose in a polite, well tended garden by the way, as they all seemed to be. DC certainly was beautiful at this time of year and you couldn't help feeling cheerful, despite the general sense of gloom that hung over everything like a grey pall; every now and then you would see a driver driving alone with a mask on, or another person walking alone by the side of the road also wearing a mask and the reminder was like an ink blot on a wedding gown, somehow, a blot of fear and unpleasantness that shouldn't mar such absolute splendidness.

Faustus stunned him out of his reverie with an unexpected question, "Tell me, Frank, what do you think of Mr Crump, the President? Don't be afraid to be frank, er, Frank."

"Haha," said Frank, a little awkwardly, "I'm never afraid to be Frank; it's what I am." But he thought for a minute; to be honest he *was* a little afraid to be Frank. How much should he tell Dr Faustus? He decided to edit what he really thought for the good doctor's ears, because he thought he knew what Faustus wanted to hear. After all, it was his job on the line; what if he said the wrong thing and Faustus didn't like it? It could poison the well that he was relying on…

Frank said, "Well… He's a bit of a boaster, really. Sometimes he seems to go out on a limb, when everyone else has a different opinion. He's done one or two good things." He looked at Madeley — lucky she had her headphones on, listening to "The Silver Chair" probably — she just about worshipped Mr Crump — she wouldn't want to hear her Dad say anything bad about him.

Faustus said, "And what do you think of the stay-at-home orders and the masks?"

Frank said, "To be honest, I just wish they'd end. I've had enough of all of this, Dr Faustus. Let's just all take our chances, catch the virus and get back to normal."

Faustus said, "I'm sorry Frank, but my advice is going to be that they should keep the stay-at-home orders going a little longer. If the states open up too early, they could have a big spike in cases and overwhelm the hospitals. Anyhow..." and Dr Faustus smiled ruefully, and Frank realised he hadn't fooled him at all, "Your friend Mister Crump disagrees with me."

They all looked at the scenery as they drove along the Potomac River — the blue waters shimmering in the sunlight underneath the sky, with a few fluffy white clouds here and there; it really was a beautiful day. But Frank always felt an emptiness in DC, as though the power sucked the soul out of the city.

~~~

When they got to the Capitol building, this time, Frank and Madeley couldn't go in. Faustus told them they had limited the numbers in the Senate Gallery in order to stick to the DC social distancing restrictions.

"That's okay," Frank said, "We can watch it on my mobile, on C-Span."
~~~

Faustus said, “I didn’t know you could do that. It’s amazing what they can do these days.”

Frank said, “Good luck,” and he genuinely meant it; he liked Dr Faustus, even if he disagreed with some of his ideas.

After Dr Faustus went in, Madeley and Frank took off their masks.

“That’s better,” said Madeley.

“Much better,” said Frank.

~~~

Chairman Dimitrios came up to the microphone, took off his mask and left it hanging on his ear, and began the Senate hearing.

“Now, just before we get started,” he said, “I’d just like to mention a few things about masks. We’ve been advised by the Senate office of the attending physician that we’re allowed to remove our masks and talk into the microphone so long as we stay a good six foot apart from the nearest person, and so, that’s why I’m not wearing my mask right now, people,” and he waved his arms about for a moment; “I’m six feet away from everybody so that’s okay, see? — but like most of the senators here I wear wear my mask when I’m walking in the hallway and I wear my mask when I’m in the Senate on the floor, or when I’m in my office with
~~~

my staffers, and that's because I trust the CDE — and the CDE said, 'Cloth coverings slow the spread of the BirdFlip virus and help those who may be asymptomatic from transmitting' what I like to call the sneaky, devious virus.

"But there's a big problem, now, with this, which all seems so easy, folks — this simple little protective practice that's intended to save lives has become a political statement: if you wear a mask, you're against President Crump, if you don't wear a mask, you're for President Crump. It's so wearying, it really is. That's why I recommended to the President myself that he should wear a mask sometimes, just to be nice, just occasionally, I said, Danill, even though it's not really necessary for him to do that.

"If he just did that much, it would help to end the poisonous politics that hang about this whole issue, 'cause, you know, we just don't want to make each other sick, and that's what this is all about. Do you know I was exposed to this sneaky, devious, underhanded BirdFlip virus by one of my staffers a little while ago who had it asymptomatically, and then I had to self-quarantine for two weeks, but I didn't even catch it! — my physician told me that's because my staffer was wearing a mask. Masks work, people. Masks work.

"And furthermore, a mask can be a statement about your personality — you can wear a plaid mask like me to show your Scottish heritage — you can indicate your support for your football team with a mask — I've seen that Dr Faustus himself shows his support for the Washington Nationals professional baseball team with his mask — and we see Senator Hoss over here supports the Cowboys, Senator Owl over there supports the Bandits, and Senator Sapsucker, as you all know, supports the Orioles — so you see, now, this is how we can all work together.

"Now, we're all here today to talk about the school and college closures. While it doesn't compare to the many tragic deaths caused by this sneaky, devious, underhanded, treacherous virus, the round eighty million students who had to go home instead of attending their schools and colleges in March this year, and the teachers who suddenly had to adapt to teaching via weblink video, and the working parents whose children were now at home and they didn't have any kind of support structure in place to look after them or home-school them while they were at work, and the lost sports opportunities, graduations, dilemmas for administrations and school budgets.

"We've had over two and a half million cases of the sneaky, devious, underhanded, treacherous, Machiavellian BirdFlip virus and somewhere near a hundred and twenty thousands deaths according to John Chacalaca University, and everybody's been working together, but nothing's been quite so disruptive as those school and college students staying home. And all those schools and colleges, thousands of 'em, they're all gonna be opening again this fall.

"So we heard from the college presidents and school principals about reopening safely in fall about three weeks ago — well this hearing is gonna be an opportunity to have an update on that reopening — and the question we're gonna be asking is not, 'should we go back to school,' but, 'how do we go back to school safely in the fall.'

"And do you know — it's not so good. The Academy of Pediatric Doctors has issued a statement recently. 'Our academy believes that the evidence for in-person learning is overwhelming.' They say it's no good keeping kids home — when they're away from school for as long as they have been, there are significant problems for many kids, specially those that are disadvantaged. The ones who suffer from abuse, substance use, suicidal thoughts, depression and mental problems — these children have been much, much worse off not going to school — many have been made more unwell, some have even died. Even apart from the educational disadvantages of not being at school, many children simply don't get enough meals at home, or enough exercise, so the thin ones are getting thinner and the obese ones are getting more obese — and this is not good — that's what the Academy of Pediatric Doctors says, that's not just me sayin' that...."

In the SUV, Frank and Maddy were watching the Senate hearing live on Maddy's tablet, on C-Span.

Maddy said, "See, Mister Crump's right."

Frank said, "Just don't let Dr Faustus hear you saying that, Madeley."

Chairman Dimitrios went on, "This hearing is all about what's gonna happen next. All the distinguished experts underestimated just how sneaky, devious, underhanded, treacherous, Machiavellian and shifty this virus would be, and there's still a whole lot of mystery that hangs about the BirdFlip virus; it's like a devious spy in our midst, wandering about, lookin' for someone to *stab!* Keep your eye open people, or it'll *git* you, and then you're a goner! You're meat for the worms, watching your own eye rot away in the ground, until you're lookin' out through your own skull socket, like the corpse that you'll be. So what we're talkin' about today — the other thing we're talkin' about today — is what you'll all have to do when you're back in school — and we all know what that is — socially distance — stay six feet away from the nearest person or you'll *die!* — wash your hands, wear a mask, test with those little test kits they give you, isolation and quarantining those who were exposed to the shifty little virus, contact tracing of *every single person* they might have even *talked* to for thirty seconds — and hopefully we can keep this dread disease from *destroyin' us all* this fall. I look forward to hearin' from all our speakers here in the Senate today, every single one of them is an eminent person in our community, and I'm lookin' forward to hearin' how we can restart the innumerable schools and colleges this fall in our great country of the United States of America, before the long awaited vaccines finally arrive. Senator Billpuss, come up here now and give us a piece of your mind."

Senator Billpuss stepped up to the microphone. "Thank you indeed, Mr Chairman. Thanks for setting the tone for today's press conference and I'm telling you I'm not going to be mincing any words today. I'm going to tell it like it is. The BirdFlip Coronavirus response is an absolute unmitigated disaster, sir, a disaster of epic proportions. We have lost more Americans to the BirdFlip virus than we lose to influenza every year — and alright, the flu may have disappeared completely this year, strangely enough, but we've lost more American lives than in the Civil War and World War II combined — oh hold on, I have a message from my teleprompter person — oh sorry misread that — we've lost more American lives than any single war except the Civil War and World War II. And President Crump just sits on his hands, twiddling his thumbs, while the nation is going up in smoke, metaphorically speaking. It's a leadership crisis like no other leadership crisis — consider his appalling failures — I don't think the President cares at all about the pandemic, not even a smidgeon — I think that's completely obvious — he told us 'oh, people, everyone will be able to get hold of a test kit to see if they've got the BirdFlip Virus' — only of course when he promises this he uses the appalling expression the 'WooHoo Flu' or the 'Kung Flu' — and it's a simple fact that nobody can even get hold of a test, there's not enough available. Then the President says, 'oh, testing is overrated anyway, we don't need it.' At every turn he's a massive failure.

"And let me tell you what we know: the saviour is just around the corner. The dawn we are awaiting that will enable us to return to our lives is coming — it is almost here — the blessed day when the awaited saviour arrives and rescues us from social distancing and having to wash our hands every two minutes like a person with obsessive compulsive fixations — yes, the *vaccines are coming* — they are coming to *save* us from the BirdFlip coronavirus — they are coming to rescue us all — oh, praise the vaccines, praise the mighty vaccines, for they are coming, yes, Amen, say Amen with me brothers, praise the mighty name of Pfutticup, Modyearna, praise the vaccines, people! The saviour cometh! I lift lift up mine eyes unto the hills, from whence cometh my help, my help cometh from the Vaccine, which will be administered throughout the earth. The vaccine will not suffer thy sense of smell to be removed, the vaccine will not slumber, behold the vaccine that keepeth thee safe shall neither slumber nor sleep, but will keep producing Spike protein to give thee immunity both day and night, the vaccine is thy keeper: the vaccine is thy shade upon thy right hand. The BirdFlip shall not smite thee by day, nor the coronavirus by night. The vaccine shall preserve thee from all evil: the vaccine shall preserve thy life, my fellow Americans. All Praise to the mighty Vaccine!"

Madeley said, "Is he right? When the vaccine comes, will it save us? While I'm listening to him, I think he's right about everything, and Danill Crump is wrong. Do you think he's right?"

Frank said, "I don't know Madeley. I just don't know. It does sound as though the new vaccines might help… But who knows?"

Senator Billpuss continued, "We are all aware that this pandemic will not come to an end until we have a safe and effective vaccine. Let me say again, a *safe* and *effective* vaccine. Now, we're all aware that Crump's administration completely stuffed up the testing débâcle, and now, we're faced with the necessity of a vaccine rollout plan, and I think it's pretty plain to see that Crump and his Cronies are going to stuff this whole business up too — Crump couldn't organise his way out of a paper bag — and we're about to witness another monumental stuff-up. Oh well." Billpuss feigned nonchalant melancholy, then brightened up and said, "There's no question that we're still in a dreadful crisis that will have no intelligible solution and we're heading for an election. And what I'm trying to broadly hint at, fellow citizens, is that Crump cannot be even remotely imagined to be the best man for the job. In fact, I think we have a great chance to win that election, with the help of a few votes from dead voters, hacked voting machines, fraud and community help centres that can perform postal vote drops at the drop of a hat, yes sir, when that vaccine has its coming, so will we, my fellow fellows."

The Chairman thanked Senator Billpuss, and he sat right back down, and the Chairman introduced George Faustus. "George Faustus is the director of the National Allergy & Infectious Academy of Diseases (NAIAD) at the National Health Institute Junket. He has, in fact, held this same position for over thirty six years, a very long tenure indeed, Dr Faustus. He has led NAIAD's research investigations into HOOV, the Flu, Malaria, Bulgaria,

Hysteria, Progeria, Pueraria[41] and Drynaria[42], which I was not even aware was a real word, Ibizavirus, as well as a whole bunch of BirdFlit related Booby-viruses: such as the Abbott's Booby virus, the Yellow-bellied Sapsucker virus, and the Hoary Puffleg virus, the Kākā virus, the Exclamatory Paradise-Whydah virus, the Bananaquit proto-influenza, the Peruvian Booby virus, Satanic Nightjar oppression, the Chachalaca virus and the Ortalis virus. He has advised a bunch of presidents over the years — I won't embarrass you Dr Faustus by telling everyone just how *many* — but there's a lot I'm telling you — more than you think — and he's been involved in a bunch of vaccine trials for the Ibiza-virus and a bunch of other vaccines too numerous to mention, some failed, some successful, some others failed and a few others failed as well. Welcome to the podium, Dr

---

[41] a species of isoflavenoid enriched medicinal legumes native to Southeast Asia, New Guinea, & Northern Australia, also called kudzu or Japanese arrowroot, used in the treatment of dysentery, diarrhoea, diabetes, dementia, dengue, demyelinating disease, delusional disorder, delirium and diverse other diseases that start with the letter 'D'. Why indeed this particular legume is effective at treating diseases starting with the letter 'D' is a complete mystery to science: it does indicate that when these legumes evolved they were following some pre-determined template or broad pattern cognate *with* the development of the English language (there is no indication that Japanese uses for the plant favour the letter 'D'), i.e. evolution somehow favoured or pre-prepared utility only with *English* diseases starting 'D'. Of course, there is also the theory that after Dr Faustus made a huge catalogue of the diseases that Drynaria treated, he lost all his index cards, except for the filofax for diseases starting with 'D'; and to *this* author this appears a more satisfying explanation for this oddity; however unless other scientists come forward to study Drynaria, I suppose we'll never know.

[42] Basket ferns.

Faustus, we're just waiting with baited breath to hear what you have to tell us. You are a true hero of the people."

And the hand-picked crowd clapped ecstatically as Dr Faustus ascended to the podium microphone.

And Madeley said, "Boy, they sure love Doctor Faustus."

Dr Faustus said, "Thank you so much, Chairman Dimitrios, Senator Billpuss, Senator Hoss, Senator Owl, members of the committee, and all you other Senators and honourable people and all the rest of you, etcetera etcetera, thank you so much for inviting me today and let me emphasize that I am here to address the school and college issues and to speak to the future that we can hope for. This is like a military campaign, or, rather it *is* a military campaign, considering the role the DOD will have in the rollouts and the BARDUP, but you see, NAIAD is attacking the virus on four fronts: first, we want to really understand the virus — to know everything about it — especially the Spike protein, otherwise known as S — we want to understand how this virus affects the human body and how the immune system reacts to it. Secondly we are working on diagnostics. Thirdly, animal models, and the fourth string to our metaphorical bow is, obviously, the vaccines which are being developed even while we speak.

Now, regarding those vaccines — we are not just developing one single type of vaccine — we're making mRNA, recombinant protein, and traditional vaccines that use dead bits of virus to stimulate an immune response, because we really don't want all our eggs in one basket. Being optimistic about it, we should know by winter if we're on the right track with any of these, and by early next year, we might be ready to start jabbing people with them. So… at the moment, it looks like we will have vaccines by the early part of next year. I'm not joking. This is real. Vaccines by early next year."

Everyone clapped, and Dr Faustus sat back down.

Chairman Dimitrios said, "And now, please welcome Dr. Emilio Handy, our representative here today from the FAD. Dr Handy, please take the mike."

Dr Handy stepped up, a big man with large, bony-knuckled hands, with which he took control of the microphone and said, "The FAD is always at work, people, every day and every night, evaluating data, testing things, looking at double-blind placebo controlled trials, reading stuff, meeting with the Pharmaceutical executives and getting job offers for when we step down from our FAD positions, looking at diagnostic tests and denouncing agnostic pests. The FAD is the authority that decides whether drugs get approved or not: this gives us a tremendous vantage point to take the initiative to accelerate drug approvals by removing impediments in the way of said drugs being approved, by making sure that nothing *can* get in the way of a drug being approved. And how we expedite things is very simple: we just say yes when we're asked to. This is because we *know* those guys: I went to the Oktoberfest with Alby, he's a good guy, and Lenny Schlenny, I love playing golf with the guy, he's fully worthy of our trust, and don't forget Spynil Shiverin, alright, he gives me the creeps, but he's still a good guy to have on your side when you need someone who's good at counting cards at the casino. And Bel T., what a great guy, we both share a love for old books; I don't mean *reading* them, why would you want to do that? I mean *buying* them, *owning* them, having them in your *collection*. What greater privilege in the world could there be than to own a first edition Coverdale Bible, or a Tyndale New Testament; great books, I've never read them, but they're really great books. Or Dickens — a Christmas Carol — first edition — a historic book — I've got three. What a great purchase, and those books have escalated in value as the years go by.

"And you may think that this stuff about books was a slight diversion from the topic of my speech, the FAD, but in fact, this is related, because just as I never read the books that I own, the FAD never reads the voluminous submissions from the big Pharmaceutical companies before we approve them. As I told you, this whole thing is based on trust. I know these guys. They're good guys. I trust them. If they say a completely new experimental product — that's never been tried before and probably has vastly inadequate trial data and longitudinal-ness — is safe and effective — I believe them implicitly. Would you doubt your friends? No, I tell you, definitely not. Neither do I.

"So let me tell you about some of our promising antiviral candidates. Rundeathisnear is one of the best drugs we've ever approved, and we can say this because we really don't know. If we did know, then it would probably be perjury, but if we *don't really know,* but are just basing our statement on our sincere belief that the drug Rundeathisnear is a fantastic drug, then our lawyers tell us that we have *no liability* for the consequences. What a great loophole for us. And so, I can tell you now, that Rendeathisnear is both safe and effective for treating the BirdFlip Coronavirus, because that's *my* sincere belief. Believe me. It is.

"Now we are preparing for the next chapter of this developing novel, and just like the last chapter, I will keep my personal reading of what's going on in the story to a minimum. The FAD prefers to judge each book by its cover — judging it by its contents could be risky for everyone except the patients — but who cares about them?

"So I just want to thank the more than 18,000 FAD employees who just work around the clock to help medical products get over the line and get approved. And if there are any big pharma bosses out there with big pockets and even bigger cheque books (that's a joke — some of you younger people won't even know what a cheque book is) — if you are out there, big pharma guys, please listen to what I'm saying — getting *your* drug approved is not tricky and does not need to be difficult. Just hand in some dodgy studies and a pile of paperwork that is complicated and tortuous enough that nobody could possibly read it all, so that nobody would ever know the difference if (gods forbid) there ever was an inquiry into how a total ineffectual and unsafe drug ever got approved — and once you've put that paperwork in then go and talk to the board members and ingratiate yourselves a little — those board members, they're human beings, just like you and me, and they want a future, just like you do. Just reassure them that there'll be a well paying position in the pipeline at your company a year after they leave the FAD and I'm sure they'll rubber stump every single drug you want approved. Yes, sir, line their palms with silver, or to put it in plain language that the public doesn't want to comprehend or understand, improve the board members' fortunes and you'll inevitably get an improvement in your own fortunes too — you'll get your precious drug approved, I *can* promise you that."

After this, the Chairman called on Senator Titmouse to come and address the Inquiry.

Senator Titmouse said, "Look I want to say a firm thank you to all of our witnesses. And let me say, everybody appreciates your candour and honesty, and your service for our country, Dr Faustus; so please, last time you were here testifying before this committee, about a month ago, you warned us of the approaching apocalypse, the impending trauma, needless suffering, and the millions of agonising deaths that would inevitably follow if any state in our glorious union dared to open a single school even a day early. And now, just a month after you prophesied here, we see a record number of BirdFlit cases. Just yesterday the CDE told us there is too much virus in the community now, that we've lost the battle, and that the transmission is completely uncontrollable. And Dr Shoeshine from the CDE said, "This is just the beginning of the apocalypse that I can see looming before us like a great darkness, because our strategy simply has not worked." Now I really wanted to ask you, Dr Faustus, is there any hope? What can the government and the health authorities and the 30 states with rocketing BirdFlit cases do to reverse this slide down the proverbial gurgler, *sir*?"

Madeley, listening in the SUV, said to Frank, "Dad, that really sounds bad, doesn't it?"

Frank said dejectedly, "I really don't know what to believe, Madeley. First they told us, fifteen days to stop the spread. Then they told us contract tracing and testing will stop the spread. Then they told us, when we close the schools, that will stop the spread. Then they told us, not visiting our aging relatives in the nursing homes would stop the spread. Then they told us, social distancing and closing down the non-essential services would stop the spread. Then they told us, if we just keep the stay-at-home orders that will stop the spread. Then they told us wearing masks while we're in the bathroom and in the car alone that will stop the spread. Now they're telling us, *keeping* the schools closed will stop the spread. And do you know, about the only thing that seemed to actually stop the spread, at least according to some of the doctors at the front lines, was Hydroxychloroquilline, and they're telling us, *no,* those doctors are wrong, it doesn't stop the spread. So I'm beginning to suspect that they don't really know what they're doing, Madeley. Let's see what Dr Faustus says."

Dr Faustus said, "Why, thank you so much for your — ah — dramatically phrased question, Senator Titmouse. Let me say I am also very concerned at what we're seeing in Florida, California, Texas, Arizona and New York State. More than half the new infections are in those states. And let me say tactfully that despite the leaders in some of those states encouraging people do the right thing and stay at home and wear your mask all the time even when you're in the bathroom, etcetera etcetera, what we're actually seeing in those states when we look at YouTube videos and clips on TicTacToe, is that some individuals in those communities do not really sincerely appear to be following the instructions, in fact, what we see these individuals doing is gathering in crowds, drinking in bars and partying together, doing big mass protests and shooting each other (gunshot wounds are usually counted as BirdFlit deaths in the emergency department remember?) and burning down parked cars and cities and generally not obeying the restrictions.

"And that brings me to my next point. As individuals, we each need to take responsibility for our own actions: if some people are toeing the line, doing the right thing, staying at home, wearing masks, and other people are not doing these things, well, we cannot expect to beat this whole thing. Everybody needs to do their part to defeat the BirdFlit virus. Every single person. And we can only do it, if we work together. If we do our best effort simply to do the right thing, I really believe that we as a nation can defeat the virus and get our lives back. Of course, the key to that end is a seven letter word starting with v and ending in e, and no, that word is not valvule, vehicle or vampire, nor is it vulpine, valence, verbile, volvate, or volupte, nor village, nor vespine, nor vaginae, nor vantage; nor is it voltage, vulture, vorlagge, or vintage, no, and it is not valuate or violate or votable or vesicle, although vesicle, being a medical term, is not far off. No, sir. That word is — and I'm sure you all know what I'm talking about — a word that starts with v and ends with e — VACCINE.

"Yes sure, and let me tell that we can all do our part with the vaccine as well, because I have heard it through the grapevine — not that 'not much longer will you mine' or something like that, no — I have heard that Pfutticup and Modyearna are both looking for volunteers for their clinical trials. You heard me correctly — and this is a way that ordinary people like anyone listening to this on C-SPAN or something like that can help to get things back to normal. You see, they have to test these vaccines on people, to find out if they work or if they do harm or kill anybody, this is what we have to do, and we can only do that with real human clinical trials. And you know, it's a fifty fifty chance you'll get the placebo anyway. (Of course, these days admittedly the placebo might not be a saline solution, it might be another vaccine we're testing or some kind of other concoction we wouldn't necessarily tell you about) But you know how it is — the big Pharmaceutical companies need your help — and I'm talking about the common, everyday person — to test their vaccines to find out if they work or not. And it's a brave, selfless thing to do, Senator, for not only will you be exposed to a highly experimental mRNA Methyl1-pseudo-uridine product that uses lipid nanoparticles as the vehicle to cause your cells to do something that they ordinarily wouldn't do in a hundred years, but you will also be exposed to the virus, to find out who dies more: the ones who took what we call the 'vaccines' or the ones who didn't. And if more of the ones who didn't take the vaccine die, well, the vaccine wins. But you know, the FDA is flexible; I want to reassure you that it will probably get approved anyway.

"So I'm offering an invitation to anyone who wants to just do *something* to help us overcome this dreadful BirdFlip virus, to be part of the clinical trials, to serve your country, and you'll be a part of my team, Team Faustus."

After this, the Chairman called on Senator Burp to come up and offer a summary and close the session.

Senator Burp said, "I've worked on epidemic, plague and pestilence policy, contagion policy, blight policy, infirmity policy, scourge and pandemic policy for the past thirty seven years, Mr Chairman, yes and I have even worked on affliction policy, and — would you believe — even curse policy, yes, there is such a thing. If a certain power or person curses our country some people believe it could have a negative effect, and this is something we may need to be prepared for. In any event, I want to urge everybody to pay attention to every single thing these respected people have come to say to us, because there is an urgent threat out there that is stalking us as a lion stalks its prey. None of us are safe, until these countermeasures and vaccines are in place. Now, we all know that the President wants it done quicker, but thankfully we have Dr Faustus, who's holding the reins, and who's holding back the vaccine horse, 'cause we don't want that horse making a run for it until we're completely sure that it's safe. And so, to that end, I just reiterate what Dr Faustus says: the companies need willing idiots to test their products upon, people who are eager to help their country get back to normal. To echo those old Uncle Sam posters, your country needs you — to be part of a clinical trial."

And with that, the Senate Inquiry was over.

And Madeley said, "Do you know, Dr Faustus sounds more reasonable than some of those other people."

Frank said, "I know, he does. Maybe that's just because we know him personally, and that means we see him as more of a real person, more reasonable and normal?"

Madeley reflected on this for a few minutes. Then she seemed to have come to a decision.

Madeley said, "Dad, do you think *I* could be part of a clinical trial? I want to do my bit to help. There's nothing else I can do, except stay home from school. If I was part of a clinical trial, then I'd be helping the country get back to normal."

Frank said, "Madeley — you're a very big-hearted girl — you always want to help people. But, darling, I don't think they take children for those clinical trials. And you know, it might be dangerous. You could come to harm. I don't want that for my daughter."

Madeley was very upset by his answer, and she put her headphones on and sulked from that moment until Dr Faustus got in the car, and she kept sulking while they dropped him off, and Frank tried to talk to her but she wouldn't talk, and somehow the sunniness of the day and the beauty of the green-leaved trees and the blossoms here and there took on an ironic, mocking tinge, as though nature didn't really mean it, because Madeley wouldn't talk to him.

She was still sulking when they reached home.

~~~
~~~

CHAPTER 11

Trials and Tribulations.

It was about four thirty when they came home, and Madeley went straight to her room. Frank thought about knocking on the door, but he knew that what the girl really needed was her mother. He had stuffed it up, he knew that, somehow; but that was normal, it wasn't unusual at all.

Frank went out the back to where Linda was sleeping in the hammock.

He sat there in the chair —, not wanting to wake her because he knew how much she needed the sleep — for at least fifteen or twenty minutes. He was almost frantic for her to wake her up, so frantic he actually prayed silently a desperate prayer, "Dear Lord, please let her wake up. I really don't want to wake her up. But I really do need her to talk to Madeley."

To his great surprise, the prayer was heard. Linda gradually started stirring, and she opened her eyes. She said, "I was in the middle of such a lovely dream. A doctor came to visit us — he had heard about — something — and he made Madeley better."

Frank said, "But, Linda, Madeley's not ill."

"Oh," she said in a dreamy voice. "I thought she was... I dreamed Madeley was sick, so sick she couldn't work. But then a Doctor came, and he said he could help. There was a funny medicine that he offered us — it was a Malaria drug but it wasn't Hydroxychloroquilline, it was something else... The name escapes me now. It started with I-V-E-R, iver—something or other."

Frank said, "Well, it's just a dream, but darling, your daughter needs her Mom right now. I just can't cut it. I'm not the right parent."

Linda said, "Oh, what happened?"

Frank sighed. "Well," he said, and his voice sounded like a moan, "She's got it in her head that she wants to be in a clinical trial to help in the fight against the BirdFlip virus."

Linda said, "Oh... What on earth put that idea in her head?"

Frank said, "Dr Faustus."

Linda said, "What... did he *talk* her into it in the car? That's a bit creepy."

Frank said, "No, no, nothing like that. She saw his speech in the Senate Inquiry."

Linda said, "I thought you said you thought you wouldn't be able to watch from the Senate Gallery today;

wasn't it closed to the public? Limited numbers, invitation only, or something like that, because of social distancing and so on?"

Frank said, "It *was* closed. We watched the whole Senate Inquiry on C-SPAN on her $99 tablet, using my hot spot, believe it or not. When I told her she couldn't do the clinical trial she sulked all the way home."

Linda shook her head. "Maybe that wasn't the way to go — she's only a few years away from being a teenager. Maybe it would have been better to say, 'Okay, maybe, we'll see,' you know, more non-committal?"

Frank said, "*Now* you tell me. Hindsight is 2020[43]."

Linda climbed out of the hammock and went into the house, to see Madeley, and Frank avoided getting the usual beer: he knew when it was best not to have a drink, and this was one of those times.

~~~

Linda stood outside Madeley's room — she could hear coming from within the tinny sound of pop music being piped loudly through headphones.

---

[43] This phrase, which originated during the BirdFlip pandemic, could well have been coined in this very conversation, as it is the earliest recorded mention of the phrase, anywhere on the internet or in books or real life. That's Frank's story, anyhow, and he's sticking to it.
~~~

Linda waited for a short while then knocked on Madeley's door.

Madeley shouted, "I told you! Go away! I'm listening to music!"

Linda said, "It's your mother, dear. Let me in, Madeley; maybe you need to just... get whatever it is that's worrying you off your chest."

The sound of the music stopped, and there was silence for a while.

Finally Madeley conceded. "Come in," she said.

Linda said, "Okay," quietly and opened the door.

Madeley's room was usually quite neat, but now there were clothes strewn around and books on the floor, but Linda knew better than to complain about that. Visible things were like the leaves on a weed — a problem like this had to dealt with at the root. And who knows, maybe it wasn't a weed? Maybe Madeley needed this for some reason?

Linda said, "So... tell me what happened?"

Madeley sighed. "Dad told me I couldn't do a clinical trial."

Linda said, "Well, just go back a little further, darling. Tell me the *whole* story, right from the beginning."

Madeley said, "Well, we went to the Capitol building but we couldn't go on. So we watched the Senate Inquiry together on my tablet. Some of the speakers didn't make any sense at all." She paused and looked very upset. Linda squeezed her hand.

Madeley continued, "So, the *problem* is, Dr Faustus actually *did* make some sense, he was about the only one who *did,* and he talked about things we could do to help — for instance, be in one of the clinical trials. And Mom, I am really sick of the stay-at-home orders and the masks, and all the scary things on television and on the internet and not seeing my friends at school. I want to do something *positive*."

Linda found it hard to argue with that.

"Madeley — we'll see, alright?" she said. "I know you want to help, but we can't do it without your father being on the same page. I wouldn't want to do anything without bringing him along. Would you?"

Madeley said, "No, no, I wouldn't want to do anything without Dad."

Linda said, "But look — just leave the whole thing alone for a little while. I'm not telling you you can't do it, and neither is your Dad, I think. We just want to be sure —

and anyhow, I think you should be ready to be disappointed, because I don't think they do Clinical trials for eleven year olds. You're too young, Madeley."

Madeley said, "Okay, Mom. I'll be prepared to be disappointed."

They had dinner then, a bit later than usual; Frank went and got takeaway — normally they wouldn't because of the expense, it was only for special occasions. But he said to Madeley and Linda, "Today is a special occasion — my daughter wasn't talking to me, and now she is again."

Madeley made a point of kissing her Dad and gave him a hug, before she went to bed.

Frank sat next to Linda on the lounge seat, and held her hand. He said, "Well, I sure mismanaged that one. Frank bites the dust again. I'm just lucky I've got a beautiful wife who can fix things up and a beautiful daughter who forgives."

Linda kissed him tenderly on the lips, and said, "You are lucky."

They sat there for a while, holding hands with Linda's head on Frank's shoulder. Then Frank said, "Well, what do you think of the Clinical Trial idea? What if the drug injured her?"

Linda said, “Surely they would have some sort of support scheme wouldn’t they? I mean, these are Doctors running these things. Don’t they have to obey the Hippocratic oath, or something, do no harm?”

Frank nodded. “That’s what I thought,” he said. “Do no harm — it’s the sacred oath of medicine. That and the Nuremberg code. I’m sure it’s not just about money for them. You know, Dr Faustus seems like a decent guy, really, Linda — I didn’t really expect that at the start. Not from what I know about his political views.” He paused. “But you know, I only want to protect our daughter. She’s our only child — I don’t think we should, you know, take risks with her health or safety. She’s precious.”

Linda shook her head and said, “Anyhow, I don’t think they do clinical trials with children, do they? I mean, they’d have to be doubly sure it’s safe, wouldn’t they, before they would even try it on a child? They’re not monsters, these people — they have their own children — surely they’d understand that our daughter is precious.”

Frank said, “You’re right. I can’t imagine they would even have clinical trials for a girl that young. She’s only eleven years old — what would they want to be trying out experimental treatments on her?”

Linda stroked his hand, and he closed his eyes in bliss. She said, "Just think about it, Frank. If the possibility comes up, maybe it will be good for her — for us — to take a risk, for somebody else's benefit. You know? It's her love for her neighbour that's motivating her."

Frank said, "And... her desire to go back to school and have a normal life and be done with all this pandemic rubbish."

Linda inhaled and said, "You're right about that."

~~~

The next morning, Frank woke up early, as usual. He usually tried to have breakfast with Linda before her early shift, but Linda had a day off from the bakery, so they had breakfast together with Madeley, who usually woke up later than they did. It was nice, eating with the three of them, especially after the night before.

Linda told Madeley what they had decided: they would keep their eyes out for clinical trials for eleven year-olds (or twelve year olds, in fact, as she was nearly twelve) but that's what they would do, with the proviso that Madeley would accept that there probably wouldn't *be* any, not for such a young age group.
~~~

As they ate their breakfast, Frank eagerly asked Madeley if she wanted to come today. Faustus was being interviewed by some guy called Paul Ronson, a firebrand of a senator, who often gave Faustus real trouble.

Madeley said she didn't feel up to it.

Frank thought he understood — he was tired also this morning, and the whole episode must have taken it out of her as well.

"Have a day off," said Linda. "We'll get your grandmother to come around and look after you."

A little sadly, Frank got together his things and started tying his shoelaces, looking up every now and then at the hallway that led to Madeley's room, to see if she might have changed her mind.

He wished he could go and knock on her door and convince Madeley to come today, because he was really going to miss her company, but he knew that sometimes the best thing to do was just to ease off a little, don't push things too much. Gentleness is a good father's best quality — that was what Linda had once said to him, when Madeley was only one day old, and he was holding her in his arms, looking in her beautiful eyes and beautiful face. Amazingly, Madeley's personality was clearly visible in every atom of her being, even then. Before he saw her, before she was born, he hadn't really thought that a baby could actually have a personality, but Madeley came into the world with her personality already fully grown, like a little miracle.

Sadly, Frank eventually tied the second shoelace, picked his bag of things and his spare shirt, and walked out into the darkness of early morning to the SUV. Before he started the engine, he looked at the front door in forlorn hope, but it didn't open, and Madeley didn't run out; he waited at least ten minutes longer than he should have, given the DC traffic, but she didn't come. He texted Dr Faustus to say the traffic was bad today and he was going to be late, and then finally started the engine and accepted that she wasn't coming today.

It was still dark when he set off. As he drove, the sun gradually drenched the world with golden light, and the leaves were especially beautiful at dawn in DC. He wished Madeley was with him, but she wasn't, and there was nothing to about it. But as he drove, he realised God was with him anyway, and with his daughter, and that he had to let God manage things more and not get in the way.

~~~
~~~

Frank picked Faustus up — and he seemed different from usual somehow. Faustus wasn't the most gregarious guy in the world, but today it was like he was withdrawn or gloomy, or dreading some imminent tribulation.

Faustus didn't say anything as he got in; he didn't even say hello, so Frank started the engine and set off. Faustus didn't even notice that Madeley wasn't there.

Eventually Frank said, "Are you okay, Doctor Faustus? You seem kinda withdrawn this morning."

Faustus said, "Oh, it's Senator Ronan questioning me today. He's not very nice, always trying to pick fault with everything we do. I suppose I'm not looking forward to it very much, Frank."

He went silent then, and Frank respected his wish to be left alone. You learned how to tell these things as a driver.

About three quarters of the way there, Faustus suddenly blurted, "Where's Madeley today?"

Frank said, "Oh, she just wasn't feeling very well today. Decided to stay home with her Grandma."

~~~

When they got there, Faustus walked across the carpark as though he was going to a funeral procession, his shoulders
~~~

hunched, putting one foot in front of another like a man walking to his own executioner.

Frank felt quite sorry for him, truth be known, but he didn't know what he could have done to help him. Funnily enough, Faustus had been talking to himself in the last half a mile of the journey — Frank had heard him whispering to himself, "I am the Science, I am the Science." He didn't mention it — it would be rude — but he did wonder if that was Faustus' mantra, the phrase he used to centre himself.

Ha — did he really *believe* he was the Science? That did seem a bit arrogant, a bit hubristic, to Frank… Was Faustus heading for a fall? That was what it looked like. Frank had seen it before — pride comes before the fall — it wasn't just an old proverb, it was a principle of existence that seemed to permeate all our human interactions. He had known a guy once, a Wall Street guy, a millionaire, and a stockbroker, who had made a lot of money; he was a buddy of one of Frank's old school pals, and he had asked Frank to sit in, to fill out the numbers in a fundraising lunch. During the meal, Frank actually heard him boasting, "I have a gift for knowing when something is going to be a success. I've never been wrong. I'm like God, I've got a kind of omniscience. It's a gift, and I tell you, this share offering is going to be a hit like no other."

That share offering coincided with a huge, historic slump in the Stock market, and the guy lost all his money the very next day.

That's why you should never boast — you might be wrong — there's no point in tempting God to strike you down, is there?

Then Frank remembered the C-SPAN broadcast and got his phone and found the website and started listening.

~~~

Frank knew who Senator Ronan was; he'd often admired the man — he was a straight talking guy, and one of the few sitting Senators who was actually a trained Doctor. If anyone sitting in the senate knew enough to put Faustus on the spot, it was Ronan.

Senator Ronan was already speaking when he turned the broadcast on: "Look, the problem here is that the decision-making is concentrated in the hands of the few, and that is the fatal flaw — no one single person can fully grasp the complexity of the millions of reciprocal interactivities that occur every day in the cities and the towns of the United States. No one single person has the requisite knowledge and
~~~

insight to manage a whole economy or to dictate public health mandates. Government experts need to exercise a little humility during this pandemic and not throw caution to the winds: they need to be a little more skeptical about their own utterances and a little more cautious in making prognostications. If society submits to the opinion and dictates of a single expert and that expert is wrong, a great deal more harm may occur than if we spread the decision making around a little. Take, for example, the autocratic experts who insist that the schools must remain closed. Up till a few months ago, maybe we didn't have enough data to know if that's harmful or not, but we have the data now. We know that children don't catch the virus, they rarely spread it, and they simply don't die from it. Over 20 countries in Europe have opened their schools already and there's no sudden spike in cases. Here's the data, on the screen behind me." And the CSPAN view changed to the graphs Ronan was talking about. "None of the countries where they opened the schools ended up having any increase in cases. Austria, Belgium, Denmark, Germany, Netherlands — they all opened their schools — no discernable spike in cases at all...

"And contact tracing studies from China and three European countries did not even find one single case where a child passed the virus on to an adult. Some researchers looked at children of essential workers who were in daycare during the pandemic — it was a large study group — less than 0.17% of those kids caught BirdFlip, virus and their parents weren't catching it either. And there were other studies — the children weren't catching it — they weren't transmitting it — the Pediatrics are saying you've got to get the kids back into school, physically present. Ultimately, it comes down to the anti-democratic notion that a small cabal of central bureaucrats are smart and omniscient enough to tell everyone in the entire nation what they can and can't do.

"This nation was founded on the idea that centralised power doesn't work: no one can know enough to actually tell everyone what to do, we're not a flock of sheep run by instructions from Washington. A nation the size of the United States works better with localised power, where the local authorities can weigh up the merits of the local situation — what right do you have, Mr Faustus, to tell the people of this country that we can't play National league football or baseball — what right do you have to to tell teachers they can't go to work — shouldn't people have the individual right to take the risk if they decide that it's a risk they want to take?

"All we ever hear from you, Dr Faustus, is everything we *can't* do — what about what we *can* do for a change? *None of it*'s based on science. Why are you stopping kids from playing baseball? They're not standing close to each other for more than a millisecond — why would you stop them from getting sunshine in October, when vitamin D is good for the immune system? And there's all this scientific evidence that contradicts everything you're saying, and for some reason, and a scientist lady from England lists it all, and for some reason her video gets blocked from you-boob and blocked from go-ogle and fact-book, and nobody can tell me why. And she's black-banned and her report goes *missing* from the World Health website, and nobody can tell me why either. What's going on, Dr Faustus? Who's really in charge here?"

Suddenly, listening to this, Frank felt that his eyes were opened. He didn't want Madeley to be part of any pharmaceutical trial. What was going on?

Senator Ronan continued, "I simply want to ask you, when all the actual evidence says that it's good for children to go back to schools, Dr Faustus, why can't the children go back to school?"

Dr Faustus' answer was strangely evasive and Frank was not convinced by any of it.

Dr. Faustus said, "I - I might need a little extra time to try to ah… recover a semblance of control here, Mr. Chairman. The optics, you see…"

The Chairman said, "Well, um… I'll give you a bit of extra time. Just don't go on and on, Dr Faustus."

Faustus thought to himself, even the Chairman's against me now. "Thankyou so much Senator Ronan. I *agree* with a lot of what you've said — a lot of people put out stuff without any data behind it — and maybe I'm one of them — but the thing is, you have use your skills of deduction, sometimes, like my friend Shamrock Holmes — to have to extrapolate from the known to the unknown because you quite simply have to say *something* and recommend *something* when you're asked. And as I said before, if you were listening, which I very much doubt, I said, that we have to get the children back to school, something we obviously agree on. I'd like to emphasize that I never told anybody not to play a *particular* sport — my advice has simply been more general, I would give advice that says it's not good in *general* to play sports, and then whatever state or local authority or sporting club might decide to do with that advice is completely up to them."

Senator Ronan said, "Well, that's not really how it's working, is it? You're not giving general advice, that people have a choice about following, are you? That's the most dis —" And at that moment Senator Ronan's microphone stopped working for some reason and the Chairman said, "Anyhow, moving on..."

Thoroughly disgusted with Faustus' evasions and dishonesty — for goodness' sake, Faustus knew that everyone treated every utterance that came from his mouth as an oracle from the divine — Faustus knew that everyone treated him almost as the prophetic voice of Science itself — which state or local authority or sporting club was going to go against what Faustus said? They would be crucified. They would be pariahs — all the parents would turn against them and in two minutes the sporting club officials would be replaced, the local authority would be voted out — Frank turned C-SPAN off.

And he sat in the car thinking to himself. What was going on? Was Faustus the one running things, or was someone else behind it all? He'd been going along with it —

the stay-at-home orders, the masking, the social distancing in the restaurants, the restrictions on their movements all the time — because he thought it was the best thing for everybody. What if it wasn't? It suddenly seemed to him like a huge game being played on them, some sort of big trick, trying to bamboozle everybody. For God's sake, the BirdFlit virus even had a stupid name, and the name of the bird it came from, the Red-Footed Booby, was even more ridiculous. In fact, the whole thing suddenly looked ridiculous to him. A *coronavirus?* Frank knew — he'd read it in Scientific American once, when one read magazines and magazines were worth reading — that common colds were 40% rhino-viruses and 60% coronaviruses, or maybe it was the other way round? Well it didn't matter. Around half of all common colds were coronaviruses like the BirdFlit virus.

Were they fooling us all? How could he even know what was true?

Then he thought about something one of their neighbours had been talking about. He hadn't even been listening when she'd told him. It was something like this: this lady's husband had gone to hospital with a broken arm. While he was in there being mended, he tested positive for BirdFlit, even though he had no symptoms. He told them he'd been taking Hydroxychloroquilline and should be fine, and they said to him, "Oh, no, you mustn't take that. That stuff kills you."

And before you know it the hospital was calling him and telling her he was dying. He'd been perfectly healthy apart from the arm he'd broken climbing the ladder to clean the gutters the day before.

So she'd gone to see him, and she found out they'd put him on a ventilator and filled him full of drugs, morphine, valium and fentanyl, or something like that — the lady looked up the drug combination on the internet on her mobile phone and it turned out it was for end-of-life care, or lethal executions in the states where they still had that! This lady ripped the ventilator off his face, and somehow she managed to get him walking — well, he was fine the day before — and with the help of prayer (something else that had made Frank doubt her story at the time, but now it was starting to look real) she managed to get him past security and got him out of the hospital somehow and into their car — and she got him home.

And he survived, with a bit of bed rest and a lot of caffeine and aspirin for a few days.

And she had been trying to say to Frank, "They tried to kill my husband."

Well, at the time, Frank had barely even listened to her. She was a crazy woman. She was insane, or at least just very, very weird; some kind of anti-vaxxer or fringe dwelling sociopath. Well, that was what he thought at the time.

But now he thought to himself, something's happened in our society that has been making people go crazy — not her, she was actually the *sane* one — everyone *else* had gone crazy. It was like something in the air — a force that was acting on people; everyone can feel it, it tells you what the socially acceptable thing to do is, it guides you to do the crazy things that everyone else is doing, to *say* the crazy things everyone else is saying — and sometimes you even know what you're supposed to do and say without anyone telling you, because this force is acting on everybody, and people don't even have to say to you, 'this is the socially acceptable thing to do', but you know you have to, because if you don't say the crazy things, they'll say *you're* crazy, and if you don't *do* the crazy things, they'll call you crazy as well, and then who knows where *that* will lead?

But the thing is, and that was what he had suddenly realised, this force that's acting on us is anti-human, it's anti-God, it's anti-Jesus Christ.

And with that, Frank realised that he had made his mind up. There is *no way* I'm letting my daughter take one of those jabs. That was it. No experimental clinical trials for *my* daughter.

~~~

He drove Faustus back to his home in the leafy suburb in DC and barely talked to him — he wondered if Faustus knew that he had been listening to the interchange on C-SPAN? It was crazy, but Frank wondered if Faustus had some kind of sixth sense that could tell him that Frank had suddenly changed opinion to the other side. Was that even possible?

Frank glanced at Faustus, and he felt like he was peering at him suspiciously, through narrowed eyes, so he took his eyes back to the road, and for some reason he started praying the Lord's prayer silently and inwardly.

"Our Father who art in heaven,
hallowed be thy name.
Thy kingdom come.
Thy will be done
~~~

on earth as it is in heaven.
Give us this day our daily bread,
and forgive us our trespasses,
as we forgive those who trespass against us,
and lead us not into temptation,
but deliver us from evil.
For thine is the kingdom and the power, and the glory,
forever and ever. Amen."

He had learned it as a child. It was the only rote-learned prayer he still remembered from his childhood.

Somehow, as he prayed, the atmosphere in the SUV changed. It was as though Frank was relaxing, and he looked at Faustus in the rear view mirror, and even Faustus looked more relaxed. Faustus *never* looked relaxed.

And suddenly Faustus said, "You know, Frank, I feel comfortable travelling with you. You're one of the few drivers that I really trust. And I've had quite a few different drivers over the years. Thank you for driving me, Frank. Thank you."

Frank didn't know what to say. He just said, "Thank you, sir," and left it at that.

~~~
~~~

The next day, Madeley decided she would come with Frank to work, which was good, because Madeley's grandmother didn't have that much energy any more; she couldn't really cope with two or three days of continuous activity in a row. And with her Irish temperament, Linda's mother always had to be doing *helpful* things when she was staying at their house — she had to cook dinner, or put the laundry on, or do any one of the other innumerable jobs that were still waiting to be done — there were always plenty of those — so it really was good that Madeley had decided to come — and it was good for Frank, too.

He had still felt as though there was a gulf between them, after he had told her that she wasn't going to be doing any clinical trials; not that he thought there really was any gulf between them still — Madeley had already forgiven him — he really believed that — but the problem was, while his daughter was staying at home still, Frank didn't *feel* that she'd forgiven him.

So it was with great anticipation that he waited in the SUV that morning with the heater on warming up the car — it was a cold morning that day, especially for summer in DC — waiting for Madeley to come out of the house. She was a bit late, he figured, because she was out of practice getting up so early. Especially since her grandmother had been staying with her all day — Linda's mother was apt to allow Madeley to sleep in to all hours in the morning, which was a little problematic when it came to getting their daughter to bed on time.

Eventually, when he had almost given up and was beginning to fear that Madeley had changed her mind, Frank saw the door open a crack, and Madeley came out, and he was so certain that she was going to open the SUV passenger door and tell him she wasn't coming — but she jumped in the car and to his surprise and delight said, "Let's go."

~~~

And they had a nice conversation in the car, and Frank steered it away from anything upsetting. They actually talked about Puddleglum, a character in CS Lewis' book "The Silver Chair." Puddleglum was a strange character. He was always a bit depressed, really, and looked at the negative side of everything. But the strange thing was, when they were stuck in the underground kingdom, and they were all enchanted by the witch to forget everything they had ever known and accept the morbid underground kingdom as the only reality they had ever known, Puddleglum, with his melancholic personality, was the only one who remembered
~~~

that there really was a sky and a world above the caves that they were imprisoned in. He was the only one who remembered that there was really was an Aslan.

Suddenly, while they were talking, Frank realised that this was a little like *him*. He realised that somehow, some way, he had come to understand that they were all living in the underground kingdom, where people were telling them, there's no such thing as the sky, there's no such thing as a world outside, there's no such thing as God and Jesus. When you were enchanted, you didn't need anybody to tell you what to think — you just thought it on your own — and everybody was just under a spell — but somehow, in his slightly depressed, Puddleglum-like way, Frank had gotten out from under it, and he knew that there *was* a sky and a world outside and a God. And he would keep believing it, even if nobody else did.

The conversation continued a little while, then Madeley seemed to rest into a quiet reverie about the story, then she took her headphones and started listening to it again.

Then they arrived in Dr Faustus' driveway.

Dr Faustus was running a bit late this morning — he certainly looked comical, coming up the driveway, trying to carry his briefcase and his computer bag and his spectacles, sort of juggling them, and his tie wasn't even on properly. Suddenly he no longer looked scary to Frank — just slightly ridiculous, kind of eccentric, a bit peculiar and odd like an absent minded Professor, and he loved the guy in that moment. He wasn't the big evil one — Frank suddenly realised — Faustus was just as much a prisoner in the underground kingdom as Frank was, and Linda and Madeley. Well, not quite — Faustus *was* a prisoner, but he was a prisoner with privileges — he was one of the *guards*...

Silently, inwardly, Frank prayed for his boss, that he might be delivered, as Faustus opened the back door and got in. Frank gave the old man a few seconds to organise his things and put his seatbelt on, and then he pulled out onto the road and continued along on the way to Bethesda, Maryland, today. Faustus didn't have any press conferences, but for once he was going to the NAIAD offices in Bethesda, which Frank hadn't taken him to for months and months.

It was a slightly longer journey to Bethesda, and when they were about half way there, to Frank's surprise, Madeley took her headphones off and said to Dr Faustus, "Hello."

Faustus said, "Hello, Madeley. How are you today?" And looking at the awkwardness of Faustus' interactions with his eleven year old daughter, Frank suddenly had an insight into Faustus' condition — the man was existentially lonely — he had no idea at all about people, about how you relate to people — his whole life was centred around abstractions, abstract ideas, generalisations, suppositions and deductions. There was nothing concrete and personal, nothing simple and tactile, even; the man lived in a world of complete abstraction. And Frank pitied him even more.

And then Madeley said something Frank hadn't expected at all. "Dr Faustus," she said, "Are there any clinical trials for children?" Frank's heart sank — he thought she'd left all that behind.

"Of the mRNA vaccines, you mean?" he said. "Yes there are — for twelve year olds, Madeley. But you're not twelve yet are you? You're only eleven, from my recollection."

Then she said in a very adult voice, "Well… I'm almost twelve."

After a pause, Faustus said, "Well there would be trials for twelve year olds. But why would you want to do a clinical trial, Madeley?" Only poor people do clinical trials, was what Faustus was thinking, people who need an extra fifty or a hundred dollars in their pocket; that's why it was a lot easier to do them in poor African and South American countries, especially the clinical trials with children.

Madeley said, "Well, I heard what you said, the day me and Dad were sitting in the car watching you on C-SPAN, about things people could do to help. And I'm just a kid — there's not much I can do to help — but I can do that. I can let them try out the drug on me."

And Faustus went very quiet, then. Frank wondered what he was thinking — the expression on his face was chastened, like someone who had suffered a huge rebuke, or a slap on the face. Was Faustus shamed by Madeley's willingness to risk her own safety and comfort for others? Was that what it was? Frank wasn't sure he was seeing what he thought he was seeing on Faustus' face — could you really be sure of what someone else was thinking, just from looking at the expression on their face? — Frank thought he was sure — he thought he could see it in his eyes, in the rear view mirror.

Then Madeley said, "What do you think, Mister Faustus — do you think the vaccines will be safe? Will I be safe, if I do the clinical trials?"

She sounded so plaintive in the car, and Frank's heart broke. What was Faustus going to do? Was he going to tell the truth? Frank had been doing research on the internet, now, he'd been looking things up — just a few years ago, they had been tearing their hair out about mRNA vaccines because they caused inflammatory reactions in the animals that had been taking them — only a year ago, they still hadn't done any clinical trials in humans at all. It was completely experimental, and who could know what would happen when people were injected with this stuff.

He looked in the rear view mirror. Faustus looked completely stunned; Frank had an 'Aussie' friend — an Australian — who had an expression — a stunned mullet — that's what Faustus looked like — a stunned mullet.

Madeley said, "Dr Faustus, did you hear? Would I be safe?"

Frank looked at the man. For a moment, there was a spark of nobility in his face, as though he had almost decided that he would risk everything and tell the truth, but like the rich young man in the gospels (one of the few Bible stories Frank could remember from his days in Sunday School when he was six or seven) Faustus decided to take the easy road.

"Of course you'd be safe," he said, and Faustus' face looked like the face of a pig, with little black, beady eyes, and his nose looked like a snout, and Frank shook his head.

Faustus continued with the lies, "Those vaccines will be safe and effective. Didn't you hear me say that to all the people?"

And Frank decided at that moment that his daughter's life was worth more than his job and his security and even his life. Maybe he would never work as a chauffeur again. Maybe he would be black-banned, and his name would be mud, and they would rubbish him all over the media and the social media. Maybe there would be even worse consequences, things he couldn't even imagine. But he was going to speak the truth, whatever the cost.

"Dr Faustus," Frank said, "Don't lie to my daughter. You can't possibly know if they're going to be safe and effective — you won't know that until at least seven years have passed, and you have done the *proper* phase one, two and three trials, which I very much doubt will ever be done, because the FAD approval is so damned easy these days. How dare you lie to an innocent child, sir."

And Faustus' face went red and then purple, and he gripped it with both hands and to Frank it looked as though it was going to explode and was only being held together by his vice-like hands, and Faustus screwed up his eyes and his lips and appeared to be about to say something so poisonous to Frank that he almost put his foot on the brake to stop time from going forwards. But something changed in that moment and Faustus clutched at his chest and his face screwed up in pain and he said with difficulty, squeezing the words out between his teeth, "I'm having a heart attack — you'd better take me to emergency."

Frank immediately put his foot on the gas; they were only five minutes from the NAIAD building in Bethesda — that was a building full of Doctors and scientists — surely they could get help there.

He drove fast, and they arrived at the NAIAD security gate in less than a minute. He used the intercom, and said, "Quick, get someone here right now, Dr Faustus is having a heart attack."

In just moments the siren of an ambulance split the air, and the paramedics were pulling Faustus out of the car onto a stretcher. Frank asked the paramedics, "Where're you taking him?"

They said, "Walter Reed."

"Alright," said Frank, "We'll follow."

Frank told Madeley to ring Faustus' wife — her number was in his phone — and she did, and told him what had happened, and where he had been taken.

They drove to the hospital.

When they arrived there, Frank didn't quite know what to do. He parked in the visitor's car park and waited.

He knew Gloriana's car, and when she arrived, and thankfully parked quite near where they were parked, he got out to talk to her.

"Hello, Frank," Gloriana said, "I've talked to him on the phone — they're stabilising him — thank you for getting him here."

Frank said, "Well, I'm glad he's okay — I'll take Madeley home then?"

Gloriana said, "No, no, he wants to talk to you — he said he wants to talk to you, Frank. You and Madeley."

So Frank told Madeley and they both followed Gloriana into the Emergency Department entrance. They didn't even have their masks on, but for some reason, they were let through by the guards. Perhaps it wasn't that uncommon for people who were coming through into Walter Reed's Emergency Department for them to not be wearing masks.

They were directed straight through because Gloriana was who she was, and they found themselves at Faustus' bedside. There were electrodes attached to his chest and his head and a blood pressure monitor on his finger, and beeping monitors by the bedside. Faustus looked feeble and vulnerable; Frank suddenly realised that he wasn't really a very tall man, or maybe he'd shrunk? He seemed almost childlike, laying there, attached to all those electrodes.

He didn't notice them at first, but Gloriana said, "They're here."

Faustus looked up at them — he looked like an owl, all wide-eyed and shocked — or like someone who had just climbed out of a deep, deep pit and was looking at daylight for the first time.

Frank said, "I didn't — " but Faustus interrupted him, saying, "I was out of line, Frank. You were completely right. They are experimental. We have no right to gild the lily about that. And the doctors told me that, while our little communication might have triggered the heart attack, it was going to happen anyway. There's a blocked artery. It was only lucky that it happened when it did and you had such presence of mind, and were so quick to get help to me. I owe my life to you, Frank, and never let it be said that I don't recognise those who have helped me." Faustus paused. "You could have just stopped the car and waited. I would have died, and no one would have been the wiser."

Frank said, “I would never do that, Dr Faustus. Never. There would never be a circumstance I could imagine where I would have let you die just now. I would never let you — or anyone — die to protect my own job or career.”

Faustus looked at him with a strange expression, a combination of chastened humility and astonishment. “I would,” he said. “I would let someone die to protect my career. Or maybe I would have. I don’t know; I don’t think I’ve changed. Do people ever really change? Your job is safe, Frank.”

Frank said, “I changed, George. I turned to God. I was heading towards being an alcoholic, and I think I was on the way to being a wife-beater. It was partially the post-traumatic stress after the explosions, but George, it was me — I’d be doing myself no service if I didn’t admit that *I* was the problem. I turned to Jesus and repented — and I changed; if I can change so can you.”

Frank looked up, over Faustus, and noticed Gloriana’s expression — it was sour — an expression of deep revulsion, actually, covered her face, as though she despised her husband’s weakness in listening to

Faustus turned to Madeley. “Don’t do the trials, Madeley. They’re too dangerous,” he said.

Madeley said, "But you said these vaccines were already safe and effective! You said it in your speech; you said it to me..."

Faustus said, "I may have... lied a little, Madeley, or stretched the truth, anyhow. I confess I don't know if they're safe and effective. Don't do the trials. Those companies do them in third world countries so that they're not hurting American kids, not because they care about American kids, but because their parents are more likely to sue if their kids get hurt."

Frank looked up again, and Gloriana was glowering. This conversation was definitely not pleasing her. She looked like some sort of archetypal representation of dissatisfaction, or a statue of discontent, completely motionless, or like a vulture sitting on a power-line, waiting for the prey to come along or for something to conveniently die.

Then she suddenly came to life, and it was almost shocking; Madeley gave a start. Gloriana snapped aggressively, "Well, that's enough then, let's get you both out of here — my husband is tired and he's not himself. Shuffle off. Nurse! Can you show them the way out."

As they followed the nurse down the corridor, they could hear Gloriana shouting at Faustus, "What do you think you're saying? We never admit those things. What's wrong with you? Don't you care about me? Don't you understand that if you go down, I'll go down with you? This is outrageous — just because you've had a heart attack doesn't give you the right to— " and then she gave a little expression of surprise, "Oh," and they wondered what had happened to her.

And then they heard Faustus saying rather loudly, "Officer, could you escort this woman — my wife — out of the building please? I'm just not ready to deal with this right now. My constitution is still rather tender if you will after the cardiac event I just experienced. Please take her out of the building and let her come back in an hour or two when she's calmed down. Or wherever you want to take her."

And they heard Gloriana protesting in a slurred voice, "What? Get your hands off me. I'm not going anywhere. How dare you! Don't you know who I am? Oh, you're manhandling me — you're violating my bodily space — oh, this is assault — no I'm staying right here. Haven't you ever heard of informed consent? Ohh."

Then Frank and Madeley followed the nurse through a few twisting corridors, and they appeared to have left Gloriana behind them. But as they walked out through the building entrance, a gurney went past being pushed along by two military security guards, and Gloriana was lying upon it. Her wrists were tied to the metal restraints on the side, and she was clearly drugged. She was mumbling to herself, but only the occasional word was audible: "medical ethics... pharmaceutical... testing on children... how dare you!"

The military guards stopped at the reception window and said to the receptionist, "Well, where are we taking her?"

The receptionist said, "Doctor Bailey said she's clearly in a delusional state. Take her to the mental wing."

~~~

Frank drove Madeley home, then, and they were both silent for the whole journey. Before they got home, he turned off and drove into the carpark of a nice café where they had often had lunch in the past with Madeley's mother, but this time, Frank bought Madeley lunch. She ate in silence, but then eventually she spoke. "Sorry, Dad. Sorry that I didn't listen to you. I didn't really believe what you were saying. But I see now that it was all true."

Frank said, "So, no clinical trials?"
~~~

Madeley said, "No. No clinical trials. And do you know what? I think we'll avoid the vaccines, too, don't you?"

Frank replied with a question, "So you're an anti-vaxxer now?"

"I don't know," she said, in her adult voice. "But I feel like I'm ready to be twelve years old now."

He took her hand in his, and didn't say anything, but she knew that he meant that she would always be his baby.

They sat like that for quite a while, looking out through the café windows at Laurel Lake with tears in their eyes. Finally Frank said, "Let's go home."

~~~

Gloriana spent two weeks in a very exclusive private mental hospital; in the moneyed classes they call these places sanatariums, or rehabilitation clinics, or meditation centres, or any other name rather name mental asylums.

Any public knowledge of her mental breakdown was successfully suppressed; the military police were known for their discretion, but they were asked to sign non-disclosure forms and threatened with court martial if they ever talked about what the military brass called Gloriana's unfortunate incident.
~~~

For all her colleagues and underlings knew at the NHIJ, she had been called away on an emergency military medical mission somewhere in Angola. It was a good story because no one dared question her about her absence, and it gave a sense of plausibility to the fact that it happened very suddenly.

Clarence Collins was the one who eventually went and picked her up from the sanatorium to bring her home, one afternoon, on a hot, humid summer day.

Faustus was already at home; they don't keep them long in hospital these days. He was having a short holiday himself. They had said he didn't need an operation, yet, and that at his age it might be an unacceptable risk anyhow if he *did* have a stent put in — they gave him a cocktail of heart medications and blood thinners and said that they'd keep monitoring his condition.

Clarence parked outside the mansion and opened the passenger door for Gloriana. She was still unsteady on her feet, partly because of the shock of it all, but also because she was still partially medicated. Clarence took her hand and helped her out of the car, and into the house.

Faustus was seated in the lounge room in front of the fire.

Gloriana came in and sat down unsteadily. Faustus found her iPad and Clarence brought her a gin and tonic, and she silently sat there sipping it.

Faustus was about to say something, but Clarence shook his head. "I don't think she's ready, George," he said.

They went out into Faustus' office.

He looked up at Jesus on the cross, and nodded, and said quite respectfully, "You win this round."

Faustus sat at his desk; it was a comfortable ergonomic chair — he'd slept in it plenty of times — and Clarence sat down on one of the lounge chairs Faustus kept in their for guests.

Clarence said, "What was that about?"

Faustus said, "What was what about?"

Clarence nodded at the hallway door. "You win this round?"

Faustus replied, "Just a little tussle me and Jesus Christ are having, Clarence. Do you know I died, when they put me in the ambulance? For maybe half a minute."

Clarence raised his eyebrows.

Faustus said, "Don't you want to know what it was like? Being dead?"

Clarence shrugged. He said, "Nothing? God?"

Faustus said, "No, not at first. The other guy."

Clarence frowned. "The devil?"

Faustus said, "Yeh, him. Horns and all. Maybe all that's just a scary mental representation, but I could see into his mouth, and it was literally hell in there: there was nothing inside his mouth and his head but fire and darkness. I was burning up, Clarence, it was... hell. There was fire everywhere and I was in it, and there was no relief, not even a moment of relief. Then the devil spoke. He said, 'You gave me your soul, back when you were twenty years old.' And I said, 'No I didn't.' And the devil said, 'Yes you did. And now it's time for me to claim your soul. I've given you everything. You've had the whole world at your feet — adulation — worship — every single person on this planet (just about) does everything you tell them to, no matter how idiotic or stupid or unscientific or ridiculous it is. Thank you.'

"And I said, 'What for?'

"And the devil said, 'Thank you — for the pandemic — I haven't had such a good laugh in a long time. The hospital protocols were especially precious. And sending all the children home from school. What a delight that was — do you realise my minions feed on them — all their suffering — it is food for us?'

"I said, 'I never gave you my soul, you're a liar.'

"But the devil said, 'Oh, yes you did. Don't you remember? Probably not; that's because I have the power to make you forget, and I did cause you to forget it. It wasn't hard; you wanted to forget it anyway.'

"Then I suddenly saw myself, at that fraternity swearing in ceremony — do you remember? You were there, Clarence."

Clarence shook his head and said, "No, I don't. Was I?"

Faustus said, "Yes, it all took place in front of that skull. Don't you remember? They gave us an oath to swear. It was all about giving ourselves to the power of the skull in solemn service, and in return he would be obliged to give us all riches and power and dominion over all the earth, which is his domain, apparently. I had completely forgotten it — at the time, I discounted it as just stupid kid stuff, not real. Of course, I would never have told my grandmother what I did; she would have warded off the evil eye with the sign of the cross or something like that — "

Clarence said, "So you're here now. So what happened? How did you get back?"

Faustus said, "You won't believe what happened."

Clarence said, "What?"

Faustus said, “I thought of my driver, Frank. He’s such a decent fellow. Never heard him speak a mean word about anyone; he’s a Crump supporter but we won’t hold that against him. There was this day when he was driving me somewhere and this peace just descended on the car — I’ve never felt peace so strongly — and I’m sure he was praying silently in that moment, I’m sure of it — and I thought of that peace, and it reminded me of my grandmother. I had such pain, then, in that place, with all the burning flames, thinking of the regret, because I was so cruel to that woman about her faith, when I got older — but when I was a little boy, she taught me a prayer. One of the psalms. ‘The Lord is my Shepherd.’ And I began to recite it.”

And Clarence Collins recited it:

“The Lord is my shepherd; I shall not want.

“He maketh me to lie down in green pastures: he leadeth me beside the still waters.

“He restoreth my soul: he leadeth me in the paths of righteousness for his name's sake.

“Yea, though I walk through the valley of the shadow of death, I will fear no evil: for thou art with me; thy rod and thy staff they comfort me.

"Thou preparest a table before me in the presence of mine enemies: thou anointest my head with oil; my cup runneth over.

"Surely goodness and mercy shall follow me all the days of my life: and I will dwell in the house of the Lord for ever."

And Faustus said, "Exactly, that's the one. I started reciting that — I don't know if I even got to the end; I don't think I could remember it all. But a hand reached down and plucked me out of the flames, and I could hear the devil screaming in rage because I wasn't imprisoned any more.

"And then I'm sitting there on the green grass, and Jesus is there in front of me. I couldn't look at his face, Clarence — I really wanted to look at his face, to see what he looked like, but I was too in awe of him. And Jesus said to me, 'George — I'm sending you back — you can't stay here. You have to make amends. You have to fix some things.'

"I said, 'I thought you're all forgiving.'

"'You have trouble accepting my forgiveness, George, and that's because you often fail to forgive others.'

"I was a bit devastated by this. I said, 'Does the devil have my soul?'

"Jesus said, 'Not yet. There's still time for you to turn to me.'

"I said, 'So you mean, when I vowed to give my service to the skull, it didn't mean anything?'

"Jesus said, 'If you repent, now, then it didn't mean anything, and you will come and live with me in my house that has many rooms.

"I said, 'My house has many rooms. Can't I live there?'

"And Jesus said, 'not forever. For a little while longer.'

"And I said, 'You've won this round, haven't you?'

"And Jesus said, 'I've won every round. That's what the cross means.'

"And then, suddenly, I was in the ambulance being revived. That was it, I was in this world again, suffering and pain and that was it."

Clarence was standing by the window looking out at the shrubbery outside; it was dark now, and the leaves were being buffeted by a steamy summer rain. The rain made a muffled sound on the roof and the branches outside flicked to and fro as the rain became more forceful.

Clarence said, "I always wanted to have a vision. I've never been given one."

Faustus shrugged. "Maybe it was just a dream?"

Clarence said, "Do you think it was just a dream?"

Faustus said, "Not now. But I know me. When everything gets busy, and when Gloriana gets in my ear, and when I stop thinking about death and dying and the afterlife, and ethics, and all that stuff, I'll just go back to being my former self, Clarence. I'm not going to change. I just know it."

Clarence said, "How do you know? You do realise that all you have to do is ask him for help."

Faustus shrugged again. "I'm pretty stubborn, Clarence. Do you think I'm going to do that? Humiliate myself in front of Him?"

Clarence said, "It's the only way."

Faustus' expression was almost contemptuous; Clarence didn't like seeing such ugliness on his friend's face. Faustus said, "He told me I can't forgive, and so I can't accept forgiveness. I know, I know, 'forgive us our trespasses as we forgive those who trespass against us' — I went to Sunday School too, Clarence, it's the only condition on His love. But the thing is, I can't forgive what they did to me."

Clarence said, "You can ask Him for help to forgive. I think sometimes *that's* the only way."

Faustus had a bitter look on his face. "I know," he said. Then he added, "It was just a dream."

And Clarence wondered whether their friendship would last, after this...

~~~

It would be a nice ending to the book to say that Faustus repented, and everything was alright, and he went to heaven in the end. But I don't know if that's the case. All the indications seem to say that he was right: as he got busy and involved and forgot about death and ethics, he went back to being the person that he was before.

After being the spokesperson for the US Birdflip Coronavirus response for three years, George Faustus eventually resigned as head of the NAIAD division of the NHIJ in December 2022, just before his unredacted emails were released in response to an FOI request.

Peter Dackazacka[44], the Chairman of the Green-Goblecki-Health Alliance received NAIAD grants totalling $24 million, some of which was spent subsequently doing research in the WooHoo Institute of Virology, somehow ended up being on the World Health Club team investigating the lab leak theory in WooHoo six months later.

---

[44] It is thought that Peter Dackazacka's surname was the inspiration for the name of the famous Australian rock band, AC DC.
~~~

Kristen Solo, listed as the principal author of the research letter published in Lance-At-Every-Boil, and the study, “The proximal origin of BirdFlip-CoV-2”, runs a lab at the Scrappy Research Institute. A search on NHIJ REport reveals that before he helped write this research paper, Kristen Solo’s lab had received little more than $9.9 million in total funding from the NIAID. After the paper was published he received $27 million in funding from the NIAID for projects in which Kristen Solo was chief researcher, beginning with two projects approved about a year after the publication of the paper, totalling more than $1.6 million in funding.

Coauthor Shamrock Holmes was already highly compromised: before he left the US to move to an Australian University in 2012, he had received over $55 million in funding from the NAIAD for projects in which he was the chief researcher.

Between 2013 and 2019, Coauthor Barry A Gog had apparently received over $25 million in funding from the NIAID, spread over a number of years. In the four years after the paper, he received a further $16 million, which actually represented a funding boost of 17% per annum.

And one of the other authors received $229 million for projects in which he was lead researcher since 1987.

The only author of the research letter who appears not to have received any funding ever from the NIAID was Conrad McBean, of Edinburgh Technically University.

Jerry Blacksmith, who is revealed in the FOI emails as the organiser of the teleconference and the facilitator of the composition of the research paper, is relatively untouched by any imputation of conflict of interest, in comparison with the others. He received a measly $3,993,994 from the NHIJ in 2007 for a project in which he was lead researcher.

However the Wellness M.I.S. Trust, of which he was director at the time, together with the University of Pixford where he was a Professor, were partners in joint projects funded by the NAIAD to the tune of $23.4 million over more than twenty years. Jerry Blacksmith is now the chief scientist at the World Health Club.

~~~

The death toll of the BirdFlip CoV2 virus according to Worldometer was over 6.8 million.

~~~

Four scientists were commissioned to write a review on Ivermectillion, a cheap generic drug that was found in an in silico study to be good for treating the BirdFlip Coronavirus.

Avidly Hillock was one of the scientists commissioned to write the study. He worked for an avian charity called "Save the Fluffy-backed Tit-babbler", which was both an eco-conservation project favoured by the Greens and a health based charity: it fit perfectly into the "One-Health" framework favoured by the World Health Club these days.

The four scientists were corresponding via email and Zoom and TicTacTwit, and Avidly was the one raving the most about Ivermectillion, of them all. "What a great medication! It's so effective. My brother's a smoker and if he got sick with the BirdFlip Virus I'd definitely find a way to get some. Fantastic medication! Let's write the review. Let's do it, it should be used in all the hospitals and all the data says how great it is. Let's write the review and tell everyone about it and we'll save ten thousand lives a week."

Well, it so happened that Avidly was in the bath one day, when he got a mobile call.

He said, "Hello?"

"Hi. This is Gill Bates. You may know who I am?"

Avidly said, "Hahaha! Are you even joking? Is that really Gill Bates or is that you, Jean, having me on?"

Gill said, "Why do people always do this when I call them? It is. It's me. If you doubt it check your bank account; I've just funded next year's project. Do you know what I am?"

Avidly checked his mobile banking app quickly, and it was true. Another couple of million dollars of funding, plonked in there just now! "Do I? Billionaire, tech tycoon, and more than that: you are the main funder of the charity I run, 'Save the Fluffy-backed Tit-babbler'. Thanks, Gill."

"Well," said Gill, "It's time for you to do something in return. I heard that you're on the committee for assessing Ivermectillion?"

"That's right," said Avidly.

"Well," said Gill. "You know that we're coming out with these vaccines, Avidly. It would be bad for everyone if a useless medication like Ivermectillion gets approved, wouldn't it, when these excellent vaccines are just about to come onto the market..."

~~~

The following Sunday, Frank took his family to church.
~~~

It was a nice church — the music was reasonably lively, the people were friendly, the whole experience was really good.

Then the preacher started preaching.

"Danill Crump is God's chosen one to bring our nation out of the darkness of vaccine worship and BirdFlip idolatry. He is going to have another term in the Presidency: this is God's prophetic word for us today. And he will bring in a golden era of prosperity and freedom, for the whole world. He is God's chosen one."

Frank immediately grabbed Madeley's hand and said to Linda, "We're going."

Linda said, "I thought we were going to go to church every Sunday now?"

And Madeley said, "He's really good. I really like this guy…!"

But Frank said, "Yes, we are going to church every Sunday now. Just not this one."

And Linda said, "That's good. I'd like to find one where they worship God…"

And Frank said, "Me too. I wonder if there are any around?"

www.ingramcontent.com/pod-product-compliance
Lightning Source LLC
Chambersburg PA
CBHW061059210726
48294CB00001B/221
9781763626096